THE SAINT OF BAGHDAD

Michael Woodman

Connlaswell Publishing

Copyright

This edition published in 2019 by Connlaswell Publishing.

Copyright © Michael Woodman 2019

The right of Michael Woodman to be identified as the author of this work has been asserted in accordance with the Copyright, Designs and Patents Act 1988. All the characters in this book, with the exception of those already in the public domain, are fictitious, and any resemblance to actual persons, living or dead, is purely coincidental.

All rights reserved. No part of this publication may be reproduced, stored in a retrieval system or transmitted in any form or by any means without the prior permission in writing of the publisher, nor be otherwise circulated in any form of binding or cover other than that in which it is published without a similar condition, including this condition, being imposed on the subsequent purchaser.

Woodman, Michael. The Saint of Baghdad.
Connlaswell Publishing.
www.connlaswell.com

ISBN 978-1-9160095-2-3

WHAT AMAZON READERS ARE SAYING:

★★★★★ "A fast paced, tense, gripping story of espionage that will keep you well up past your bedtime."

★★★★★ "…a complete thrill ride starting on page one."

★★★★★ "Incredibly well-written, this is a book that gives us the readers great moments and a feeling of loneliness when it ends."

★★★★★ "A genuinely exciting and intriguing story by an expert storyteller."

★★★★★ "I had no intention of reading it cover to cover in one day but I did!"

★★★★★ "The plot is absolutely brilliant, and the characters are highly believable and realistic."

★★★★★ "Full of action and suspense, this novel takes you down many twists and turns and leaves you wondering who to trust."

★★★★★ "…a page turner from the gate. I read it in two sittings."

★★★★★ "It is difficult not to get engulfed in this kind of storytelling. Terrific start to the CJ Brink series."

★★★★★ "A must read. Loved all the players. Wonderful women. Devastating losses. Brilliant writing."

ABOUT THE AUTHOR

Michael Woodman was a thriller-writing sensation in his teens, signing multi-book deals with major publishers straight out of high school.

His spy novels ended up on bestseller shelves on both sides of the Atlantic, but their young author was oddly troubled. His hero went on dangerous missions to exotic locations, but Michael had never been anywhere or done anything, and he wanted a thriller-writer's bio like the authors who inspired him. So he quit writing imaginary adventures and took off looking for real ones.

Since then, he has traveled in over 50 countries and had extraordinary careers and adventures on four continents. He now lives in Spain with his wife, Elizabeth, and he's back at the keyboard with a new hero for a new age.

Find out more at michaelwoodman.com.

PROLOGUE

Iraq, May 2009

Is it me?

The blindfold comes off and it hits me when I see the black hoods, the webcam and the jagged-edged knife.

Is it me?

Sunlight is streaming through a hole in the roof and hitting the dirt floor like a spotlight on a dark stage. The webcam is staring at it. Stark. Expectant.

It's showtime.

But who's the main event?

CJ, Declan, or me?

We're huddled in shadows by the wall. I'm nursing a head wound with blood trickling down my neck. That would be frightening in any other world, but here it's oddly comforting.

It's not me. It can't be.

Why crack open a guy's head when you're about to hack it off? It makes no sense. Even for these guys.

But if not me, then who?

CJ is piled in a heap at my side. He's lying on a stack of rubble and bleeding bad. Worse than me. He's fiddling with the cuffs at his back. Maybe he's found a pick. Some old nail in that pile of debris. It can't be CJ. Same logic as me. Why beat a man senseless if you need him live on camera reading from a cue card?

It must be Declan. They haven't touched him yet. Strange. He's the VIP, the IT expert we were guarding when a hundred cops showed up and arrested us. Only they weren't cops. And we're not prisoners. We're not hostages either. At least, not me and CJ. A hostage is worth something. We're expendables. Me especially—I'm American. They won't get jack for me. As for CJ, he's an equally worthless Brit. If we were French or Italian, they might trade us for a suitcase full of used bills. But all they'll get from our guys is an IOU scribbled on the business end of a Hellfire missile.

Two hooded stooges drag Declan in front of the webcam and gut-punch him down to his knees. They hold him there and check back with the movie director—the guy with the knife. His name is Jahil. Jihadi Jill we call him. Easy enough to recognize even under the hood. Big. Another Brit. And that's obvious as soon as he opens his mouth. From somewhere "up North" according to CJ. Manchester or thereabouts. A once-upon-a-time soccer fan, maybe. City or United? Blue or red? Now pure black.

The fourth guy is Hussein. He's working the laptop and the webcam. He calls out to Jill. There's something wrong. Declan's not roughed up enough. Or maybe he's roughed up too much. I can't figure it out. Either way, he's not ready for his close-up. The stooges rip at his shirt until Jill sees something dangling from the rags. He grabs it and holds it up like a rare jewel in a shaft of sunlight. It's a sliver of black plastic. A memory card. He gives it to Hussein and steps back into the limelight as the stooges hold Declan steady.

"What's on the card, my friend?"

Declan's eyes blaze up at the masked face. "It's blank. I swear."

"So why was it sewn in your shirt?"

"It wasn't. It was in the pocket. They missed it."

Jill glances back at Hussein, who slots the memory card into his laptop and buzzes through menus. Jill crouches, his mouth at Declan's ear, his voice a hoarse whisper. "I really want to know what's on that card." He strokes his blade down the Irishman's cheek and blood drips from his chin onto his rag-strewn chest. "So I'm going to cut your throat extra slowly to give you plenty of time to answer."

"Okay," Declan says, his eyes tracking the blade as Jill eases it away from his face. "Secrets—"

"Bullshit." Jill cracks him on the head with the butt of his knife. Declan groans and his body wilts, but he doesn't quit.

"They faked this war. I can prove it. You can break America's heart with this. It's a propaganda goldmine. The Vietnam War was won by a photo—not a bomb. When America saw that naked kid running—"

"A photo? They've seen hundreds of photos. And videos too. They don't give a damn about what their soldiers do. The world's moved on. Atrocity is the new normal. And it gets prime time."

"This is different. Way beyond top secret."

"You said it was blank."

"I lied. It's in a hidden partition."

Hussein calls out to Jill. He's found something on the card. He's pumped, fingers jabbing at the laptop.

But Jill's not convinced. He looks down at Declan.

"You're a liar."

Declan turns to Hussein and pleads for his life, howling in pidgin Arabic studded with English computer words. I catch bits of it, but the mishmash of languages makes no sense to me. Hussein is buying it, but Jill's still not convinced. They shout and rage at each other until something breaks and silence hangs in the emptiness.

Jill is looking at us now.

Me and CJ.

He barks out orders and the stooges drag Declan offstage, banging him up against the wall until he crumples to the floor. There's been a change of plan. Something on that card. A ticket to ride for the Irishman. Suddenly too precious to kill.

It's me.

I see it in Jill's eyes. That's all I can see behind the mask. But it's enough. Sooner or later, it had to be me. I'm every jihadi's wet dream. That blue passport works its magic every time. A real American. Box office. Even better—a former US Marine. The stooges drag me in front of the webcam and its empty lens stares at me. They pin me by the shoulders and Jill lays into my back with his knee. Ribs pop and pain gags in my throat. CJ bellows and leaps to his feet.

Crazy James. He's going for them. Cuffs or not.

Take it easy, buddy. Or they'll kill you too.

Hussein leaps up and knocks CJ to the floor. It's the last thing I see before Jill hits me again and I tumble into darkness. They shake me, bring me back.

The room is quiet—a slice of time missing.

CJ is sitting with his back against the wall. His eyes are on mine, his shoulders shifting, hands still working the chains behind his back. This guy never gives up.

Jill is at my shoulder, hauling my head back by a handful of hair. The stooges are wrestling a sheet of plywood inked up with propaganda. It's a jihadi teleprompter, and they're trying to stand it up straight where I can read it. I'll spare you the fine print. But it's not much of a sales pitch for the USA.

"I'm going to tell you a secret," Jill says. "Remember the Deer Hunter game we used to play? How I'd spin the cylinder, stick the barrel to your head and drop the hammer?" He leans in closer. "I was faking it. I used to palm the live round. And we're doing the same thing here. No one has to die. Just read what's written on that board. Hussein can fake the rest. Snip, snip. We'll cut and paste video of some other poor bastard's throat getting cut instead of yours. You're more valuable to us alive than dead. I respect you, Alex. You were a US Marine, a warrior like me. You're a prisoner of war. Not a hostage. I don't want to kill you. Help me out here. One way or another, I need that video. I need America to see and hear a decorated Marine telling them the truth."

"He'll kill you anyway." CJ struggles to his feet, but Hussein kicks him back down.

Jill tucks the blade under my chin and the stooges aim my head at the message board. "Read it."

"Sure. I'll read it," I say. "I don't want to die. You don't need the knife. We can do it like you said. Hussein can patch in the blood and gore from some other video. Then we can do a deal for Declan's card."

"Smart move, Alex."

Jill and the stooges step back and stand in the darkness as Hussein triggers the camera and its red light winks at me. Fear is creeping into my bones, but

I suck it up. Nothing to lose now but pride, and mine's not going anywhere. I breathe it all in. The last of my life. The warmth of the sun. The burn in CJ's eyes. I'm glad he's here. My buddy. My witness. I nod to him and off I go. I can hardly believe it. I'm straining forward like I'm reading the board and trying hard to get it right. But hey, guys, listen up… I'm singing "The Star-Spangled Banner."

The stooges are frozen. Even Hussein. Maybe their English isn't up to the task. It's the craziest thing, but I smile. Jill launches himself at me as CJ leaps to his feet. He's done it. His hands are free. He's on his way. Jill's knife is at my throat. Hussein goes for CJ and they grapple. Hussein keels over, his head dangling on his chest. Jill is cutting. One more line. I can make this. CJ and the stooges are fighting and guns are blasting. I hear it all, but faint, as if from some distant room. I'm in full song. One more line. I hear it. The knife saws into me. The stooges fall. CJ's coming.

O'er the land of the f-r-e-e…

Part One

LONDON

ONE

Eight Years Later

CJ was sitting up in bed, eyes shuttering mechanically, taking endless snapshots of the same room.

Tubes, wires, life support.

The landscape was always the same and always haunted by the strangest things, like that mirror on the dresser at the end of his bed. It was mounted in an ornate wooden frame—a strange thing to find in a hospital. But then this wasn't so much a hospital as a hospice, a waiting room for warriors.

Most of them were waiting to die. Some were waiting to forget. But CJ was different. He was waiting to remember. That face, for example. That face in the mirror. Colors swirling in glass. Tones and textures painting a portrait of a severed head.

Whose head?

His eyes closed, his world folding in and out of darkness until hurrying steps brought him back to light. Different steps. Not the hospital staff. Doctors and nurses padding around in sneakers and sensible shoes. Those were everyday steps going about their business. Hardly worth the listen. But these steps were driven. Boots and heels. Clickety-click. These steps had a goal, and nothing was going to get in their way.

The door opened and she swept into the room, dumping flowers on the dresser and propping a satchel against the nightstand.

"It's me again," she said, taking his head between her hands and angling it up so he was looking directly at her.

He shuttered once. Another snapshot. Auburn hair cut in a bob, goofy smile, and freckles like raw sugar, tumbling off her nose onto her cheeks.

The mystery woman.

In CJ's mind soup, she was the constant.

She let go of his head and slid onto the chair.

"No change, I see."

She picked up her satchel and rummaged inside.

"They told me not to expect the Hollywood movie version. But if I'd had any idea…" She pulled a phone out of her bag and flicked her finger over the screen as she continued. "In the movie, the beautiful and brave woman—that would be me, by the way—sits by the hero's bed. He's comatose, like you were when they wheeled you in here. But she's patient and loving. Like I am. She holds his hand and croons soothing words." She grabbed his hand. "Like this. And sure enough, it all pays off. The hero's eyes pop open. He's lucid and coherent. And thank God for that, because he's the only one who knows the secret that'll save the world." She waited. She always did. But there was nothing happening on CJ's end. No twinkling eye. No wrinkling brow. So she went back to the phone and he went back to the mirror, where the head was now dripping blood onto the flowers.

"The real-life script has a few more pages," the mystery woman continued. "After the coma comes PVS—a persistent vegetative state. That's doctor-speak for potatohead. Although that's not a word I'd use in front of them, so don't quote me. They tell me that talking to you like this—rambling on as I do—is beneficial." She looked up again. "What is it with you and that mirror?" She pulled his head back towards her. "I don't like to be rough. But no pain, no gain. You're a soldier. You know the routine." She tapped her phone. "Today's goal is one more point on the Glasgow Coma Scale. You're a number eight. Moderate. One more point and you're a *Mild*. So what I need from you is"—she consulted the phone again—"*confused conversation*. I think we can manage that, don't you?"

She edged the chair closer and leaned forward, peering into his eyes like an ophthalmologist checking his retinas before thumbing through more pages.

"We've had *incomprehensible speech*, two points—that's basically just groaning—you excelled at that. And we've had *inappropriate speech*—although I think that 'you wankers' merits more than a miserly three points. In some parts of Dublin that would pass for articulate speech."

His eyes flickered. Bits and pieces adding up. Something happening. The face in the mirror was part of it. And the woman's voice. Not the words, but its music. The lilt of it. The soft tone and sinuous threading. Something was weaving all these things together. It was the sun, splashing the woman with light and spilling it all over the bed. That puddle of light and the throat and its blood. Echoes and images were sparking forgotten pathways and breathing new life into numb neural networks. But then it was all gone. It was all too much. His eyes closed and his chin eased down onto his chest.

"CJ. Come back." She stood up. "Is the sun too strong?" She shaded him with her body and squeezed his hands. His eyes opened, lingering on her face before darting around the room like a newborn baby sampling the forms and colors of a strange new world.

"That's better. Beautiful. Eye movement. Listen to me, CJ. I've seen the scans. They had to patch some bits and do some rewiring. But you've still got enough of that gray mushy stuff"—she tapped his head with her knuckles—"to be halfway normal. The problem is the software. Too much bad data jammed up in your buffers. If you were a computer, I could reboot you. But you're human, so it's more complicated."

She went to the window and was drawing the curtains when a sound stopped her.

"Bagre…"

She whirled around.

"What? Again."

His eyes rolled into the sunlight bathing her silhouette.

"Bagde…"

"Baghdad. Holy Mother of God." She rushed back to the bed and held his face between her palms. "No. It's not Baghdad. It's Surrey. You're home." She shifted her hands aside, framing his withered face.

"Surre."

"This is an official miracle. Wait." She whipped out her phone. "That's not confused conversation. That's oriented. Four points. Well, not quite. The patient knows who she/he is, where she/he is and why, the year, season and month. That's too severe. There are plenty of people walking around out there who couldn't handle that one. But you've got the where. So let's go for the who. What's your name?" She waited, her face drifting closer to his.

"We're going too fast. Let's start with an introduction like we've just met. My name is Enya O'Brien. Do you recognize me? I'm Declan's sister. His twin. Not identical. He always used to say that he got the brains and I got the beauty." She made a clown's face, but it drooped into a frown as she glanced over at the call button. "I should tell the doctors. You'll be needing medication or tests or something. But let's nail this orientation thing first. I'm going to start recording now." She fiddled with the phone. "So what is your name?" She waited, fidgeting.

He swung his eyes back to the dresser, to the mirror and its head, and she followed his interest.

"You like the flowers? The colors?"

"Alex?" His voice was faltering, testing itself as much as querying the object shimmering in the glass.

"No. Your name is not Alex. That's confused conversation. Two points. We did that months ago. Hold on."

She took off her leather jacket and used it to cover the mirror, and she dropped the flowers on the floor at the foot of the bed, where he couldn't see them.

"Now let's try again," she said as she settled back in the chair. "What is your name?"

"Alex." His voice was clear this time. No doubts.

"Forget Alex. He was the other one. The American. Poor man. I shouldn't be the one to tell you. But he's dead."

"Deh." He stared at her as she fiddled with her phone, his mouth open, his jaw slewing off to one side.

"I've turned off the recording. Let's take a shortcut. I'm going to tell you who you are. We can rehearse it a bit. Then I'll turn on the recording and we can pretend it's all happening live. It's a bit sneaky. Like reality TV. But that's the world we live in. Everything's fake. Your name is Christopher James. CJ for short. CJ. Got it? My name is Enya. So what's your name?"

"Alex." He called it out like a summons, twisting back to the covered mirror. Enya leapt from her chair, caught him by the chin and dragged him back.

"He's dead, I'm telling you."

"Alex?" His voice was muted now, her words filtering into meaning, but one that made no sense.

He went quiet after that.

She glanced at the call button. But as she went to use it, he jerked up off the pillows.

She yelped and hopped back, hands at her mouth.

He was crawling out of bed, his limbs tangling in tubes and wires. She grabbed him and pushed him back down and they struggled until he fell back exhausted.

"My poor darling," she comforted him, stroking his forehead. "Your friend Alex died in that room with my brother. And so did everyone else."

More fragments of meaning. Pieces of a jigsaw. But still no box top to make sense of it. CJ's body melted into the sheets and his eyes blanked over. Enya stepped back. Nothing else to do now but call the doctor. She dropped her phone in her satchel and was about to do just that when the bed jolted. It actually moved, shaken by his body, rattled as if in some invisible hand. She reached out to touch him, to calm him. But he knocked her aside, his tremors morphing into spasms and foam streaming from his nose and mouth. The bed frame groaned and shook as the cables and tubes that had nurtured his life snapped out and whirled above him like angry snakes. Enya screamed, a wailing summons for doctors, nurses, someone, anyone. Then she pinned herself against the wall and fumbled for the call button, locking it down tight and closing her eyes.

TWO

Six Months Later

The door was open, so CJ walked right in. Not so easy for a big man on crutches. More like right side first, swinging one crutch through the doorway, then sidestepping like a crab.

Doctor Sam was studying a computer screen, her face loaded with concentration. "Hey." She looked up and broke out a smile, studying his movement as he shunted across the room and eased into the patient's chair. "Good job," she said, settling back and waiting while he arranged the crutches on the floor. "I got your request."

"And?"

"Do you think you're ready for the street?"

"In a few weeks. When I get my legs back. Why not?"

She nodded as if he'd made a good point, but followed it up with a sigh that said something else.

"Tests okay?" He was dreading the answer. Blood, scans, samples—there'd been months of them. He was desperate to get the update even though it was certain to be a good-news-bad-news bulletin.

She checked her computer while his eyes roamed her cluttered desktop, landing with a thump on the plastic brain at its center. The brain was mounted on a stand, modular, with different-colored sections numbered with black digits in white circles. It was a brain built for teaching, a perfect brain—unlike his own—easy to pull apart and slot back together. It was the sort of brain she could use to explain things like why he couldn't feel anything he touched.

"Excellent," she said. "The physio is off the charts."

That was ducking the question. He already knew the physio was working. He could see the results in the mirror. His muscles were bulking back to normal and his face was filling out.

"What about the psych stuff?"

"Encouraging," she said.

Nicely put. The E-word. All by the book.

"Off the charts the wrong way," he said, thinking out loud on purpose, dangling half a question like a baited hook.

Doctor Sam was lost in the computer screen, but she didn't miss the hook.

"Physio is easier to measure. That's all." She pointed at the screen. "All I see here is progress. Trust me."

No question about that. He trusted her. It was Project CJ that made him wary. Ever since he'd come back from the dead, he'd been a guinea pig with a team of stakeholders that read like the expert speaker list at a neuroscience convention.

She turned to the brain on the table, and he edged forward as she disassembled it piece by piece. "You have no unilateral neglect. No apraxia. That's trouble organizing your movements. No agnosia. No trouble recognizing familiar things. Like a toothbrush. I hear you're even shaving yourself now."

"I have been for weeks," he said. "And I'm wiping my own arse too."

She stopped in a freeze frame, red number two suspended in space. "I'm sure the nursing staff are so disappointed."

She stifled a giggle, leaving CJ to figure out why. He hadn't meant it as a joke. Humor was one of the many social interactions he was still struggling with. He'd meant it as a point of information and her repartee caught him off balance. He stared at her, disoriented. Then it came to him. He'd made a joke, albeit unwittingly, and they shared a welcome laugh.

"So here's where we are and how we got here," she said. "Bullet fragments and splinters of steel. Some of it couldn't be removed. So your brain healed around it. Vision, hearing, touch." She held up the relevant bits. "Each of the five senses links to a zone, and these multisensory areas blend all the data together with balance, time, and proprioception—that's how we orient ourselves in space. We call the result a percept. We use it to figure out the who, what, and where of our situation."

"I know who I am and what I am." He spread his arms. "And here I am in this room with my doctor. My only problem is…" He was going to say touch, but he might have said blank spots in his memory, or confusing memories with dreams. He might have said a lot of things. But none of them was the only problem. His eyes drifted down to the bits of plastic on the table. "When my brain healed, what went wrong?"

She stepped out from behind the desk and took his hand in hers, holding it up like an exhibit. "Look at these knuckles. They aren't normal. This thick shiny skin here"—she ran her finger over the scar tissue that joined all four of his knuckles into a single cicatrix—"how did you get it?"

"Practicing martial arts. Punching a lump of straw called a *makiwara* every day after school."

"Damage. That's how you got it. Damage and healing. The body self-repairs. It adapts and remodels. And not just the skin, but the bones too. If I scanned your hand, I'd see microfractures that healed, making the bone denser, stronger." She went back to her chair. "Skin and bones are very good at self-repair, but the brain isn't. Growing back brain cells is one of medicine's Holy Grails. Even today, we're only at the stage of trials and experiments. But in your case, you were in a military hospital with its own rulebook and you weren't expected to live."

"So they took risks?"

"They removed some brain tissue. They cultured it and injected the cells they'd grown back into the damaged areas along with an ambitious cocktail of drugs."

"Like stem cells?"

"Not exactly. My guess is that it contained D-cells, doublecortin-positive cells. They're similar to stem cells but behave differently. In recent experiments, they've used them to repair damaged brains, with remarkable results."

"Experiments? On trauma victims like me?"

She hesitated. "Human brains are similar to monkey brains in that—"

"Monkeys? They're only testing it on monkeys now,

and eight years ago they tried it on me! Where does that put me on the evolutionary scale?"

"But it worked. Your brain healed. Only like your hand, it remodeled itself. It adapted. Stronger and faster in some ways, but problematic in others."

"So where am I now? Is the healing done and dusted?"

She pointed at the computer screen. "That's not what these results tell me. Your brain is continuing to grow skills and efficiencies. Your hearing and vision are so remarkable we had to repeat the tests, and your dexterity and coordination are extraordinary." She threw up her hands. "That's why we need more time."

So this was it. Not the graduation ceremony he'd hoped for. More like a half-term report card.

He pointed down at the brain bits.

"Why didn't the touch part heal?"

"It did. Physically it's intact. But somewhere along the line, your body adapted to pain by ignoring it. Painkillers like morphine don't block pain. They just stop you suffering from it. Somehow your nervous system is actuating similar pain tolerance, but it's also interfering with these other sensations. Cold, hot, tickle, itch and so on."

A file on the desk rattled and she snatched a phone from under it. She glanced at the screen, then tossed it aside.

"Sorry," she said. "I turned it off. But it has this emergency thing. If someone keeps calling, it puts them through."

"Maybe it's important."

She shook her head.

"We could try hypnotherapy," she said. "And I could teach you how to use self-hypnosis."

CJ liked that idea. He was done with drugs and here was something that put him in the driver's seat.

"Could it help me remember too?"

"You don't have amnesia. Remember what?"

"That last day."

It had been troubling him from the start. He could play everything back like a video from the day they were taken hostage. But that last day was patchy and hit a blank screen when Alex had a knife at his throat.

"It's probably for the best," she said. "Self-protection. You buried it and tossed away the map."

"Can you help me find it?"

"Why?"

He shrugged. He didn't have an answer. But that didn't make it any the less important. They always got to this point when he pressed her. He wanted to explain why the events of that day were so important. But every time he tried to put it into words they choked up in his throat. Anger? Guilt? He didn't know why. But whatever was doing the choking, it was the one thing that could still hurt him.

"Thanks for everything." His mood shifted, suddenly frustrated, done with it all. Doctor Sam. The hospice. He reached for his crutches and struggled to get out of the chair.

"Stop." She jumped up.

He let go the crutches and they clattered to the floor. That was so undoctorly. The way she said it— blasting it out like a friend or a lover, like somebody who actually cared.

"Your sanity is the issue. You have to build your own route back to these memories."

"But it's taking so long."

She picked up a file and shuffled through its pages.

"If I help you, will you stay longer here?"

He nodded.

She pulled a note out of a file.

"I was contacted by someone in the Foreign Office. Julian Ashford." She looked up. But CJ shook his head. "He's put in a written request to see you a number of times, but I've always denied it on medical grounds. He called me again last week. Some sort of follow-up. Box ticking, I suppose. He knows more about that last day than I do. All I have is medical reports."

"Thanks, Doc."

CJ reached across the desk and as they were shaking hands, her phone rang under his arm. He picked it up and passed it to her, noting the caller ID was a single word: Him.

"Why don't you take the call?" he said. "We're about done here."

"No," she said. "There was something else important."

"I can wait," he sat back down.

She hesitated, then walked out the door and headed down the corridor. CJ levered himself up with the help of the chair and after looking at the crutches, he tried his luck without them. His goal was the bay window overlooking the gardens. He slid along the desk before stumbling and falling onto its broad windowsill. They were just baby steps, but they were important. Another triumph. He looked out the window at the winter sun filtering through gray clouds, then down at patients jogging behind a physio, doing gentle laps around the pond. He tapped on the window, but no one looked up.

There were piles of magazines stacked at each end of the windowsill. He checked a few, their covers trailing contents with teasers like *5 Ways to Improve Lithium Tolerance*. He set them aside and pulled himself up against the wall noticing a framed photo hanging there. A family shot. Mother and father standing like bookends on either side of two kids. The girl was a younger version of Doctor Sam and the boy was obviously her brother. He towered over her. Military. Not in uniform. But CJ had no doubts. Her arm was snaked around his waist and she was leaning into him, sheltering under a thick arm laid like a cape across her shoulders. Their faces were alive with the soft edge of sibling love. Her lost brother. No idea why, but CJ knew for a certainty that he was on the other side with Alex.

He looked around the office. Just the one photo. No shot of her own family. No picture of Him and their brood of kids. The family whose welfare was now the topic of a testy exchange down the corridor. He didn't like to eavesdrop, but there was no real choice. Doctor Sam was right about his hearing. His post-trauma world was a jungle of sound, his refurbished brain switched from single to multitrack and the power button amped up to max. Their conversation, like their marriage, seemed to be winding up, so CJ hurried back to his chair. He didn't want her to see him stumbling and falling. He made it just in time, catching the corner of the desk and sliding along it until he could flop into the chair.

Doctor Sam apologized for the interruption and made an excuse about a family emergency. His instinct was to tell her to dump her husband and be done with it. But he kept his mouth zipped. It was none of his business, and she would read his comment as another example of his socially inappropriate behavior. He'd been told about that. Warned, even. It was a symptom of his PTSD, she said, a reflex of his retread brain and its iron-man scaffolding.

He waited while she fiddled with the controls of her chair, adjusting the seat and muttering like it was the major problem in her life. All theater. And not very convincing. CJ wanted to tell her to have a good cry. But he kept quiet about that too.

"You okay, Doc?" She looked up and flashed him a game face before sorting out papers on her desk. "I'm really looking forward to working with you on the hypnotherapy," he said. "And I want to thank you for everything you've done for me. I know I'm a lucky guy."

She stopped fiddling.

"Thank you, CJ."

"Was there anything else?"

She leaned back in her chair like she didn't need notes or bits of a plastic brain for this part.

"According to your sister—"

"My sister?"

"Half-sister, I mean."

Whole or half, any fraction of sister was news to him. But he let it go. There was only one candidate for his sister role, and he had no need to ask who it was.

Enya!

"She told me that you're still getting those…" She paused, scouring her doctor's dictionary, no doubt, looking for the kindest word.

"Delusions?" he suggested to help her out. "Hallucinations?" He had to say something, anything to mask the stream of anti-Enya abuse wobbling in his throat and looking for the exit. The sister lie, he could live with, but sharing confidences with Doctor Sam was an outrage. He'd told Enya everything—the medicines he was skipping, the tests he was faking. Worse yet, the H-word. Hallucinations. This wasn't about dodging medicines or faking tests. This was the biggie. Seeing the dead. He'd lied about it, telling her that it was all in the past.

"I see we made adjustments to your dosages last month." She was peering at her computer screen. "I thought that had done the trick." CJ kept quiet. "I'm talking about Alex."

"It's not a big deal."

"Can you see him now?"

He thought about lying but then nodded.

"Where is he?"

"He's standing next to you. Just to your right. He's reading my test results on your computer, and that's not so easy when you're decapitated. Even for a Marine. So he's dangling his head in front of the screen, and it's dripping blood on the keyboard."

Her eyes swiveled towards the computer, dragging her head shakily in their wake until she caught herself and snapped it back.

"Do you believe in ghosts?" she said.

He shook his head. He was never going to fess up to that. He was a Marine, a ghost-maker, not a believer. There had to be a scientific explanation.

"What about the metal stuff in my head? Could that be acting as some kind of antenna, picking up signals?"

"I'm not following. Radio waves? Like FM. The BBC."

"Not exactly."

"Then what?"

There had to be a good way to put this. CJ glanced back at the brain, but that didn't help.

"I read that psychics have solved murders by contacting the dead. So what if..." He stopped short, pulled up by the horrified look on her face, and let her finish the sentence.

"What if you've been transformed into a psychic? You're asking me—a psychiatrist—if shrapnel in your head could be picking up radio waves. Like Instagrams from the dead?"

CJ winced. Laid out like that—clinical, cold—it sounded crazy. And there was worse to come.

"Cee-Jay." It was just one word said quickly, but she stretched it into two that seemed to go on forever.

Splat!

Reality 101.

There are no ghosts.

She went back to her computer, and CJ went back to shrinking into the fabric of his chair.

"Impressive CV," she said. "Special Boat Service. Combat. You saw men die." She looked up at him like it was a question.

He nodded. Barely perceptible.

She went back to the screen. "And some you killed?" This time she didn't wait for a response. "Have any of those turned up in your life lately?"

"I get the point."

He was ready to move on, but there was no chance of that.

"Are you straight?" she said.

He stared at her as if her question had been addressed to someone else. But she waited him out, staring right back.

"As in gay?" he said finally.

"I'm your doctor. Knowing these things helps me."

"You're asking me if Alex was my lover?" He tried

to say the word with a straight face, but it was hard. Alex was shaking one fist and waving his head around with the other. CJ tried to read his lips, but it was tough with it bouncing around like that. Something along the lines of…

Your goddamn what!

"Did I say something funny?" she said.

"Not at all." CJ shook his head. Without Alex's performance to clue her in, she'd obviously read his reaction all wrong, and he was eager to sort that out. "I've served with gay men. No worries about that. It's just that Alex wasn't one of them. We were mates. That's all. Buddies. We met in the Iraq War, when the US Marine Expeditionary force was put under the tactical command of 3 Commando Brigade. I was a serving Royal Marine officer back then."

"So how did you both get to work for the same security company?"

"I got an invitation to join Tratfors from another Brit, an ex-army officer called Masterson. Alex was back in California at the time. There was plenty of money to be made. So I called him."

"You invited him back to Iraq?"

He'd never thought of it like that. The implications. But now she'd said it, the what-if at the heart of her question was spelled out for him in neon.

"Are you okay, CJ?"

He nodded, struggling to stay in focus.

"So you worked together as a team in Iraq?" she said.

"We were in CPP. Close Personal Protection. Taking care of VIPs. Me and Alex and two Boers. South Africans. We were a team."

"And you were all taken together?"

He nodded again.

"What happened to the South Africans?"

"We were separated. They were killed some months later."

She waited. A solemn beat. But not to respect the dead—he could see that. She was figuring out how all this patched into his reformatted brain and fueled his Alex "hallucination."

"Do you ever see the South Africans?"

He shook his head. "Just Alex."

"How about the men you killed? Any ghosts?"

"Just Alex."

"Starts to make sense, doesn't it?"

"Only if you're God. Or a psychiatrist."

"These apparitions—do they trouble you or comfort you?"

"They clear my head. They remind me that someone in the Iraqi administration leaked our visit that day. Everything. The identity of the VIP. The nature of his job. The exact time we were due at the ministry. How else could one hundred Shia militia with vehicles, guns and cop uniforms show up? That's not exactly spur-of-the-moment stuff."

"So how do you feel about that person?"

"If you could bring him into the room here with us, I'd be delighted to show you." He pointed down at the crutches on the floor. "Legs or no legs."

Doctor Sam's face clouded over, and CJ cursed his lack of control. Anger was fine so long as he could keep it on the inside, driving his motor. But showing it off to Doctor Sam was a no-no, another sidebar in his medical report, another milligram or two of something to hide under his tongue.

They left it there, with Doctor Sam recovering her

cheery face and hitting a few upbeat chords as she keyed in her notes. CJ thanked her and hauled himself up on his crutches. He crabbed his way through the doorway and shuffled along the corridor with Alex striding solemnly at his side, his head resting on his palm with the fingertips of his other hand holding it steady. It reminded CJ of a statue he'd seen in some old church on a school trip to France.

Back in his room, CJ lay on the bed, closed his eyes and played the meeting with Doctor Sam back like a video.

The medical stuff was interesting. A bit scary in places. And the monkey part was a bummer. But all that was coded communication. What Doctor Sam was really telling him was that all those doctors and scientists were guessing. They had no idea how he'd gotten like this, or where he would end up. He was a New Age Columbus, a psych-sea navigator, lost without a compass. At least she'd been honest. He wasn't part of an experiment. He was the experiment. But what about Alex? Could he really be a concoction of CJ's own brain, a spectral fusion of guilt and busted synapses? CJ doubted it. If Alex was just a hallucination, then why were his visits so rare and always chosen to coincide with important events?

Julian Ashford.

That was today's event.

Someone from the Foreign Office, she'd called him.

After all these years, they were sending a spook to debrief him. She'd written it off as box ticking, but she didn't know Her Majesty's Government like CJ did. To her, it was the benevolent nanny who took care of us all. To CJ, it was more of a wicked stepmother with a strict set of rules that you broke at your peril. This was no box-checking exercise. More like an agenda. And with multiple requests driving it forward, it had to be a priority on the to-do list of someone very important.

He pulled himself up off the bed and made it to the dresser without crutches in a single wobbling step. He was reaching for the TV remote when he noticed a note on his scratchpad. *Panorama 8.30.* He picked it up and stared at it. No question. It was his handwriting. But he had no recollection of writing it. He looked back suspiciously at Alex, who shrugged and tapped his watchless wrist, then pointed at the TV. It was almost 8:30, and the BBC's flagship investigative journalism show was about to begin. CJ turned it on, stumbled onto the bed and settled down to watch. It was news alright. But not news to CJ. Foreign aid, corruption, fraud. It was the same old, same old. They quoted 28.9 billion dollars as the running total for Iraq. That was a lot of zeros—and a few more than CJ remembered—with little or none of it traceable. The report followed a journalist swaddled in Kevlar as he was hustled by anxious security agents from one perilous rendezvous to the next. CJ followed it all with professional interest, noting the latest crop of Iraqi politicians, jostling for a piece of the pie. They were all recycling drain-the-swamp speeches scripted by the crooks they were replacing, and CJ was about to doze off when a snatch of video jolted him wide-eyed. It was some new politician arriving at the ministry building where they had been taken. He drove into the square and headed up the steps surrounded by security, pausing and turning towards the camera to deliver a soundbite.

That was their square, their steps, their ministry.

The news story continued, signing off on the segment with a footnote about their own hostage taking ten years earlier.

"That's us, mate," CJ said. "Not even a page in a history book. Just a bleeding line and a half."

He switched off the TV. The program had triggered an echo that he couldn't get out of his head.

Doctor Sam's question.

So how do you feel about that person?

He'd shot back an angry response. But even then, he'd downplayed it. The unedited version was homicidal. He'd sworn it to Alex. He was duty bound now. No wriggle room. Not that he wanted any. He just wanted to get on with it. But all these years down the road, could he still make good on his promise?

He crawled down on the floor and lay on his back. The first step had to be recovery, getting his strength back and getting out of the hospice. He pulled his heels up to his buttocks, crossed his arms on his chest and did crunches until he was too weak to lift his head. It dropped back on the carpet and his eyes closed, his thoughts patching in and out before fading to dark... *spooks, secrets, Alex.*

THREE

One Month Later

Catching up. It was a full-time job for CJ, and his new laptop was his launchpad. He was hunched over it, sitting at a tiny desk in the corner of his room. He could have done it much sooner by using the computers in the library, but there were too many eyes down there—nosy eyes—and he wanted privacy.

The world he found through the laptop's lens was still recognizable, but in the years he'd been AWOL, it had rebuilt itself. New technologies and new rules. But most especially, new gods. Social media had been in its infancy back then, and smartphones hadn't been half as smart as the computers now lining everyone's pocket and purse. He browsed through pages of new gadgets and technologies before moving on to politics and major events. He already had the big picture from the TV news, but he wanted to drill down on the detail. It was all interesting stuff, and he soon had plenty of fodder for a lively debate in a pub. But CJ had more important catching up to do. He wanted a snapshot of the kidnaping and the events around it. According to Declan, his job had been to update the accounting software to stop the thieving. So CJ started by compiling a list of potential scammers made up of the Iraqi politicians and administrators who'd been running the show at that time. But he soon gave up. There had to be a better way. The list was infinite. Besides, there was someone far more interesting he needed to check out.

CJ Brink.

He typed his own name into Google and scrolled through the results. There were a lot. Mostly tabloid newspapers and social media comments calling him a hero.

Bravo!

No complaints about that. But he was looking for details. He wanted the fine print on what had happened that day and how he'd been found. His appointment with Julian Ashford was pending, and he didn't want to walk into it like a dummy. He was thinking about that meeting, as his eyes scanned the search results, when he noticed a disclaimer at the bottom of the page. It said that some search results had been removed due to EU Data Protection Law. That was something else new.

He copied and pasted it into the search bar, and thirty minutes later he was an expert on the right to be forgotten, an EU law empowering individuals to get search results about them removed. That was all well and good. But he hadn't asked anyone to remove his results. So who had asked and why? He did the research. Google had a removal process, but it wasn't algorithmic. It involved human judgment on an application made by an individual, but not necessarily the individual. That gave it flexibility according to Google. So maybe a UK government letterhead might work, or a statement signed by a doctor.

But why?

He took his wallet out of the jacket hanging off the back of his chair. Money was no issue for CJ. His bank accounts were still stuffed with the rich pickings of his dangerous but highly paid profession. So all he'd had to do on his recovery was get new plastic. He checked out some security blogs before signing up to a VPN, a virtual private network based in Switzerland that touted its independence and no-logging policies. Minutes later, he was in the USA—at least his IP address was—and he was drilling through additional pages of results. But as he scanned through page after page, he realized that what he was really looking for was something that he hoped never to find. That video. The one recorded by Hussein. The one of Jahil sawing through Alex's neck.

Could it possibly exist?

The camera had been rolling, but what had happened to it since? Had it died that day along with Alex and everyone else, leaving nothing but the shot-up laptop? Or had it survived, rescued by insurgents and posted with pride on some dark corner of the internet? He switched the search to video and went for it, trying different keyword combinations, using Alex's name as well as his own. But that video was nowhere to be found. Either it didn't exist, or the security services had gotten hold of it and buried it in a top-secret archive. He was disappointed, but he was relieved too. He'd come a long way since his minestrone mind soup days, but they weren't so far behind him that he could take chances with his sanity.

He checked his watch. It was Saturday afternoon and Enya was due. She came every Saturday as a rule, but he hadn't seen her for over a month as she'd been working in the US. It was tough for him to admit it, but he'd missed her. He was about to shut down the computer and head downstairs when he noticed some Arabic scrawl at the bottom of the page and he clicked on it.

No. It wasn't that video.

Not the one he was looking for. But it was more than good enough to do the same job—to fire his rage and steel his determination. Some Iraqi bystander must have captured it with a phone. It was just a snatch. Twenty seconds or less of jerky images, blurring in and out of focus.

CJ was running. He was in a debris-strewn street of bombed-out buildings. He was soaked in blood, the white of one eye barely visible in the red mush of his face. In one hand was a Kalashnikov and in his other was the severed head of Alex Solo, held by a scruff of his hair. Alex's teeth were bared in a snarl and his eyes were wide and sparking with incongruous life.

CJ stiffened up, his fists balled, his heart exploding as a groan rippled up from his guts into a deep-throated roar. In an instant, he was back there, and that same feeling hit him, the force that had fueled his strength that day.

Save Alex. Kill 'em all. Never stop.

He snapped down the lid on the laptop and leapt to his feet. He was sweating, wet with it. For a moment, he thought it was blood and the flashback ran in his head. He stumbled backwards on his newly reconstituted legs, knocking the chair aside and grabbing the dresser to catch his fall. He struggled, determined not to lose it, digging back into the strength he'd found that day. He pulled himself together and was cleaning himself up when he recognized a familiar sound, filtering it out of a myriad of noises. A car engine. Nothing special about that. But this was the one he'd been listening for, the gutsy growl of Enya's souped-up Mini Hatch. He threw on his jacket and went downstairs to meet her. He'd made great progress since he'd last seen her, and he was looking forward to showing her what his new legs could do by taking her on a brisk walk around the grounds.

She was still outside parking the car when he reached the reception area, so he went to the desk to talk to George. He was one of two receptionists who alternated the early and late shifts. He had his head down, fiddling with a phone in his lap, his face hidden by curtains of black hair. CJ would have known it was George from the other end of the corridor as the sticky aroma of potent pot oozed out of his pores.

"Hey, George."

"CJ." He looked up and tapped his phone. "Chelsea are playing."

CJ leaned over the counter. "I've got a favor to ask. Can you print me out a list of all the visitors I've had since I've been here?"

"I can tell you now. It's a list of one. Your sister."

"No, I mean way back. Those first weeks. Before they all knew I was in a coma." CJ had made some great friends in the Marines, and some of them had surely come by. But there was a more compelling reason to get that list too. He wanted to know if any government types had come calling.

"Okay. Sure." He nodded at Enya as she pushed the doors aside and strode into reception.

CJ and Enya hugged each other, full of smiles, then headed outside. As they walked, Enya talked about her trip, and after a few circuits of the grounds, they sat on a bench by the pond. It was a genteel moment, and CJ was enjoying it. Too bad he had to wreck it. No choice about that. First there was the sister thing, lying to the staff. Then there was the Alex thing, shooting her mouth off about his "hallucinations." He had to bring it all up, but he didn't want it to degenerate into a confrontation. It was such a lovely afternoon. So somehow, he had to transition from this genteel moment to a prickly one and get back to genteel without any broken bones. That was the challenge. The prickly part was unavoidable. Months of Enya O'Brien had taught him that. Freckles and smiles she had aplenty, but all that was camouflage. Underneath it, she was Ms. Pushback, and whatever he started, she was bound to finish.

"Why do you keep looking at me like that?" she said, suddenly aggressive and he hadn't even started yet.

"Like what?"

"Sliding your eyes over me like a crocodile sizing up its next dinner. It's creepy."

He grunted out a blast of air like a boxer heading into the twelfth round. He hated that, the way she read him like he had a public announcement scrawled on his chest.

"It's your goddamn mouth."

"What?" Her hand darted up, fingers hovering inches off coral-pink lips, her face clouding with confusion. But then it dropped away and she looked him in the eye.

"To hell with you. I was right to tell her. It's not

normal to see a dead person. Even your best friend. Wake up! Your mind's not right. You shouldn't lie to your doctors. It's plain stupid. You should thank me for looking out for you."

"That's what sisters are for, isn't it?"

She did a double take on that before her eyes drifted away to the pond, where a drama was playing out between angry ducks.

"I had no idea you were comatose when they brought you in here. I wanted to ask you about my brother, but the receptionist—it wasn't George—it was that blond bitch with the permed hair, the one who looks like a refugee from a sixties girl band. She said to me *only relatives are permitted*, and she said it like... *piss off, Irish*. So I told her I was your sister, and she said... *he's an orphan and an only child*. She was calling me a liar. No other way to put it. That's when I became your half-sister, and even then I had to browbeat her into submission. And after all that—what a letdown. You were a potatohead."

"But you kept coming back?"

"I had no choice. I made the mistake of asking your doctor about your prognosis. And she was like... thank God, a relative. All sorts of questions and decisions. About a year later, some pen pusher wanted to pull the plug on you to save a few measly pounds. So they asked me for permission. And by the way—I said no."

"Really?"

"No, I made that part up. But I would have said no. And the half-sister stuff is true."

"But it's still not enough to explain why you kept visiting me all these years."

"I'm Declan's twin. The day he died I didn't even know he was dead, but I fell ill. They thought I'd had a stroke. I posted a selfie online with one of the nurses as soon as I came around. You can check the date on it if you don't believe me. You don't have a sister or a brother. You can't even understand what it means to have a sibling. Never mind a twin. We had our own language. When I started a question, he'd finish it. When he thought something new, I'd say why not before he even opened his mouth. Part of me died with him. That's how it feels, and I can't accept it. You were the last person to see my brother. You're all I have left of him."

CJ nodded and let it lie. If he pushed her any further, he'd be seeing the back of her for the last time, and he didn't want that.

"I'm meeting a guy from the Foreign Office next week," he said.

She snapped her head around. "A spook?"

"I'll get their report. All the details."

"Suitably redacted, no doubt."

"Why do you say that?"

"You tell me. You're the conspiracy theorist. Treating me like I'm some kind of Mata Hari. You want a conspiracy? Then ask him how one hundred Shia militia moonlighting as police knew exactly where you were and when you'd be there."

That stopped him in his tracks. It was like hearing an echo of his thoughts.

"I had a different question in mind," he said.

"Like what?"

"Like finding out who in the Iraqi administration had the most to lose from Declan plugging the leaks in their accounting software."

"So you knew what he was doing?"

"He told us. More or less. Millions of dollars a week

were draining out between the zeros and ones. So he was installing some kind of fix."

"And you think the Americans would be stupid enough to tell the Iraqis what he was doing?"

"They had to know. Surely. It was their ministry."

"They were expecting a routine upgrade. That's all. They were purposely kept out of the loop. The allies had gone down that road already. They'd sent a team of Iraqi accountants to the UK to train them in forensic auditing. After that, the thieving went up exponentially. They had effectively trained them to steal better. Besides, it was impossible for anyone in the Iraqi government to know."

"Why?"

"Because Declan was planning to fly back here to the UK from Afghanistan the day you picked him up in Iraq. He only agreed to take the Iraq job while he was waiting in the departure lounge in Kabul. I know it for a fact because I was planning to pick him up at the airport, and he called me to cancel. Tratfors switched him from that commercial flight to London to a military charter to Baghdad."

CJ thought back to the sequence of events that day. They'd picked Declan up from a military flight. That was true. And the next day they'd gone to the ministry, which was closed for some religious holiday. It was last-minute for them. It always was. But he'd assumed it had been all planned in advance for Declan.

"When you picked him up that afternoon," she said, "did you know that you were headed to the ministry the next day?"

CJ shook his head.

"So you didn't know, Declan didn't know, and no one in the Iraqi administration knew. But one hundred militia knew. You want a conspiracy, forget me. Smoke that one."

She was right. That changed everything. That list of Iraqi politicians he had so carefully compiled was a worthless sheet of paper. It had always seemed like everyone in Iraq was bent. He couldn't count the times he'd escorted engineers to fix oil pipelines cut by the same people who were demanding compensation for losing their oil supplies. Oil scams were everywhere. But they were petty compared to the white-collar crimes. Accountants. The guys who counted the money. Who shifted it from this column to that with zeros getting dropped here and there and mysteriously reappearing who knows where. That was big money, and with Declan O'Brien plugging up the holes it was natural to assume that the tip-off had come from some local guy on the take. But now there was a new prime suspect, and it was a cardboard cutout of someone inside the UK or US defense or intelligence establishments. They both sat in silence, eyes on the still life landscape of the pond. It made no sense. Why would allied intelligence set up a player on their own team?

Unless…

"They found a memory card in his pocket," CJ said.

"Declan?"

He nodded.

"That'll be it. Your spook friends. That'll be what they're after."

"It saved your brother from the knife. When they found it, they switched him for Alex."

"Didn't matter much in the end, though, did it?"

"He made a deal with them. I thought he'd seen me trying to escape and was pitching them some bullshit to buy time."

"What kind of bullshit?"

"The card was encrypted. He said he'd show them how to get into it. Jahil wasn't buying it. So Declan tried with Hussein, switching to Arabic."

"You speak it?"

"Not enough."

"Do you remember what he said?"

"The English bits. Washington. The CIA. Stuff like that. He said he'd give them the password."

"And did he?"

"I don't know. It was Arabic and I was working on the cuffs. Then all shit broke loose. Alex started singing the US national anthem, and Jahil went for him. I broke free. Something hit me and it all went blank. But I kept on going somehow."

"Nothing else?"

"It was Arabic mixed with computer jargon."

"Like what?"

"Canary. Is that an IT word?" She took her time, her face wrinkling and her eyes darting from one side to another. "What does it mean?" he said.

"It's a detection thing. Like a canary in a mine. When the gas leaks, the bird dies first. It's a trap to catch hackers or people sniffing around in places they shouldn't be."

"Was that his job, installing canaries to catch the scammers?"

"I have no idea. But even if it was, why would he tell them? Why would terrorists give a damn?"

"He said it a few times too. It sounded like cat and canary. I thought it was about us. Like birds trapped in a cage."

"Sounds like he was delirious. Or else you were.

Either way, I'd skip all that stuff when you meet the spooks. You mention the CIA, secrets, and passwords and they'll swing you by the balls until they break off."

"I doubt it. Nobody gives a damn about the Iraq War these days."

"All the same, I'd plead brain damage and take the Fifth."

"You want a coffee?"

They squeezed in one last lap of the pond, then made it back to the cafeteria before dark. Enya went to their table, the one where they always sat in the corner by the window. CJ fetched two coffees and two butter croissants from a wall of vending machines, surveying the room while he waited for his change to drop. There was just one couple seated at a table dead center. The man's back was stiff, and the woman was reaching across to him, her hands wrapped around his. No words. Eyes intense. Another sad story unfolding in a storybook room of tea and cakes. CJ gave them a wide berth as he threaded his way back through the tables to Enya. Then they too sat in silence, pecking at their croissants and sipping their coffees. She supped hers in micro-sips, elbows on the table, the mug inches from her mouth, hands wrapped around it like an oriental cup with no handle.

CJ felt good. Better. Talking about it had helped. That last day. The axis day. When his life had turned on a roll of dice. And the rest of their conversation had turned out better than expected too. The prickly part. She'd lied to get into the place, but the half-sister story made sense. Or half-sense at least. And she was right to challenge him for questioning her motives. How could he second-guess the love of one twin for another? The circumstances of her brother's death were traumatic, and she wanted answers. It was natural. A woman as smart and willful as Enya was never going to accept the waffle churned out by government spin masters. CJ was her only hope of getting to the truth. Too bad that it was buried under bits of metal inside his head. So that left just one topic unresolved between them. Something they never talked about. The something that was happening between them. Every time they met now, they had a disagreement, a squall that soon blew itself out, followed by a contented silence as some odd emotional redrafting edged them closer together.

But where was it all going?

"Don't you have a life?" he said. "A boyfriend?" It wasn't meant to come out like that. Jagged and ugly. But there it was again. Sublime thoughts minted in crude coinage.

"Does that pass as flirting in your world?"

He reached across the table and tweaked the gold heart hanging from her neck. She knocked his hand away and held the locket up, her eyes swiveling down on it.

"I was fourteen. Insanely drunk. And an uncouth pig of a boy..." She trailed off. "You know the rest. So Declan caught me crying about it the next day. He hugged me and told me jokes and made me laugh. He bought me this and told me that a man with a golden heart was waiting somewhere for me and all I had to do was find him." She dropped the locket and gulped the rest of her coffee, suddenly in a hurry. She gathered up her satchel and gave him a sisterly kiss on both cheeks.

"You can get back to your room okay?"

He nodded and she turned to leave, but he snatched

her hand and pulled her back.

"Thanks for coming."

It took her a while, and he was ready for a sassy rejoinder. But it never came. She smiled and ruffled his hair. Then she zipped up her leather jacket and left.

He watched her through the window as she made her way in and out of patches of lamplight, through the garden and into the car park beyond the trees. He listened as her car door shut and its engine fired. And he followed the sound of it fading into the matrix of night noise. The silent couple were still there, sharing some loss. CJ couldn't remember what exactly and he didn't want to. There was too much loss around this place. He desperately wanted out. To be out there amongst everyday people with everyday things to lose. Jobs, opportunities, lovers. Not arms, legs, testicles, minds.

"Alex." He jerked back, his chair screeching on the tiled floor. Alex was right there, sitting in Enya's chair with his head resting on her empty plate, his blood soaking into the crumbs of her croissant.

CJ glanced at the silent couple. They were still holding hands across the table, but now they were staring at him. CJ coughed and adjusted his chair like that was what he'd meant to do all along. But then he gave up the charade. It was all too important to worry about what anyone else thought. He hadn't seen Alex for weeks, and Enya's explosive revelations had shaken him. In Iraq, Alex had been his wingman, and now he needed him more than ever.

"The militia? Who told them?" he said, his voice a hard-edged whisper. "MI6? The CIA?" He waited, but there was no answer. No sonorous voice booming from the grave. Alex just knitted his eyebrows and shrugged. CJ balled his fists and squeezed them against his face. There had to be a way to communicate with Alex. If he could see him, then why couldn't he hear him?

A solution came to him suddenly like an epiphany.

Or was it a memory?

Yes… it was a memory.

They'd done it before. They had actually communicated. They'd used a coin. The more he thought about it, the more the details flooded into his head. CJ had stuck the coin up against a door and Alex had held it there, suspended as if by magic. They could do the same thing against the glass. They could work out a system. Affirmative and negative. CJ could pose questions and Alex could move the coin accordingly. He dived into his pocket and took out a coin, jamming it against the glass.

"Ready," he said. "Just hold it steady when I take my finger away." Alex's head floated up off the plate, his brow furrowed, his mouth agape. "One, two, three. Go."

CJ took his hand away and the coin fell and bounced off the windowsill. CJ and Alex both watched it roll across the table and drop onto the floor, where it weaved around checkerboard tiles and scribed a wobbly circle before falling flat at the feet of the silent man. He looked down at it, but he didn't move. CJ looked back at Alex, but he was gone. Of course he was. Doctor Sam was right. He had never been there. He was just a 3-D image cast by a projector in CJ's mind. And there was worse. He'd never used a coin to communicate with Alex before. That was nonsense. It was a scene in some movie. It took him a moment to remember. Ghost. With Patrick Swayze and Demi

Moore.

His stomach heaved and the room swirled, with the silent couple staring crazily at him as he danced around them on a carousel horse. He closed his eyes, hiding behind squeezed-shut lids until the worst of it passed. He levered himself up off the table, stumbled out into the corridor and leaned against the wall, his arms shaking. The corridor was empty. Not just empty. Void. No people. No ghosts. Just CJ Brink. Survivor. A loneliness engulfed him, stealing his breath, its strangling fingers reaching for the root of his sanity.

Knock, knock.

The door was right there. All he had to do was open it and step through and he'd be home free, comforted in the blessed arms of madness.

He cracked his head on the wall. Hard, loud. Its echo reverberating in the empty corridor. The movie thing had happened before. Scenes from movies showing up in his head like memories of a personal experience. The root cause was dreaming, according to Doctor Sam. The brain consolidated memories while dreaming, and CJ had binding and linking issues that resulted in his dreams and memories getting mixed up. The movie thing was a side effect of that. In Iraq, they'd had no internet at first, just a DVD player and a limited number of DVDs. So they'd played the same twenty movies over and over. Doctor Sam's theory was that scenes from those movies had showed up in his dreams during his prolonged vegetative state and gotten hard-coded as personal experiences.

He pulled himself off the wall and dragged his mind back on track. He had the truth now. It was someone on our side. But who and why? CJ strode down the corridor, taking bold, confident steps. He didn't know who had tipped off the militia, and he had no idea how to find that out. But he did know what was coming their way. Something to sweep away the cold loneliness that had pinned his back to the wall. Something to keep him alive and sane. Something warm.

Payback.

FOUR

The conversation was on the terrace. Not heated, but intense. Bodies forward. Elbows on the tabletop, hands almost touching. A man and a woman. A couple. But a long way from lovers. More like a well-drilled team.

The man sprang up as CJ approached, all smile and bonhomie. He had pouchy jowls and a sharp nose, so the smile was quite an event. They shook hands and he introduced himself as Julian Ashford. Then he presented the woman.

"Alicia Colby."

"Hi."

One word was enough. American.

She stayed put. Almost. Lifting her butt an inch or two as she offered him her hand. She was younger than Ashford. Thirties. With soft features and a measured smile, and she took her time about that handshake, stony eyes never leaving his.

CJ sat between them, taking the seat with a view, looking out over the lawn towards the pond and up at a feeble sun skulking in clouds. Ashford followed his gaze, taking in the parklike grounds.

"Charming place," he said.

CJ gave him a look. Charming was not his first choice of words. His eyes drifted back to the path by the pond where an orderly was walking a paraplegic soldier in a chair.

"I guess we should talk about the weather next," Colby said, perking her smile up and nodding at Ashford.

He turned to CJ and winked. "She's taking the mick out of us locals. It's her first month at the US embassy in London and she's still getting used to our ways." They both chuckled about it like their exchange was part of an ongoing joke. It was all very awkward. And it didn't get any better. They spent the next five minutes asking him about his health as if they didn't have access to his confidential medical records. It was all theater, a performance calculated to put him at ease, all part of a plan. But that was okay. He had a plan too and putting up with their bullshit was part of it. Make nice. That was the first-act plan. He needed two things, and the first was information. Later, in Act Two, there'd be plenty of time for the second—confrontation. And Ashford was setting the stage for that perfectly with all this fake bonhomie coming across like broken fingernails scraping on a chalkboard. He was saying something about CJ's heroism and exemplary service record when CJ raised his hand, palm out like he was stopping traffic.

"Who are you people?" He wanted it to sound friendly, but from the look on Ashford's face, it must have come out more like a challenge to visiting aliens. "MI6?"

"Gosh, that makes me sound so important," Ashford said. "I was in Iraq when you were taken, so they thought I might be useful in helping you get back on your feet."

That was all the answer he was likely to get, so he took it as a yes.

"And you?" He snapped his head at Colby.

"I was in Iraq too. An MP in Baghdad. I was there at the hospital when the surgeons sawed open your skull." She waited. CJ leaned back in his chair. This was more like it. "They cut out a piece of bone about yay big." She measured it with her index finger and thumb. "They did that because your brain swelled so much it was sticking out of your head. They figured you for a Humpty Dumpty. I guess you know what that is. But they took their best shot. They cleaned as much junk as they could out of your head. Pulled bits of lead out of your belly and chest. Shot you up with God knows what, then sewed you up." She shook her head. "It's hard to believe that you're the same guy."

"We're lucky to have Alicia," Ashford said. "When she left the military police, she got a liaison role at the US embassy in London. She was part of the forensic team, one of the first on the scene."

CJ took a closer look at her. An MP. He should have picked that out. Those watchful eyes, hoovering up every detail, and that athlete's body hidden discreetly in a loose-fitting pantsuit.

"Where did they find me?" He aimed the question at the American.

"A ditch. You were unconscious." She looked over at Ashford and he nodded some sort of approval. "You had both arms wrapped around the head of Alex Solo." CJ's eyes dropped to the table, reaching into the gap but finding nothing. He remembered Alex on his knees with the knife at his throat. All he had after that was the video he'd found online. He had no recollection of a ditch. But it wasn't difficult to connect the dots from the crazed and bloodied runner with a Kalashnikov and a severed head to a half-dead body in a ditch.

"And the site that I ran from?"

"We found Alex's torso and five bodies there," she said. "We'd like you to talk about that if you can."

"I have memory issues. I was hoping you could tell me. You worked the forensics."

She hesitated. Cops never like giving information. All their reflexes are geared to getting it. But then she said, "O'Brien and two unidentified insurgents had multiple gunshot wounds, inflicted by .308-caliber rounds. We found one gun in the room, and one with you in the ditch."

"Who did I kill?"

"I don't think it's that simple," Ashford said, his voice cut with alarm. "There was a fight, bullets spraying everywhere."

"He's right," Colby said. "The bullet trajectories were consistent with random fire, like a weapon discharged in a struggle for its possession."

"Even so. My gun. Who got hit?"

More silence and sharp looks.

In the end, the answer came out of Colby.

"All three of them."

CJ nodded, his face drifting down to the tabletop like he needed a moment to deal with it. And he did. He needed to make another futile effort to remember and also to shoo away the shadow of guilt. He didn't shoot O'Brien. They'd fought for the gun, and Declan had caught a bullet in the chaos. He had something else to think about as well. Act Two was pending, and this information was a gift. All he had to do was work it into the script.

"Is that how it was written up?" he said. "I've got no liability for O'Brien's death even though my gun killed him?"

She shook her head. "Absolutely not."

"Perish the thought, old chap." Ashford reached over and patted him on the shoulder. "We're on your team. We're here to protect you, not blame you."

CJ acknowledged his gratitude with a dip of the head. "And what about the other two insurgents?"

"Hussein Ahmed," Ashford said. "He was on our target list. A recruiter, propagandist. Their computer guy. His neck was broken."

"And Jahil?"

Another logjam.

Why so timid?

Most likely Doctor Sam had put the squeeze on them. Conditions, promises. Stern lectures about his fragile mind.

"The details aren't important," Ashford said. "Jahil Hazem was the number three most wanted terrorist in the world and you killed him with your bare hands. That bastard is now rotting in hell. Bloody good job. Well done."

"It was close-quarters combat," Colby said.

CJ was about to raise the curtain on Act Two when a man appeared carrying a tray loaded with tea and cakes. VIP service. That was new too. Ashford poured the teas and inspected the cakes while Colby kept her eyes on CJ.

"Why don't you talk now?" she said. "Anything you like. Start anywhere. End anywhere. We have nothing special to ask." She turned to Ashford. "Do we?" Ashford was lounging back in his chair, a cup and saucer perched on his belly. He was looking bored, like he was watching a game of cricket. He shook his head.

Nothing special to ask.

CJ thought about that. A nothing so *unspecial* they'd sent two intelligence agents, handpicked operatives with detailed knowledge. Colby had stressed her military background to make him feel comfortable, and Ashford had explained her away as working in a liaison role. But she'd obviously moved on to intelligence. And given her military background and the fact that she was hanging around with Ashford, she was most likely assigned to some special activities CIA group. It looked like Project CJ was shifting gears from science research to intelligence operations.

Cue Act Two.

"I have your guarantees." CJ flipped a pointed finger from one to the other. "There's no comeback on me about O'Brien's killing."

"I don't get it," Colby said. "Why would there be?"

"Because I've been lying. I do remember. I've been faking holes in my memory for the doctors. They're not cleared for this." He waited. All eyes on CJ. "They hacked off Alex's head. Then they grabbed O'Brien. They were going to do us all. Three beheading videos. Like a movie festival for fanatics. But when they got O'Brien on his knees, he broke down. It was pathetic. Alex died like a hero. But O'Brien was a coward. He begged and screamed. He promised them secrets if they'd let him live. They didn't believe him. So he whipped out this memory card he'd kept hidden. It was sewn in his shirt."

"Did he say what was on it?" Ashford leaned in

close.

"He said something. I wasn't paying attention. I was working on the cuffs. Top-secret stuff, he said. How they could bring down the government with it. But it was encrypted."

"Did he give them the password?" Colby said.

"Give it to them? He wrote it down for them. They took off his cuffs and he wrote it down. He became their best mate. After Alex gave his life like that. I was enraged. That Irish bastard was ready to throw us all under a bus to save his own skin."

"So what happened?" Ashford said, tea and cakes forgotten.

"With all this distraction, I'd been able to get my hands free. I grabbed a Kalashnikov off one of them and blasted. I made sure I got that son of a bitch O'Brien first. I got two more until they were on me. That's the last thing I remember. Based on what you say, it must have turned into a brawl and Marine training saved the day."

CJ watched as his unexpected confession worked its way through their systems like a mega-dose of narcotics. They didn't move. They didn't react. They just stared at him. CJ helped himself to some tea and a chocolate cake. "I suppose you were wondering about it all," he said, wiping chocolate from his lips with the back of his hand, "because you must have found the note with the password as well as the card."

The numbing effect of his startling revelation was beginning to fade, and Ashford and Colby were coming back to life. They looked at each other, then back at CJ, but said nothing.

Ashford's phone buzzed. He checked the screen, then left them on the terrace and walked around the lawn, poking in a message with one finger, leaving CJ to wonder about the timing of that call.

It was quite a coincidence.

Could it be that the wicked stepmother was listening in to their conversation?

Almost certainly.

Colby had recovered her composure and patched up her poker face. "Tell me about the run-up to the job," she said, shuffling her chair closer to CJ.

"We picked O'Brien up at the airport, and we went to the hotel bar that night and had some beers with him. The next morning, they woke us up at five thirty and told us to take him to the ministry."

"Who's they?"

"Sami. The interpreter. But he was just the messenger. Masterson was our boss. He showed up when we were kitted up. It was a quiet day. No gunfire. We were in Toyotas. Beat-up Land Cruisers like the locals. The Boers were in front. Me and Alex were behind with Sami and O'Brien. There were a couple of guards outside the ministry. Sami showed them our paperwork and we went right in. Alex and me. And O'Brien. The Boers stayed outside on point."

"And Sami?"

"He came inside with us."

Ashford rejoined them. He seemed distracted, fiddling with his cup as he topped up his tea. CJ was glad he was back. He was just killing time with Colby. He needed both of them there for the final scene.

"The militia showed up about an hour later. That's the mystery part of the story. Sixty minutes to rustle up a hundred guys in police uniforms with Kalashnikovs and vehicles. Some sort of record that."

So that was it. He'd said it. Casually enough. And it

was still half an inch shy of an accusation. But Colby read the subtext like it was on a billboard.

"You think you were set up?"

"What would you call it? Coincidence?"

She glanced over at Ashford, who shrugged it off.

"They must have been on standby," he said. "They knew O'Brien was coming sooner or later."

"Who's they?" CJ said.

"The Iraqis. The government. It was their ministry. Something leaked out. Is that what you're saying?"

"They didn't control the timing. You did. So who did you tell?"

It still wasn't an accusation. At least, not an explicit one. Not taking it word by word. But CJ laced it with aggression, and it hit Ashford with the jolt of a hangman's noose.

"CJ." Ashford arranged his elbows on the table and leaned towards him. "You were a distinguished officer in our armed forces. And although you were working for a commercial agency when this happened, as far as we're concerned, you deserve all the support you'd get if you were still commissioned…" CJ let him drone on uninterrupted, and he'd gotten to conspiracy theories and something about kicking them into the long grass when Colby interrupted him.

"It's a can of worms," she said, her hand reaching out to touch CJ's arm. "Word got out. That's all we'll ever know. So many years down the road—it's not the time to open that can."

"Did O'Brien tell you about his assignment?" Ashford said.

"Sure. He was installing canaries. Software traps to catch the scammers." CJ shot the answer out, delighted to recycle his newly acquired IT jargon into a fresh batch of bullshit. They exchanged a look loaded with innuendo. "Then the Shia police walked in. But softly-softly. Like it's no problem. Alex spoke a bit of Arabic. More than me. But we weren't getting anywhere. So we went outside to find Sami."

"I thought he went inside with you," Colby said.

"He'd gone outside for a smoke. But when we got down there, he was nowhere around. It was just the Boers. And suddenly we've got a hundred guns pointing at us. We were disarmed and bundled into the back of a van. Then we got split up in three groups. The Boers, me and Alex, and O'Brien. He was taken off by himself. We were moved every few days. We never saw the Boers again. And we never saw O'Brien until we were swapped."

"What happened on that day?" Colby said. Now all the questions were coming from her. Ashford had lost interest, his mud-colored eyes flitting around like his mind was elsewhere. It occurred to CJ that these two might be on the same team, but shooting at different goalposts.

"They drove us for hours," he said. "Then they pulled us out of the van and took off our blindfolds. We were in an open space between bombed-out buildings. O'Brien was there already. Then more vans showed up, driven by Sunnis. They dragged out a bunch of Shia militia prisoners. Nine of them. And they traded them for the three of us. So we ended up as prisoners of Al-Qaeda instead of the Shia militia." He looked back and forth between them and shifted his chair, about to get up. "Is there anything else? I have a physio session."

"Just one more thing." Colby stopped him. That hand again. MP training. Firm this time. "Enya

O'Brien. She's been a frequent visitor."

It was a comment, but they were both expecting an answer.

CJ smiled. "I think she fancies me."

Colby slid her hand off his arm. "And what girl wouldn't? But it's strange. Especially in light of what you told us about her brother."

"She doesn't know about that. She's not responsible for him. I felt sorry for her. So I lied to her. I told her he was a hero. What I told you—that's for your ears only." He pointed at Colby. "You told me they'd be no comeback."

"And there won't be," Ashford said. "No one's going to open an enquiry. Forget that."

"It's an odd situation, though," Colby said. "You were hired to protect her brother, but he was killed. And yet she befriends you and even lies to the staff here to get close to you."

"She wanted to ask about her brother, and they wouldn't let her in. So she was a bit sneaky about it."

"So many visits," Colby said. "And so many years. I'd call that motivated, not sneaky."

"What did she ask you about her brother?" Ashford said.

"Just how he died. They were twins. Carbon copy DNA. It's natural. Why are you so interested?"

"We're just concerned about your welfare," Ashford said. "You're safe in here, but—"

"You're kidding me." CJ stood up, scraping his chair noisily back over the tiles. "I survived the Iraq War, covert operations behind enemy lines, and years of Al-Qaeda's hospitality. Plus, I got my brains blown out and grew them back. And you think I'm going to get slotted by Freckle Face."

"She's a woman with an agenda," Colby said, stabbing her point home with a jab of her index finger. "You can trust me on that."

"Thank you both for coming," CJ said. "All points noted."

He felt their eyes drilling into his back as he walked off the terrace. Enya was right. Their nothing special was the memory card, and he had to thank her for that. She'd inadvertently given him the Act Two gambit. The moment she'd said, "You mention the CIA, secrets, and passwords and they'll swing you by the balls"—that was when he got it. That was exactly what he wanted them to do. Or at least, take their best shot. It was the only plan that made sense. If the suspects were inside the US/UK intelligence community, then they were untouchable. He'd have no chance of sniffing them out. He had to flush them out. That meant taking risks and going on the offensive, and today's massive disinformation dump was the opening salvo. As expected, it had knocked them sideways. Even Colby had maxed out her incredulity seismometer. As for Ashford, CJ had read it all over his face… *this guy must be brain-damaged to make a confession like this.* Exactly. It was perfect casting. He'd wanted to come across as angry and confused, but naive and trusting. Someone with a damaged memory who was still recalling way too much. A cannonball rolling loose on the deck. First they'd worry, then they'd plan. Exactly what direction those plans would take depended on what they knew about the card and on whose desk his disinformation dump ended up. He was counting on the guilty party having no choice but to stop that cannonball.

There was a van outside the entrance with

something about medical waste written on it. CJ turned back there to check the terrace. Ashford and Colby were gone, replaced by a thrush finishing off the cakes. Inside at the reception desk, there was a delivery man showing some papers to Enya's friend, the sixties girl band reject. The delivery man was brandishing a dispatch note while the receptionist was digging into emails on her computer. CJ wanted to know if George had left him the list of visitors he'd asked for. He was going to interrupt her—it was a simple question—easy to answer. But she'd probably report him for being rude or disrespectful or—God forbid—inappropriate. So he went back to his room, where he was changing into his gym kit when he heard a car start up. He glanced out of the window and saw a Ford Mondeo leaving the parking lot with Ashford and Colby on board. He noticed the van he'd seen downstairs too. It had pulled up at the end of the building, and two men in baseball caps were hauling a medical waste bin down a ramp. CJ knew what it was because it was written on the side in huge red letters. CYTOTOXIC WASTE. He had never come across the word cytotoxic before, and he wondered what it meant. It sounded terrifying, the last trash bin in the world anyone would poke around in looking for a leftover sandwich. He made a mental note to check on its meaning and made his way to the gym. But ten minutes later, in a heavy sweat on the rowing machine, the note was already forgotten and his thoughts were revisiting the charade he'd played with Ashford and Colby. A job well done. Now all he had to do was catch the first bugger who made a grab for his balls.

FIVE

After dinner, CJ passed by reception and picked up the visitors list. George had removed Enya's visits, so the list was short. Eight names, with the most frequent visitor being Phillip Masterson, the Tratfors man who had run their unit in Iraq. He'd visited every year in January, and on each occasion he'd left a note to be informed if there was any change in CJ's condition.

Phillip Masterson?

That was a surprise. They'd been friends. Sort of. But not buddies. They'd fought in the same war. And they'd been part of the same security team, although Masterson's role was invariably administrative as in *anywhere but the firing line*. CJ had always felt that Masterson looked down on him because he'd come up through the ranks, whereas Masterson was "officer class." Class wasn't supposed to mean anything in modern Britain, but for people like Masterson, it still meant something. CJ speculated about his motivations. A regular visit. Once a year. Maybe it was a legal thing. Insurance papers that needed a signature, something like that. CJ made the call. Phillip was out. This was explained to him by a woman with a posh accent who broke away from their conversation twice to tell someone called Ophelia to leave Snuffly alone.

CJ left a message that he would call again and moved on down the list.

Six friends. It was a sad commentary on his life. All of them from the war. He got through to three of them, the ones who had left numbers that were still good. All three conversations followed the same pattern. A joyous moment when they realized who was on the line, followed by incredulity that he was still alive. It was all sincere stuff and CJ didn't doubt any of it. Voices and names that took him back to a warmth of camaraderie he'd all but forgotten. That was followed by invitations—no dates, no times—just a stream of *we must meet up and we must do this*. But then, he'd hear voices in the background. Wives, sons, daughters. And their tone would change, and the conversation would drift away from the good old days and bounce around real-life topics. The school run. Parenting. Pregnancy. He'd taken a snapshot of the world with his laptop that morning, and he'd learned that it had moved on. These old comrades had done the same thing. So everything was left as it was, warmth and amity intact, with promises to meet that everyone knew were made to be broken.

He turned on the TV and watched journalists raging about Brexit and the US president's Twitter feed, but he soon got bored. So he muted the sound, closed his eyes and worked through the self-hypnosis routine he'd learned from Doctor Sam. By this point, he'd learned it by heart. All he had to do was throw some switch in his head and he could hear her voice. Not her normal speaking voice—this one was deeper, warm and frothy like a cup of hot chocolate on a cold winter's night. It led him down to a river and he walked by its waters before turning off into woods filled with sunlight. His legs swished through banks of wildflowers until he reached a giant oak tree with a door in it. He opened the door and went down a spiral staircase inside the tree and into a room where he sat at a table with a glass of milk and a saucer with two pills on it. One blue, one red. This was the creepy part, a page from one of those spooky Alice books. He finished off the session and tested his sense of touch by scraping the remote on the soft skin of his belly. There was definitely some improvement. He could sense something more, the beginning of tactile. All he had to do was keep at it.

Where's Benjie?

Benjie was the night nurse, and he was late.

CJ got off the bed and opened the door. Benjie's medication cart was tucked against the wall outside his door. But there was no sign of Benjie. Maybe he'd forgotten something and gone back for it. CJ left the door open and sat on the bed to wait for him. He'd be back soon enough to serve up CJ's late-night supper of three pills. Then they would reenact the same routine they went through every day. He'd give them to CJ and turn away to check his handheld computer while CJ faked taking them. Benjie was responsible for ensuring that all patients took their medication, but after several confrontations with CJ, they'd worked up this box-checking charade. CJ's room was at the end of the corridor on the second floor. So he was the last stop on Benjie's nightly round, and after he palmed the pills and slugged back a mouthful of water, they would hang out and talk soccer.

CJ heard wheels grinding in the corridor.

That was odd. The medication cart was already there. He got up to check it out but stopped when a face appeared in the doorway. A face he'd never seen before.

"Mr. Brink?"

CJ nodded.

Who else?

The man was British. That was even more odd. A British male night nurse. They had to exist theoretically, but CJ had never met one before. Benjie was a Filipino and like all the other nurses he came from an agency staffed exclusively by Eastern Europeans or Filipinos. Plus, this guy wheeled the cart in, then shut the door. *Why?* Benjie just brought in a paper cup with the pills.

The man rolled the cart up to the bed and broke out a cheesy grin.

"Where's Benjie?" CJ wanted it to sound like friendly interest—not a challenge, but the way the guy looked at him, he knew he'd gotten that part wrong.

"Flu." The man picked up a computer. "The agency sent me instead." He poked the screen with his finger. "Your usual." He passed CJ a paper cup.

CJ checked its contents.

The usual alright. Three pills. Pink, white and green.

The man was still fingering his computer.

"I've got to give you a shot too."

"I never have shots." CJ set the pills aside on the nightstand.

The guy noticed, but he said nothing. He just popped out that cheesy grin again. "Another war hero who's afraid of needles." He smirked, pulling out a tray with a syringe in it. "It's all been prepared by your doctor." He ducked down and pulled out something else from a lower shelf, a folded white cloth, stiff like a starched napkin. He laid it on top of the cart, picked up the syringe and flipped an air bubble out of it. All very professional.

"Right or left?" He swung himself around the cart and towered over CJ.

"I don't care." CJ rolled up his sleeve. It wasn't the needle that concerned him. It was the queasy feeling in his belly. This was all wrong, but he couldn't put his finger on the why of that.

"I promise," the man said. "You won't feel a thing."

Amen.

And that was another thing. Here was a nurse with his medical record in front of him who didn't know he had no sense of touch.

CJ straightened his arm and the man checked his veins.

Here we go.

"Do you know what cytotoxic means?" It came out of nowhere. Totally random. A challenge question like a sentry in an old-time war movie. CJ had no idea what the answer was. But surely a real nurse would know.

The man jerked back and his cheesy grin blanked over. His head spun down, eyes on the cart. The starchy napkin. His hand went for it. And that was where it all fell into place. The profile. That stern mask of a face. CJ had seen it before, wearing sunglasses and a baseball cap. This was the driver who stayed put in the delivery van while his partner sorted out the paperwork. The man drove the needle at CJ's throat and grabbed the napkin with his other hand. CJ batted away the needle and kicked up between his legs, slamming his shin into the man's groin. He dropped the needle and arched over, and CJ thumbed him. Both hands. Thumbs like spikes right up into his eye sockets. The napkin and something heavy clattered to the floor, and the man stumbled back. CJ tackled him, his shoulder colliding with the man's hips and crashing him into the wall. There was no follow-up, other than the crunching sound of the man's head against the wall.

CJ stepped back, panting, pleased with himself. He was still out of shape, but he was getting it back. He looked around the room. The unused syringe was lying on the floor, and there was a pry bar close by the fallen napkin. He checked the guy for a pulse. It was strong. He'd be back on his feet in minutes. Groggy, but still dangerous. CJ fetched the syringe and crouched next to him. He cleared the air bubble again. He didn't want the man to die of a stroke brought on by a gas embolism. Whatever was in that syringe, he wanted to see a live performance of its effect. He straightened the man's arm and slapped the elbow joint to bring up a vein. It was easy. The guy's heart was thumping, and CJ soon had a fat vein pulsing. He snicked it with the needle and emptied the syringe. Then he went back to the bed and waited. One minute. Nothing. But two minutes never came. Halfway through that second minute, the man kicked out with one leg like he was shooing away an inquisitive animal. Then his body stiffened and went limp. CJ checked his pulse again.

It was gone.

Wow!

No other word. CJ sat on the floor and thought back to the morning's theater on the terrace. He'd wanted a reaction, but he'd been thinking more along the lines of an urgent summons delivered by four large men in tight suits who stumbled across him late one night on a dark street. That would lead to a meeting in a country house with some old boy right out of a John Le Carré book, someone way up the food chain from Ashford and Colby. He'd offer CJ a glass of fine malt, and they'd talk about its peaty heritage before playing a cat-and-mouse game of who knows what.

But this?

It was inconceivable that this dead assassin was linked to his provocative lies. There was no way it could be connected, for a host of reasons. Timing, for one. The cytotoxic van would have needed to be parked outside the hospice while they were talking on the terrace. Ashford's coincidentally timed call was suspicious. But the idea that they had assassins waiting in a van outside the gates was ridiculous. Those lies were a bushwhack. They couldn't possibly have foreseen them. Besides, Ashford or Colby might have been in Iraq at the time, but it was most improbable that they were part of a conspiracy back then and also spearheading a debrief ten years later. And if that wasn't enough, there was the sheer gall of it. This was not MI6's style, and certainly not their operational area. This was England, not some anything-goes foreign place like Baghdad, or France.

CJ stood up and checked the corridor.

Nobody. Silence. Just the usual buzz of late-night TV shows coming through doors down the way. There was only one oddity—a wheelchair right outside his door. He looked back into the room, piecing it together. Plan A was the needle. CJ would be found dead in the morning. No sign of foul play and not too many questions. He was, after all, a guy with brain damage who'd spent years in a coma. The pry bar and the wheelchair had to be plan B. If CJ refused the shot, he'd get whacked on the head before getting the shot. But that crack on the head would need too much explaining. So he'd get poked in the wheelchair and stuffed into a cytotoxic bin. If plan A worked, the next morning, the hospital staff would find CJ's dead body and a missing Benjie. If CJ's death was found to be natural, then they'd think that Benjie had panicked and done a runner. Or if they suspected foul play, then they'd blame him and the cops would go looking for him. CJ thought back to the exchange between the receptionist and the van driver. Something about an email. They must have hacked into the hospice's mailbox and posted an official-looking delivery notice. Hardly rocket science. Half the hospitals in the UK had had their computer systems hijacked by ransomware earlier in the year. Dumping a fake email into a mailbox would be simple for these guys.

He went back to the man and checked his pockets. He found a phone, but he couldn't get past the PIN. Grateful for all the catching-up studies he'd done, he grabbed the man's hand and stuck his thumb on the Start button, and he was soon combing through his messages. Today's job was being done for a client identified as the Duke. He checked back through previous messaging cycles and flashed on the call sign Tang0, the military code for a target, written with a zero at the end instead of the letter O. That had to be the signal for mission accomplished. *The target has been zeroed.*

He took the chance and sent the word in reply. After that, he took his time. And it was way into the night when he pushed the wheelchair down the corridor to the elevator. The TVs were silent, the corridor in darkness, with motion detectors popping lights on and off as he passed. The world was sleeping. There was no overnight medical staff other than the night nurse, and the CCTV in the dormitory corridors had long since been disconnected, following incidents linked to big-brother paranoia in disturbed patients.

In the basement, he wheeled the night nurse along an avenue of gurgling pipes and boilers. He'd never been to the basement before, but the geography of the place was obvious. The hospice was built on a hill and at one end, as the gradient fell away, the basement squeezed out from under the building and was used as a delivery and loading zone. CJ pushed open its access door and stepped onto the loading platform, where he found the two cytotoxic waste bins. They had small wheels at the back and handles at the top so they could be wheeled like a dolly.

CJ checked the first one. No surprises. Benjie's eyes were wide open, looking up at him through the dim light. He'd been folded up like a contortionist and jammed butt first into the bin. He'd been strangled. Some sort of bloodless garrote. And there was a chemical smell drifting up out of the bin. Chloroform or something similar. CJ closed the dead man's eyes. The poor bastard had a wife and kids in Manila living off his paycheck, and now he was about to disappear. CJ closed his bin and locked the seal. Nobody would find him. It was a beautiful plan. He had to give them that. No one was going to look in those bins. That was the awesome power of cytotoxic. No one knew what the hell it meant, and no one but CJ Brink wanted to find out. He dragged the fake night nurse from the wheelchair and stuffed him unceremoniously into the second bin. He dropped the spent syringe in after him and sealed it shut. Heading back to the second floor, he left the wheelchair at the night nurse station, returned the medications cart, then went back to his room. It was a mess. So he tidied it up and lay on the bed.

One thing was clear. His days at the hospice were over. Someone had tried to kill him. Not good. But they'd failed, and their failure was a blessing. The adrenaline rush of combat had left him surging with energy. He'd done good. He'd been slow and labored about it. But somehow the right action at the right time had bubbled up through layers of busted brain.

He slept fitfully and was waiting by the window when the first staff arrived in the morning, the catering crew, braving the last of the winter's night to get the kitchens fired up for breakfast. Then came the admin and medical staff, arriving in dribs and drabs. It was all as per usual until shortly after the late-rising sun appeared, when the routine was broken by the cytotoxic van collecting the bins.

Tang0 had worked.

He watched the van leave the grounds and disappear beyond the trees. With no car, he didn't have much choice about letting it go, and until he got out of the hospice, he didn't have much choice about being an easy target either. Whoever set this up had huge resources, and this failure wouldn't faze them. They'd just try again. Rinse and repeat until he was cleaned. And the next time, they wouldn't underestimate him. They'd make sure they got it right.

SIX

"Nice color." CJ squeezed himself into Enya's Mini and hunted around for the safety belt.

"Volcanic orange," she said. "Like me."

She dropped the clutch and they zoomed out of the parking lot and onto a blacktop cut between banks of green. CJ shoved aside the shopping bag at his feet, containing his laptop and all his worldly goods, and made himself as comfortable as a big man can get in a small car.

"So, a free man at last," she said. "That was rather sudden. What happened?"

"A miracle. An unexplainable medical event. I just woke up today normal."

"That would be a miracle. So what did Doctor Sam have to say about it?"

The answer was "a lot." But the good doctor had been more concerned about maintaining his treatment and setting up outpatient services than keeping him in the hospice.

"She thinks I'm ready."

"Is the hypnotherapy working?" She reached across and squeezed his thigh. "Feel that?"

"I'm getting there. Bit by bit."

"If it doesn't work, you'll have a hell of a life."

"I'll never feel pain again."

"And you'll never know if you left the stove on until you burn your arse leaning on it. And what are you going to do with your hands when you slide off your girlfriend's pants? Not to mention the other bits. It'll be like making out with a blow-up doll. Only you'll be the doll. Not her."

"Thanks for the reminder."

"I'm just trying to be helpful." Enya pulled out of country lanes and onto city streets. "So where are we going?"

CJ shrugged. He had big plans. But this wasn't a day for big plans. This was a day for small pleasures. He was out of the hospice at last, with a set of wheels rolling under him.

"How about the next pub?"

"Out of the question. You're still on medication."

"I've switched to organic. Real ale. It's full of bio-organisms."

"It's full of something. And so are you."

"Come on, Freckles. I need a beer."

"I'm responsible for you."

"You are not my sister."

"So who else have you got?"

She had a point. But he ignored it, downing the window and flicking his eyes at the passing traffic.

"And don't sulk. Be a man."

"A what?"

"I'll take you to that place in Acton you told me about." She fiddled with the satnav. "What's the address?"

"It'll be a dump. I need to get it cleaned."

"Then my place it is."

"Just one drink on the way."

"Enough with the pub. I need to see how you react to alcohol before we go out in public. I'm not having you go apeshit on me in a pub." She checked him out with a sidelong glance. "And cheer up. This is a great day. We'll pick up some pizzas. I've got some wine at home. It'll be just the two of us. Very civilized."

"Is that what you think? I need civilizing? I'll go apeshit?"

"Correct on both counts," she said, holding on to her straight face long enough to check out his reaction before laughing and punching his thigh. "Lighten up, CJ. Let's have a party. I bought you a present."

"What?"

"It's a surprise."

And so it was. Not the present. That was yet to come. But Enya's place. She worked in IT. Or so she said. But she'd always painted herself as a digital grunt, unlike her brother, the digerati prince. So CJ was expecting something modest, a cramped bedsit, or a scruffy apartment shared with a few roommates. But after threading through the suburban streets around Richmond Park, they ended up in a penthouse with views of London through floor-to-ceiling glass. CJ stood by the windows, his eyes drifting back and forth between the tumbling bundles of gray above and the swaths of green below that fell away to a broad valley nurturing the serpentine Thames and its great city. Enya was at his side, her arm snaked around his waist.

"At night, it's even more magical," she said.

He laid his arm across her shoulders, and they stood

like that for the longest while, bodies oozing into each other like two cells in a petri dish becoming one. CJ was feeling it all and going with the flow. But the thought seed planted by those cynical spooks was starting to sprout. Ashford had rubbed him up the wrong way from the get-go, dismissing him as a brain-damaged grunt. But Colby had impressed him. She knew what he'd been through. She'd taken one look at him and decided to skip the bull. That showed good judgment. And so it was her verdict on Enya that was troubling him.

A woman with an agenda.

The pizzas were cold by the time they dragged themselves away from the window and sat at a smoky-glass table cluttered with pizza boxes, glasses, and bottles of wine. His was red. Hers was white. All sourced from a temperature-controlled cabinet running along the wall. CJ wondered about that cabinet too. Most of his friends were dead, but the ones he could remember had beer in the fridge, not liquor vaults stuffed with auction-grade wine.

"Ashford and Colby say you're going to kill me," he said.

Enya flopped back in her chair, white-knuckling the armrests.

"You're not even joking."

CJ poured her more Chablis and waited while she guzzled it, shaking her head in disgust.

"They think you blame me for your brother's death," he said.

"They're sick. What did they ever do for my brother? Or for you?"

CJ took care of his own glass, swishing the wine around before lifting it to his nose and sniffing it.

Strange, that. He'd never done that before. Was it in some movie?

"I'm not going to kill you. I wouldn't know how even if I wanted to—which I don't. I'm a pacifist by the way."

She stood up unsteadily and fetched a box from the closet. She'd already drunk most of her bottle, and wine was wobbling her steps and reddening up her cheeks.

"No time to gift-wrap," she said as she gave it to him. "I know you were planning to check out the new models, so I jumped the gun."

It was a phone.

CJ swept aside the crust of his pizza to make room on the tabletop and ripped open the box.

"I can't accept this. It's too much."

"I'd like to say you're worth it. But that has yet to be validated." CJ swallowed the rest of his protest and turned his attention back to the phone. "The PIN's 1234. You'll have to change that." She watched as he logged in. "I wanted to test it to make sure I wasn't giving you a dud, so I put my number in your contacts. In your favorites, of course."

They nestled on the sofa and CJ played with his new phone, scanning his prints and downloading apps.

"Get that one." She pointed to an encrypted messaging app. "So we can chat without your suspicious government friends listening in on us."

"Ashford is hardly my friend."

"He came to see me too. Him and his American girlfriend. She's scary. They caught me downstairs as I was coming back in. It was like, *we know where you live, bitch.*"

"What did they want?"

"Answers. About Declan and me. His work. About our company."

"What company?"

"It's just a tax dodge. Everybody has one."

Her phone rang and she checked the screen, then answered it with a theatrical groan. "This had better be good," she said to the caller as she stood up and walked towards the door. "Was this before or after the database synchronization?" She swung back to CJ and signaled a timeout with five fingers before disappearing down the hallway.

CJ set his phone on the coffee table and paced around the room, peeking in cupboards and drawers. Most of them were stuffed with the bric-a-brac of urban life, miscellaneous items not yet qualifying as trash and needing a halfway house as a staging post. One cupboard in particular was bursting, its shelves stacked with DVDs. He checked a few. They were all movies, stacked according to genre. Sci-fi on the left. Romcoms on the right. He smiled. He'd been looking for a hidden agenda, but instead he'd found the bookends of Enya's world. Blowing kisses and blowing up aliens. He checked the bottom shelf. Cables and connectors. And something so strange he had to pull it out to verify what it was. Not a DVD player, but a VCR. And as he pulled it out, a tape slid off the top. It was another movie. But not just an old movie. This one was antique. He read the title with a jolt. *The Cat and the Canary.* The cover dated its vintage with the original movie poster rendered in melodramatic comic book style—an evil green man with his hands at the throat of a terrified woman. CJ opened the box and took out an invoice. It was a 1927 silent movie sent all the way from California. She'd bought it online from some store billing itself as the world's greatest archive of the Golden Age of Cinema. The invoice was dated a week or so earlier, and she'd paid a fortune for courier delivery—more than the cost of the tape. He could hear Enya down the hallway finishing up on her call. He slipped the invoice back in the box with the tape and closed the cupboard door.

Cat and Canary.

It was such a random thing. He'd mentioned it in their conversation by the pond. And it wasn't a lie. Declan had said it. Or something like that. She must have researched the phrase online and zeroed in on this Stone Age movie.

But why?

He was back on the sofa fiddling with his phone when Enya marched into the room, reeling off sentences peppered with obscure IT jargon and familiar Anglo-Saxon expletives.

"Forgive me, CJ, but part of my job is to babysit men who get paid as much as me—and sometimes more—for knowing half as much. It grieves me to bail them out time and again."

"All forgiven," he said, papering over his suspicious thoughts with a jolly tone.

"You want a coffee?"

CJ nodded and they went into the kitchen, where he left her at an espresso machine and went in search of a bathroom.

All the doors off the hallway were open—all except one, a door by the entrance with a key in the lock. It looked like it might be a closet or a cloakroom. CJ turned the key and peeked inside. It was a room alright. But only just. Sized like a walk-around closet. A room sitting in half-light behind shades, a room humming quietly to itself.

CJ slipped inside.

The source of the humming was a cabinet in the corner of the room. It was glass-fronted and temperature-controlled like the gourmet wine rack. But this one stored a different kind of treasure—industrial-strength computers, heavy-duty geek hardware, slabs of metal with winking lights, the kind of special computers they use to run the internet.

He slunk out, securing the door at his back with the key. The next room was an office, or at least thinking about being an office. It was partially furnished in oddly contrasting styles as though someone had started with one design concept and abandoned it for another before giving up undecided. The centerpiece was an antique bureau, all dark veneers and gilt-bronze hardware, and sitting on its green leather top was a silver laptop, sleek and incongruous. The only other furniture was a steel-framed bookcase in battleship gray jammed up against the wall like a certificate of incompleteness, empty save for a seated Buddha smiling from the top shelf. Enya's bedroom was the next stop on his tour. It was a snapshot of the other Enya, the one he hadn't met yet. No tomboy iconography here. No gender-neutral nothing. This was a girl-cave gone crazy. Its bed was a patchwork of hand-crafted throws and rugs, its dressing-table landscaped with bottles and jars like a cosmetic Manhattan, and its nightstands stocked with Italian and French fashion magazines. It was a room apart from the rest, like a personal niche she'd carved in someone else's apartment. Most likely Declan's.

When he got back to the lounge, Enya was curled up on the sofa cradling her coffee.

"What are you going to do?" she said as he walked into the room.

He sat a few feet away and supped his froth, wiping the excess off his upper lip with the back of his hand.

"When?"

"Now. After. Whenever."

He supped some more, wondering what he could tell her. They were bound at the hip, their fates spliced together by pain and loss. She had to be a part of his plans. No question. But how could they work through this whiff of mistrust that surrounded them?

"You can stay here if you want," she said casually like she was offering him another cup of coffee.

"You've only got one bed."

"What are you—ten years old?"

"That's not it. I'm still a bit messed up…"

"You mean the touch thing. We can work on that. You'll be a bit out of practice. But all you need is a blue pill in your tank and a sympathetic woman to start your engine."

"Blue pill?" CJ slopped his coffee cup down on the table. "She told you about that too?"

"Who? About what? It's nothing to be ashamed of. A lot of young guys use Viagra these days."

CJ groaned. Now she thought he had ED on top of his other problems and no way to explain the misunderstanding without sounding like an idiot. He grabbed a tissue from a box on the table and mopped up the spilled coffee.

"Not that blue pill… it's complicated. I need time."

"So what do you want to do?"

"Let's talk about the elephant over there." CJ nodded at the corner of the room.

Enya glanced that way before looking back at him

and cranking up a stare.

"The timeline? Declan?"

CJ nodded. "I agree with you. It couldn't have been anyone in the Iraqi administration."

"Have you checked Tratfors' website lately?"

The answer was yes. He'd spent hours poring over it, but he'd ended up with more questions than answers. He picked up his phone and fingered his way to their site.

"What is *A Geo-Political Defense Platform?*" he said.

"It means that if you're a megabucks corporation or some government agency and you want to screw some foreign government or maybe a competitor's business, then type out a number and a string of zeros on their checkout page and they'll take care of it for you."

"In my day, they were just a guns-for-hire outfit."

"They moved on. At first it was black bag stuff for government agencies that needed deniability. But my brother introduced them to the digital universe. He showed them how easy it was to compromise people online, to set them up and fake things."

"I thought he was Mr. Nice Guy."

"It's not like it sounds. It was an adventure for him, a challenge. But then it became an addiction."

"I don't get it. NSA, GCHQ. They don't need Tratfors for that stuff. They've got plenty of hackers on the payroll."

"They do now. Weaponized digital tradecraft is a career path in the intelligence community. But back then it was different. The geeks knew their place. They were snoops and codebreakers. Declan was way ahead of them all. He was brilliant. They all wanted him. I had to bang down the door to get into Trinity College. But he got an invitation from MIT and a plane ticket."

"So how did he tie up with Tratfors?"

"He wanted travel and adventure. They offered him both. No rule book. And money? George Bush wrote a check for eighty-five billion dollars for the new Iraq. And that was just the down payment. There were suitcases stuffed with it."

"I know. I delivered plenty of them."

"Then you'll understand how they seduced him. Armed guards. Private planes. Luxury hotels. Secret missions. Two-thousand-dollar-a-night hookers. *Is two enough for you, Mr. O'Brien?* It was the ultimate video game. Spooks and warriors. Heroes and villains. And real bodies to keep the score."

"You make him sound like a monster."

"He was never evil, just naive."

"If he was so useful, then why set him up and get him killed?"

"I was hoping you could help me find out."

"How?"

"Why don't you ask Tratfors for a desk job? Something where you get a computer on their network."

"So you can hack their servers?"

She shrugged. "Can you think of something better?"

"What I think is that you lied to me about that memory card they found."

"I did not."

"Come on. You were twins. *When he started a sentence, I'd finish it.* That's what you said."

"You think I'm lying?"

He thought back to their conversation by the pond. She had been so interested in what her brother had to say about that card. If she knew what was on it, then that didn't make sense.

"Maybe not," he said.

"Then what about my plan?"

"We'll see. I fixed up a lunch date with my old pal Masterson tomorrow. He was running our unit back then."

"So ask him for a job."

"I want to hear what he has to say first."

"That's a pathetic plan."

"What do you expect? He's going to confess over a pint of beer and a plowman's lunch? So what happens then? I kill him with the cheese knife?"

"I didn't say anything about killing anybody."

"But you agree that there's something dirty here, and someone at Tratfors or one of their clients knows what. And you're asking me to find out who and why. But what do we do then? That's a question that needs an answer, or there's no point in looking."

"So you agree to help me at least?"

She was skipping his question, so he ignored hers.

"We could always rate them on a guiltometer," he said. "Eight to ten, we kill them. Four to seven, a maiming. Two or three, a beating. One or less, we show mercy and let them off with some harsh rhetoric."

"You're just taking the piss now. I can help you. Don't you see that? Like tomorrow. I can fix you up with a wire and a hidden camera."

"Jesus." He did a double take. "A wire? It's old chums having a chat. A nice pub lunch. No maiming. No killing. And no wires. Just a few loaded questions slipped in amongst all that fuzzy warmth."

"Well, good luck with that, darling." She grabbed her keys and stood up. "We'd better go and clean up that flat of yours. I've got work tomorrow."

SEVEN

It had all the makings of a good day. The sun was out, and two old comrades were in Canbury Gardens on the south bank of the River Thames downstream from Kingston Bridge. They were sitting at a table on the pub terrace overlooking the river with two pints of ale in front of them. There were war stories to tell, tales of battles won and brothers and sisters lost. There'd be truth to bend and lies to paper over. But here at least, in this oh-so-British setting, it could all be done in a civilized fashion. That was the plan anyway, and CJ needed to act his part. He had to find out who and where their fateful-day assignment had come from. But something about Masterson was all wrong, and it was grinding him up the wrong way. He'd always been a condescending prick, but now he was creepy too. CJ could feel his crafty sidelong glances measuring him like calipers whenever he looked aside. Here was a guy with something on his mind, and it wasn't the pie and mash on the lunch menu.

"Good to be back, eh?" Masterson proposed a

toast, raising his tall glass. CJ nudged it with his cheery-looking tankard before chugging away. "So what's next? That place you bought in Acton must be worth a fortune now."

"Yeah… turned out to be hell of an investment strategy. Buy a flat in London. Then get banged up by terrorists and spend the best part of the decade as a vegetable."

Masterson chortled. "Same old CJ, eh? Still got your sense of humor. That's wonderful."

CJ's eyes drifted down to the river, where a crew of schoolgirls was sculling past the island at its center, but his mind was on Masterson and those sidelong glances licking his face like a snake's tongue.

"By the way…" Masterson leaned across the table, something confidential coming. "I made damn sure they kept paying your salary every day you were taken. Five hundred a day. The bastards wanted to put it in escrow in case you came back in a bag. I went to bat for you on that one. It's all in your account."

"Thanks, Phillip."

"No need for thanks. There's more to watching a guy's back than taking care of him in the field."

"I appreciate that."

"And you got a clean bill of health from the hospital, I take it?"

"Squeaky clean. As my old buddy Alex would say."

"God. Alex. I'm so sorry about that. We were all close. But you two were like brothers."

CJ swung his chair around and read the daily specials scribbled up on a board.

Masterson said, "What are you planning to do with your life now?"

CJ shrugged. "I was thinking about going to

California. Alex has family there. He died like a hero. They need to know that."

"Good for you."

"I heard Tratfors moved their HQ there. Maybe I could look in on them."

"They'd be delighted. I called Preston yesterday and told him we were meeting. We were wondering if you'd consider coming back into the firm."

That was an offer right out of Enya's dream scenario, but CJ had other plans.

"I don't know…"

"Hear me out. We're not talking about picking up a gun. Alex is not the only hero. You ripped apart a room of Al-Qaeda thugs with your bare hands. And what about that incredible video? It was all over the web. You must have seen it already. Running through bombed-out streets with Alex's head in one hand and a Kalashnikov in the other. It scared the shit out of the locals. They even made a poster. It was all over the world. Artists. Graffiti. The Yanks loved it. Alex was in the Corps. You know what those boys are like. *Semper fidelis* and all that crap. Believe me, you'll never need beer money anywhere close to a US Marine."

"So that qualifies me for a job with Tratfors?"

"You're the bionic man. You came back from the dead. You're courage, loyalty, strength. In a word— make that three—Tratfors' new spokesperson."

CJ stared at him.

"Me?"

"When I say spokesperson, I don't mean in ads on the telly. I mean you'll be our closer. We'll wheel you in to shake hands with the big shots. They'll love it. You can tell them a few war stories. Drop a few buzzwords. We can teach you all that. Anomaly protection. Kill chain. Threat intelligence. Crap like that. They eat it up. And the money? I'm not talking about five hundred a day. I bought a bloody house in Virginia Water. Indoor swimming pool. Tennis court. A croquet lawn. I've got footballers next door and Silicon Valley types up the road. We grossed over a billion last year. And most of that ends up in our pockets."

"Who's *our*?"

"The big dogs… ruff, ruff."

"Kowalski?"

"Sean, of course. He's strategic director now. We've all got these fancy monikers. I'm director of operations, EMEA. How about that?"

"Congratulations. And thanks for the offer."

"Promise me you'll think about it. I don't need an answer now. But it's there…" He slapped the table. "You just pick it up when you're ready."

CJ double-checked the chalked-up menu like he was a lot more interested in getting lunch on the table than picking up the offer.

"What do you reckon?" he said. "Shepherd's pie or steak and kidney?"

Masterson blinked, still swooning on his own hype.

"I'll stick with my usual prawn salad." He stood up, holding out his hands as if to keep CJ pinned in his seat. "I'll get it. What's it going to be?"

The conversation shifted to food over lunch. Food, pubs and beer. But mostly beer. And after lunch, they were relaxing, watching a rowing instructor drill her team on the tow path below the terrace, when CJ said, "Where did that job come from?" He tossed it out casually, like it really wasn't a grenade with the pin out.

"Which job?"

"That morning in Baghdad."

"It was a… God, so long ago now I'd have to think back. Yes. Sean called me the day before. In the evening. I told Sami to fetch you right away. But he said you were in the bar. So I left it till the morning. Good thing in the circumstances."

"And Sean got it from?"

"It must have come from the Yanks. Some agency. Or from Preston. He's still top dog by the way."

CJ went back to the rowing crew dragging a stiletto of a boat down to the river, and Masterson went back to his snake eyes. Lick, lick. "Still trying to piece it all together," he said. "I don't blame you."

"So you didn't know about it until the evening before, but the militia must have known about it for days."

Masterson cycled a series of quizzical looks on his face, then nodded vaguely as though he wasn't wholly convinced.

"It may have leaked out," he said. "Someone at the ministry. Unless…" He let it die, his attention roaming back to the busy life of the river as though the rest of that sentence was either not worth saying or better not said.

"Unless what?"

Masterson was huffing and puffing, putting on a real show.

"You should be moving on," he said, "Making up for lost time. Even if something did leak, the bugger responsible is long gone. You can't possibly go back to Iraq. And if you start a vendetta there, you'll kiss your future goodbye. So forget it. Think about our offer. Easy street."

"I still need to hear the end of that sentence."

Masterson puffed some more, then squeezed it out.

"We had our suspicions about Sami. He knew about it the night before."

"Sami was a Sunni. If they took him, he'd be the first guy they'd kill."

"But he was fetching kebabs when they showed up. Or so he said. That was mighty convenient. But there was more. His brother went missing before you were taken. Then he mysteriously reappeared after it happened. We thought the militia might have grabbed his brother and traded him for the info. But it turned out that the brother was with some sick cousin in Fallujah and his phone was broken. Sami denied it all of course. But we kicked him out anyway. No one trusted him after that."

"So what happened to him?"

"MI6 gave him a job or two. He must have done well on that because he got his asylum application approved in a week. He set up a kebab shop in North London. Or so I heard."

"Where exactly?"

"Even if I knew—which I don't—I'm not sure I'd tell you. I don't like the way this conversation is going."

"Meaning?"

"It sounds to me like you're gunning for Sami. That hospital might have given you a clean bill of health, but I'm not so sure I do."

That was it. He was edgy. Time for the litmus test.

"I wouldn't sweat it," CJ said. "I've got plenty of medication." His eyes locked on Masterson's. "I got a lifetime prescription from Tango, the new night nurse."

It was that easy. Masterson didn't scream. But CJ heard it anyway. He didn't stick an *I'm guilty* note on his forehead either. But that too was plain to see. All he did was stop from the inside out. The mental equivalent of slamming into a stone wall. And that split second of nothingness when he was fumbling for the restart button on his brain was as good as a signed confession for CJ.

Masterson looked away, checking his chunky Rolex.

"Goodness. Already. I'm going to have to love you and leave you. My wife is shopping at the mall. It's Ophelia's birthday tomorrow. Our daughter." He winked. "You're only six once."

So they were pals again, the night nurse reference misheard perhaps, sucked away by the breeze and now skimming the waters with the athletes pulling on their oars.

They both stood up. CJ offered his hand and Masterson gave it a soldierly shake. "Listen to me, old boy." He aimed his index finger at CJ's face. "You bloody well forget this detective nonsense. Stay clear of Sami. Get focused on your future. That offer is on the table. The next time I want to see you is in my office, saying 'where do I sign?'"

"You got it, mate. And in the meantime, I'll get to work on those buzzwords."

"That's more like it."

CJ watched him hurrying back to Kingston, a man marching through the sauntering many. He sat back down and finished his beer, relishing each mouthful. Then he took his pie crust down on the tow path and tossed it to a family of ducks. But he couldn't get the image of marching Masterson out of his head. That soldierly striding was telling him something. Masterson was army through and through. Sandhurst. And then on to The Regiment, as he called it. He'd always pause before saying the word to let you know that any other regiment was some sort of fake.

The Regiment.

CJ remembered the day Alex had arrived in Iraq and he'd introduced him to Masterson. They were all at the bar when Masterson had launched into a discourse on the American War of Independence through the eyes of his illustrious Thirty-Third Regiment of Foot. He knew his history alright, starting with the Battle of Long Island and working his way through to a skirmish at the Guilford Courthouse. But it was hard not to notice that all the encounters ended in the same way. More or less. Sometimes the Americans retreated. On other occasions they withdrew. And once or twice they *retired from the action.* But in every battle fought against The Regiment, the patriots lost. CJ was embarrassed. He'd invited Alex to join him at Tratfors. Now this. He could just see Alex adding a codicil to The Regiment's history by pasting one of its former officers to the bar. But CJ needn't have worried. Masterson's rant might have come across as anti-American. But Alex was smart enough to see the real issue—the fraternity between him and CJ. They were mates, buddies. British or American. Whatever language you coined it in—it was obvious. They had everything good friends share. Including respect. Something Masterson would never get from either of them.

When the pie crust was all gone, the ducks abandoned CJ and looked for pickings elsewhere. He was watching them scatter when it came to him, echoing across the years from that hotel bar in Iraq. A point of history. The thing that was stuck in his head. It was the footnote that Masterson had added to his tedious monologue.

On the orders of Queen Victoria, the illustrious Thirty-Third Regiment had changed its name to the Duke of Wellington's Regiment.

He looked back through the trees towards Kingston.

A job for the Duke.

But the marching duke was long gone.

EIGHT

CJ was in his Acton flat, draped over the dinner table combing through restaurant reviews on his laptop. The table was squeezed in one corner to make more space, and two of its chairs were out of action, jammed up against the walls. But that didn't matter. CJ only needed one chair. There was only him. And there only ever would be. Or at least, that had been the plan when he'd bought it. His Acton flat, a solitary nest, a place to perch between overseas gigs, a parking spot for his hard-earned cash. Two rooms, a bathroom and a kitchen squeezed into an area hardly big enough for a single good-sized room.

Sami's Gourmet Kebab House.

It had to be that one. Apart from the name, the location was right and so was the menu. He dialed the phone number and listened to a message about a temporary closure for remodeling. It was unmistakably Sami's voice, his flowery antiquated English promising that London's premier kebabs would soon be available again.

CJ left a message and continued his investigations back at his computer, moving on from restaurant reviews to the Tratfors Our Team page. Preston, Kowalski, Masterson. They were all there, a catalog of serious faces oozing authority. Not a smile in sight. It might not be easy to figure out what these guys were selling, but it obviously wasn't used cars. He worked his way through their portfolio of exotic offerings, drilling in deeper than he had on previous visits. In addition to CJ's specialty—close protection—they had added counterterrorism, private and corporate investigations, technical surveillance and counterespionage. With all of the above on sale to governments and corporate clients in the oil and gas, mineral extraction and infrastructure development sectors. CJ clicked away through page after page like a Googlebot sniffing out secrets. Pathfinding. It was another new buzzword. New to CJ anyway. He read the blurb… Got a dream? Any prize. Anywhere. We can make it real. He followed the link. More buzzwords. He was digging his way into *corruption mitigation strategies* when the phone rang.

It was Sami.

"Mr. CJ. Is it true—you can walk and talk?"

"More or less. But I'm still not getting anywhere. And I'm still not making any sense."

"I can't believe I'm talking to you. God reached out his hand and brought you back from hell."

"But he left Alex there."

"No. Not hell. Paradise. *Inshallah.*"

"Do you ever think of those days?"

"I try not to."

"Not even way back before the war, when you were flying jets for Saddam?"

"I was dropping bombs on our neighbors."

"But you had everything. Status. You were a somebody."

"Flying jets! That's nothing. Do you realize that you are speaking to the proprietor of the eight-hundred-and-fifty-second best restaurant in London according to TripAdvisor?"

CJ chuckled. He'd forgotten Sami's artful sense of humor.

"Congratulations."

So far, so good. The conversation was upbeat, amicable. But Sami was too smart not to smell what was coming down the line.

"Mr. CJ, why did you call me? To talk about happy memories? I think that conversation will be a little short for us."

The moment sat there. Uncomfortable.

"I saw Phillip Masterson yesterday."

"And he said?"

"You don't keep in touch?"

"Why would I? They sacked me. They refused to support my application for asylum. I had to beg my way into this country."

"They didn't fast-track you?"

"Is that what he told you?"

Another awkward moment. But no answer.

"I asked him about that day, the day you got lucky and popped out for lunch just before a hundred militia turned up and pointed guns at us."

"Praise be to God."

"Who sent you to get the kebabs?"

"It was you."

"I didn't send you."

"Indirectly. You remember our conversation on the

drive to the ministry? We were talking about food. Alex was dreaming about a steak from Nebraska. He was teasing you, taking the mickey. Saying how Iraq was Brit heaven because every meal was lamb. And you were fighting back, singing the praises of the shawarma we used to get from Haziz's place. We passed it on the way. So after Mr. O'Brien started work and I went out for a smoke, everything was calm, so I buggered off to fetch lunch. I wanted to prove to Alex that you were right—the best shawarma in Baghdad. But when I got back, you were all getting pushed into the van at gunpoint. For a moment, I thought it was a paperwork issue. That maybe I could translate and sort it all out. But I'm Iraqi. And a Sunni. We haven't survived this long by trusting what we see, or taking chances with Shia militia. I ran like hell. What else?"

CJ was playing it all back in his head. He remembered their good-natured squabbling in the car. He used to argue with Alex about everything. Beef versus lamb was a perennial, along with the correct definition of the word football. Poking each other with a stick was their major form of entertainment. He'd all but forgotten about that.

"When did you learn about the job that day?"

"In the morning. The same time as you. I hopped out of bed and answered the phone. Then I woke you all. Why do you ask?"

"Nothing."

"Mr. Phillip told you something different, perhaps."

"It's not important."

CJ listened to Sami's breathing. Steady. Rhythmic. Like a man at peace with his conscience.

"I'm sorry to hear you had a tough time with the asylum people. Did you get your whole family over?"

"My wife and kids. Thanks to God."

"How about your brother? Did he make it?"

"My brother?"

"The one from Fallujah."

"My father had two daughters and one son, and you are talking to him."

CJ stood up and paced the room, two strides this way and two strides that. Then he sat on the windowsill and went to speak, but Sami beat him to it.

"When was the last time you had a kebab?"

"That sounds like an invitation."

"I'd like to spend some time with my British brother. And what better way to do that than over a nice lamb kebab and a cup of tea at my place?"

"I thought it was closed."

"The kitchen still works. And there won't be any customers or staff to bother us. So maybe we can chat about those unimportant nothings that you discussed with Mr. Phillip."

They made a date for the following day. Then CJ paced some more, his tiny living room a makeshift cage. It was getting dark when he settled back on his perch on the windowsill. He peered out through glass streaked with dust and rain across the road at a pub garden, its empty tables and chairs forlorn under a canopy of leafless branches.

Phillip or Sami?

One of them was lying. Phillip Masterson was a fellow countryman, an officer descended from soldiers who had fought in Britain's wars for hundreds of years. But any bias CJ might have felt based on that was oddly skewed. There was something heartless about Masterson, whereas Sami was all heart. An old rogue. But with loyalty coded deep like a reflex. On the other hand, he was an adept survivor with an abundance of guile. As one of Saddam's lieutenants, he might have ended up on the wrong end of a rope instead of the proprietor of a London kebab shop, boasting about online reviews. CJ's gut was telling him that it was Masterson, but what was the motive? It made no sense. Having an important VIP taken while under its protection was bad news for Tratfors.

He set the phone aside and lounged back against the window, shuffling through memories back to the time when he'd first met Sami. They'd been a close-knit team up to that point. One Brit, one American, and two South Africans. No problems, no issues. And suddenly there was a new boy in the class—an Iraqi who'd once dropped bombs for Saddam—and he was not just an interpreter. Sami was Mr. Fixit, a go-to guy for whatever they needed. Tratfors recruited him when they were hired to take an Italian journalist to an interview in Fallujah in a neighborhood that was a no-go area even for their heavily armed ex-military crew. They were all Westerners and this was a job that needed a local. So Sami was hired along with his two Kalashnikov-toting sidekicks.

The whole team had planned to travel in convoy to the outskirts of the city, where Sami and his men would take over, ferrying the journalist on the last leg through the dangerous city streets. The convoy was made up of three vehicles. The Boers in front. CJ and Alex with the journalist in the middle. Then Sami and his henchmen at the rear. Several hours into the drive—in apparently empty desert—they'd been ambushed by twenty plus gunmen and Sami's truck had disappeared in a cloud of dust followed by a torrent of expletives from CJ and Alex. No one bothered to ask. It was obvious. They'd been set up by Sami and co.

Their attackers were gutsy, but lousy shots, and the Tratfors team was able to pin them down and beat a retreat. But the insurgents didn't give up, and they were soon in a chase, pursued by half a dozen vehicles. That was when Sami reappeared, popping up on their flank and laying down heavy fire. He'd driven a wide loop, correctly assessing the situation and recasting the battlefield matrix. They were still outnumbered. But their attackers were caught in a crossfire in open country, and it wasn't long before their shot-up trucks were screaming off over the horizon. Sami had earned his stripes that day, and CJ and Alex had learned that their rush to judgment was a mistake.

The phone lit up with an incoming call.

"Hey, Freckles…"

"How did it go with Masterson?"

"I'll take you through it later."

"But you did see him?"

"We had a pub lunch down by the river."

"A perfect day for it. I bet the row club was busy."

"Yeah, people all over. Too many witnesses. Otherwise I'd have done him with the cheese knife."

"Very funny. I'll expect a full report when we meet. How about tomorrow? A real restaurant. One with stars. My treat."

"Sorry. I can't. I'm seeing another old mate."

"Anyone I know?"

"Let's just say I'm going to have a lot to report on."

"Why so coy? We're still a team, aren't we?"

"Sure. But it's all spinning in my head right now. I need to think it through first. I'll update you. I promise."

They fixed their date and rang off, but CJ kept

staring at his phone. That conversation bothered him.

The perfect day for it.

Enya's line kept squeaking in his head.

She was talking about the sun. In London, that was always worthy of note. No problem with that. But then she'd mentioned the row club. How did she know that? All he'd said was *a pub lunch down by the river.* Not which pub. He didn't even say where. There were plenty of pubs on the river. It could have been in Richmond, Teddington, Chiswick. Many of the pubs had gardens and terraces. But not like that one. Not built right over the tow path next to a rowing club.

The phone?

He'd been suspicious when she'd given it to him. That was serious money. But he'd checked it out for sneaky apps and adjusted all the privacy settings. It was clean. He was sure of it. But what else could explain Enya's amazing sixth sense? He sat back at the table and used the laptop to research his phone's operating system, ending up at a geek's forum, where he found a list of the processes running on his phone when it was brand-new. Then he logged into his phone and downloaded a techie app that listed all active processes. So he ended up with two lists, the new phone list and his actual phone list. He swung his head back and forth between the laptop and the phone comparing the lists and looking for discrepancies. His phone had seven additional processes. He fetched a notepad from the kitchen drawer and scribbled their names with a pencil. Some were obvious. He'd installed a few apps, and some of the processes were named accordingly. He struck them off the list. There was just one process left and it didn't take long to hunt down its origin. It belonged to a geolocation app that parents used to keep tabs on their kids. But that was puzzling. There was no such app on his phone. Enya must have stripped it down to its core functionality, then buried the code in his phone so that it was masquerading as something else or piggy-backing on some legitimate process.

He left the table and stood at the window, looking down on the street. He'd always been wary of Enya. Too many questions. And too many convenient excuses. But now that wariness had a bedfellow. Respect. She was crafty and clever. But what did that make her? A useful ally or a grievous enemy?

The darkness beyond the window had turned it into a mirror, and he could see his smiling face in it. A while ago, that might have been Alex's face. But he hadn't seen his old friend since that night in the cafeteria when he'd teetered on the edge of madness. Maybe Doctor Sam was right and some synapse had self-repaired, burying Alex's ghost under scar tissue. Or maybe CJ had accepted the truth. He'd invited Alex to Iraq. There was no way around that. Had he purged his guilt that night by choosing the path of redemption through revenge? Or was all that medical stuff nonsense and the parapsychic theories he'd so readily dismissed closer to the truth. CJ had no answers and he didn't need any. He had a certainty. Alex was still there. He could feel his presence. He was just invisible now, switched to stealth mode to keep CJ on the right side of insanity and avoid another Hollywood stunt like that coin fiasco. Death had transformed him into an ethereal wingman, feeding CJ with counsel and strength as he'd always done in life. CJ turned back from the window and looked at the empty armchair across the room.

"We can do this, mate," he said. "You and me. We're going to find every last son of a bitch. And you know exactly what we're going to do to them."

NINE

He took a taxi. An old-fashioned black one. No Uber. No phone. And he got it the old-fashioned way, strutting along the street and flagging it with a screeching whistle. He wanted to chuck the phone. Chuck it at Enya, ideally. But he'd reined all that back. The phone was in his pocket. But it was off. And it was going to stay that way.

He paid off the driver a few blocks from Sami's place and walked the rest of the way, running a routine reconnaissance on the High Street and its neighborhood.

Sami's Kebab House.

CJ slid under the scaffolding outside and tried the door.

Locked.

He peeked through the boarded windows and checked his watch. It was almost six. He was early. Stores were closing and sidewalks bustling. He meandered up the street and back along the other side, peering into shop windows, a tourist in his own country, comparing it all to the archived snapshot in his head. A betting shop, assorted franchises including a McDonald's and a Starbucks, a dry cleaners, half a dozen charity shops and a convenience store. CJ idled inside the latter, reading the headlines on newspapers and magazines before picking out a bottle of red wine.

Shopping done, CJ walked the street again and took a turn at the end of the block, finding an alleyway parallel to the High Street running behind the stores. He walked down it, checking the parking and loading areas behind each store. On the other side of the alley were the fences and walls of private homes. He stopped behind Sami's place and looked up at the three-story brick building. The floors above the restaurant had windows with curtains and lights popping on behind them. Flats. Residential apartments with their own access door at the edge of the property. There was only one car parked in the parking area, a beat-up Volvo. CJ walked around it and approached the restaurant's back door. It was half-open, like someone had just popped out to fetch supplies.

He stopped.

Something.

He edged closer. It was Arabic music. A call to prayer. It was coming from inside. Strict Muslims pray five times a day. But that wasn't Sami. Besides, if he was praying, he was spoiling dinner, because the smell of scorched lamb was unmissable. CJ looked through the doorway, where a hallway led to the kitchen. There was an office on one side and a storeroom with refrigerators on the other.

"Sami?"

CJ stepped inside and peeked into the office—a cluttered desk, a filing cabinet topped with a fan and a pile of papers. All that was there. But CJ saw none of it. All he saw was Alex. Not his ghost. Not a shimmering reflection in half-light. But the real thing. Alex alive. But not well. The star of the show. On his knees. A knife at his throat. It was a video playing on a computer screen. It was the video he had searched for and thankfully never found. He froze, unable to move his eyes from the screen, watching as Alex's life hosed out of his throat with every beat of his heart. Then the picture danced. Walls, blackness, bursting light. CJ's hands like claws. Hussein's dead eyes as he keeled over. Bodies. Flashes of gunfire and smoke. Then Jahil rearing up, and his own ragged body charging him down.

CJ stumbled back, twisting like a coil, arms curled in front of him, fists at his face, stifling his scream. He whirled around and punched the door, poking his fist clean through the plywood on both sides.

He strode into the kitchen.

Sami.

It could only be him. He was sprawled on the floor, head and shoulders stuffed in an oven. CJ dragged him out. There were deep cuts all over him. Blood everywhere. He rolled him over. His throat was cut, but bloodless, the wound already sealed by the heat of the oven, his face a grid of black stripes branded by heat rings. CJ surveyed his own blood-strewn arms before looking up and catching the blinking light of a camera in the restaurant beyond the kitchen. Someone had swiveled it around to record the kitchen instead of the cash desk. He turned and ran out the back door.

Here they come.

No sirens. But the whine of turbo-diesels in a hurry was unmistakable above the background hum of dawdling traffic.

Rapid response. Armed police.

Whoever had set this up had made sure of that. They were just seconds away. He ran to the door leading up to the flats above. It was locked and stoutly made. He stepped back and came at it with a kick that blew out the lock and the hinges. Shards of wood poked out of the frame and the door rested like a ramp on the flight of stairs directly behind it. CJ scrambled over it onto the steps. He heaved the door back up and wedged it in the doorway. It wasn't going to fool anyone for long. It might pass cursory inspection from a distance. But anyone closer than a few yards would see the trailing bits of wood. He skipped up the stairs to the top floor. There was just one door. It was flimsy, and he busted through it with a body check.

Hallway, bathroom, bedroom, kitchen.

They were all empty.

In the living room, an old woman was sitting in an armchair watching TV. Her eyes flicked up at him and her hand jerked up protectively, its veins thick as bones.

"Don't worry. I'm harmless," CJ said.

Her eyes took him in, then went back to the TV, where a naked couple in a medieval room were having sex doggy style on a four-poster bed. CJ darted across the room to the window just as a BMW X5 skidded into the loading zone below and armed police poured out of it. He was planning to open the window and climb up on the roof. It wasn't much of a plan, but it was the only one he could think of that didn't involve jail time. It might work. He might get lucky. But the first part was tricky. Getting out of the window and up onto the roof. No way to do it without being totally exposed. And there had to be more cops. One car wasn't enough. Overwhelming force. That was their motto. His instincts were telling him to wait. They'd find the busted door and be streaming up the steps soon enough, but first they'd get bogged down in the restaurant.

He looked back at the old lady. She was draining a glass of sherry, her knobby hands shaking, her eyes still on the screen.

"Sorry about the door, luv." CJ pulled four fifties from his pocket and dropped them on the table next to her half-empty bottle.

He checked back at the window. A Range Rover had joined the BMW, and more cops were disappearing into the restaurant. He slid open the window and crawled out onto the ledge. Both of the response vehicles were parked too close to the building for anyone inside them to be able to see him. Even so, he had seconds to get this right. He braced himself with his arms stretched out on the brickwork on either side as he figured out how to do this. His options were few in number and all of them bad, especially the most likely—ending up in a pile of busted bones on top of a cop car. He eyed the gutter above. It looked out of reach. And would it hold two hundred pounds? His guess was no. But there was only one way to find out. He turned around, shuffled his heels off the ledge and launched himself upwards. His fingers grabbed the gutter, but they slipped, and as he fell, they caught the ledge he'd been standing on.

He looked down. Cop arms. Cop legs. He could see them right there in the car. He could hear their voices too. Some sort of report going down over a blessedly noisy radio link. He walked his legs one way on the wall, then kicked off and swung back the other way, casting himself loose and falling at an angle that gave him a shot at a drainpipe. He caught it with one hand, his knee cracking the wall beyond it and skidding down it until his fingers jammed against a flange bolt pegging it to the wall. He was feet from the cop car with more voices coming from inside the kitchen. He looped his hands behind the pipe and walked up the wall. The pipe held. And so did the gutter at the top as he levered himself up onto the tiled roof.

He lay flat against it and peeked down at the yard below as two more cop cars pulled up. Patrol cars. The cop in the Range Rover went to each of them in turn and they headed off to block the alleyway at each end. But as he headed back to his vehicle, he noticed the busted door to the flats above. He went over for a closer look. They'd be inside in minutes and up in the old lady's apartment. They'd check the roof for sure. But they'd need ladders, or a chopper or a drone. Or else they'd get access to a building with line of sight to the roof. It would take time. But not much. He crept on all fours, heading back to the side street he'd walked down to get to the alleyway. He lay flat when he got there, peeking over the edge, looking for a way down, but there was nothing. Not even a drainpipe. Just three stories of pure brick.

Darkness was closing in and men and women were hurrying home on the nearby High Street. He scooted up the roof and hid between a chimney and a dish antenna, a big one. Most likely it was a community feed shared by all the flats in the block. It was a good spot to hide, invisible from all but close inspection. But neither the darkness nor his newfound hidey-hole was going to save him. He had to get off that roof. He was crouched with one hand on the dish, his eyes following the cable that ran from its base. It was molded to the roof in a rubber channel, then tacked to the end wall, where it disappeared into a hole in the brickwork.

But where did it go from there?

It had to run through the cavity wall and get terminated in some sort of single-cable distribution system. It looked like a regular coax cable. If so, there was nothing anchoring it except a few tacks and a bit of crimping at the other end. It might work as a buffer, like a poorly tethered rope, breaking his fall as he dropped down the side of the building. He shuffled back to the edge and surveyed the side road below. It was residential, parked cars and plane trees with an occasional pedestrian on their way home. CJ disconnected the cable and wrenched it free of the studs tacking it to the roof and down as far as the hole where it disappeared into the wall. Then he measured the distance from the hole to the ground with his eyeball ruler. The stretch of cable he'd pulled out looked good for some of it. He wrapped the end of the cable around his forearm and rolled off the edge. It all worked. Up to a point. But his eyeball ruler was spot-on. That point was not far enough down the wall. He checked the drop. He'd only made it about ten feet below the hole and that left a long way to go. He might not suffer the pain of the fall, but no one runs with broken legs. His eyes darted towards the pulsing cop lights at the end of the alley. The car was tucked around the corner and out of sight, but not by much. His only hope was the winter-bare branches of a nearby plane tree. If he could swing out far enough, he might be able to grab one of those on his way down. He kicked himself off the wall.

Once. Twice.

Then it happened.

What exactly? He didn't know. Something inside the building. Something breaking. Or something spectacular like a wired-up box whizzing across the room and slamming into a wall. On CJ's end, it was a lot less dramatic. He just dropped fifteen feet in an instant. He looked down.

That's more like it.

He let go of the cable, landing in a crouch and tumbling forward onto his hands. He pulled himself up and hurried away from the flashing lights and buzzing radio in the alleyway and stepped out onto the High Street. He'd made it. And no one even stopped to stare or shoot a video. A man hanging by a cable off the side of a building. But passersby on the High Street never glanced his way as they crossed the quiet side street. They were all wearing blinders and had more important things on their minds. Home, the pub, the kids. Some important him or her. London was changing shifts and CJ walked invisible through the crack between work-hell and home-sanctuary.

He crossed the High Street, slipped into McDonald's and went to the bathroom. He washed Sami's blood from his hands and arms and his own blood from his knee where he'd cracked it against the wall, cleaning it all up through the hole in his now-fashionably-ripped jeans. He looked in the mirror to inspect his handiwork. *Awful.* He looked like the loser of a gang fight in an abattoir. He hid in one of the cubicles and locked the door. He had started the day looking for a murderer. Now he was one, according to the police—or at least he soon would be. So where was he going to go? He was trapped in a McDonald's toilet, his Acton flat a no-go zone, totally out of options.

Except…

Wonder Woman.

He pulled out his phone and turned it on. He had to contact Enya and explain the seriousness of the situation. He needed rescuing. No questions. No debate. She had to drop everything and fly. Beyond that, he wanted to tell her the truth. That he'd found the bug on his phone and that he was pissed off about it. That was a lot of explaining and he couldn't risk a long conversation sitting on a McDonald's toilet with needy diners popping in and out to relieve themselves. Besides, CJ was into cryptic. He gave it a moment's thought, then squeezed it all into three words.

Find me. Bitch!

There was no way she could resist an intriguing summons like that, and he could count on her overactive intelligence to fill in all the necessary blanks. He dropped the phone in the trash on his way out, then crossed the road and picked up a newspaper. Time to kill. He bought a latte and a croissant in Starbucks and hid behind his newspaper, dunking his croissant and chewing on it thoughtfully, his eyes on the Golden Arches across the street.

TEN

She was outside McDonald's, pretending to read a poster promoting their specials. But what she was really doing was checking out the diners inside. CJ scooped her off the window, kissed her, and marched her away from the patrol car sitting across the street in front of Sami's restaurant. It was theatrical, over the top. That was the way he planned it. She had to get the message. They were a couple meeting after work and heading for the pub.

"Where's the car?"

She picked up the urgency in his voice and flicked her head, and they turned into a side street, his arm around her sweeping her onward. It would all be on CCTV and it would all get sifted out in the days ahead. But the cops wouldn't know who they were looking for yet. Not unless they'd been told by whoever had tipped them off, and that was unlikely as it would stink of a setup. So he was still a person or persons unknown for the next twenty-four hours at least, maybe forty-eight. CSI technicians in white suits would already be hoovering up his DNA. And the restaurant's CCTV system would soon be coughing out his likeness. If that recording was complete, it would show his entry into the kitchen and his discovery of the body and it would exonerate him. But whoever had set this up would have accounted for that. No doubt the footage would be damaged, with only a few grainy images surviving, like a shot of him standing over Sami's body, dripping with his blood. Add that to his DNA, his medical record, and Masterson's lying through his teeth under oath in his best officer-and-gentleman accent, and he'd be convicted in a blink.

He waited until Enya was inside the car before slipping into the passenger seat. The side street was empty. Rows of cars parked curbside in front of two-story houses. They drove off in silence, Enya punctuating her gear shifts and wheel turns with sidelong glances at CJ. She drove south and picked up the Westway, where they got snarled in traffic, shunting along, their silence weightier by the minute until Enya burst it with an avalanche of words.

"It's not like you think. I apologize. I shouldn't have done it. I know that. But it was for your own good. I wanted to make sure you were okay."

CJ kept his eyes on the road like he was too disgusted to look at her and made no reply.

She worked the gearstick and rolled them along a little further, measuring him with constant looks.

"It was completely wrong of me. I'm ashamed." She waited, then said, "Are you going to tell me what happened back there?"

"Just drive."

"Where?"

"One of those hypermarkets that sells phones."

"And then?"

He didn't answer. He didn't know.

"The cops back there," she said. "Was that to do with you?" He said nothing. "The interpreter, that's his place, right?"

"Drop me at the market. You can head on your way then."

"What am I? A taxi service? I apologized. A gentleman would accept it and move on. I made a mistake. I'm trying to make up for it. I've got a place no one knows about. You could stay there."

"Just find a market."

She nodded as though that was the end of the debate, but he knew it wasn't. When they escaped the traffic, she headed south across the river and pulled into a Tesco, parking in its huge lot lit with sodium lamps. As she cut the engine, she noticed the stains on his jeans and jacket.

"God Almighty." They were black in the orange glow of the lights. But she didn't need a color palette to work out what they were. "Is he dead?"

"I didn't kill him."

She took a while to process it all, staring out across floodlit concrete.

"Maybe I should leave you here and go like you said."

"He was dead already. And there was this video playing on a computer. Alex getting beheaded."

Her eyes widened, whites flashing in the eerie light.

"That's it. It has to be Tratfors or their spook cronies. Who else would have that video? It never went out on the web. Propaganda killings like that get canned and streamed later. They would never risk streaming it live. It's too easy to trace. And you killed all the terrorists."

"Unless Sami was part of it?"

"You think he was?"

He shook his head. "Someone put that on his computer."

"Tratfors could fix that in their sleep."

"They're not the only ones."

"You mean Ashford?"

"I was thinking more about someone else." He turned towards her. "Someone who could hack a phone with a find-me app without leaving any trace."

Thwack.

He took it on the jaw. It was that fast and no way to stop it. He parried her second shot. But she landed the third—a good one—a stabby punch to the soft ribs that she drove home with a grunt.

"You disgusting bastard." She reared up over him, gulping mouthfuls of air, her face contorted with rage. "Get out of my car, or I'll call the police."

But CJ stayed put.

She'd passed the test with straight As.

He waited until she slid back down in her seat and resumed nose breathing before he continued.

"The prosecutor will argue that Sami was implicated in the hostage taking. There's a case for that and the video proves it. They'll say I tortured him, and I got to the truth along with the video. I watched it and freaked out. So I stuck him with a knife a few hundred times. Exhibit A. The CCTV image of a bloodstained maniac standing over the butchered body. Exhibit B. My medical record. Early discharge from hospital. PTSD. Talking to ghosts. They won't jail me. They'll pity me. I'll get sectioned under the Mental Health Act. Whoever set this up would be well pleased with that. I'll be certified crazy. It's better than dead. Who's going to believe anything I say?" CJ looked around the car park. He went to get out, but she grabbed his arm and stopped him.

"I believe you," she said.

They stared at each other, letting their eyes do the talking until she let go of his arm. "You better grab some new clothes at the same time," she said. "And don't be too long."

With CJ's new wardrobe sitting on the backseat and two new phones in his pocket, they pulled out of the parking lot.

"So where are we going?" CJ said.

"Do you trust me?"

That was a black-and-white question worth ducking. The answer was gray. But he'd already collected Enya's knuckle print on one side of his face and was not anxious to decorate the other.

"Sure I do."

Enya smiled and headed west to Surbiton, where she pulled into an underground parking entrance off a narrow side street and waited for an electric gate to roll up.

"My secret hideaway," she said. "It was my first buy-to-let, but after some tenants trashed it, I signed up for that BnB thing and made it a holiday rental." She drove down the ramp and parked. "No one's going to look for us here. It's owned by my other company. The offshore one. And I'm not even a director of that. I use a nominee. Some lawyer in Belize."

"Jesus…"

"What?"

"Nothing."

She cut the engine and pecked his bruised cheek.

"I'm a resourceful woman."

CJ nodded. That was unarguable. But Colby's word was motivated, and his was sneaky. In the end, all three of them were right, and the sum total of their wordage was dangerous.

They left the parking lot through a PIN-locked door, took the elevator to the fifth floor and entered an apartment with rooftop views. CJ scouted its spacious living area and open-plan kitchen, adjusting the blinds and checking a locked door that led out onto a balcony running alongside the bedrooms.

Enya went to the wine rack, a folding concertina of wood on the breakfast counter and picked a bottle.

"I give them some starter booze. They're on holiday after all." She pulled the cork and found two jumbo-sized glasses in a cupboard.

"You'll be needing this." She gave him the glass. "It's not going to win any gold medals, but it's made from grapes at least." They touched glasses and drank. "You'd better clean yourself up before you sit anywhere. You can use the guest bathroom off the hallway. There's a man-size bathrobe in the second bedroom. I'll stick these things"—she waved a hand at his torn jeans and bloodied shirt—"in the trash."

CJ stripped down to his pants.

"Masterson led me to Sami like a pig with a ring in its nose. You should have seen the performance he put on. And I was fool enough to get suckered." He handed over the pile of clothes. "Find out where he lives."

"For what? So I can be an accessory to murder?"

"I didn't kill Sami. I told you."

"And I believe you. But I think you'll kill Masterson."

"I need him alive and talking."

"To tell you what?"

"Who's pulling his chain and why."

"And you think he'll tell you?"

"One way or another."

CJ disappeared into the bathroom with his wine, emerging twenty minutes later wearing a blue bathrobe and carrying an empty glass. Enya was slouched against the wing of an armchair, fingering a tablet computer, her legs curled underneath her. CJ fetched the wine bottle, topped up their glasses, and lay full-length on the sofa opposite with his head propped up on cushions and the glass perched on his belly. The TV news was on, the soundtrack muted. He read the headlines scrolling across the bottom of the screen.

Incident in North London. May be terror-related.

"No one mentioned your name." Enya looked up from the computer. "No mugshots. Most wanted. That kind of stuff. Just the usual. Nothing for the public to worry about, etc."

"Did you get the address?"

She nodded, still looking at her tablet and swiping through pages. "It's a beautiful property."

"You got pictures?"

"I've got the floor plan too. It's still up on the website of the estate agents he bought it from. Six million, they were asking."

She joined him on the sofa and they worked through the photos of Masterson's estate until she stopped at one of its imposing facade.

"Look at that," she said. "The beautiful things that only blood can buy."

He put his arm around her and hugged her. She let him do it, her body limp in his arms, her face tender.

"Maybe we should run away and forget it all," she said. "I hear tell that Venezuela is a garden spot for fugitives."

"You're not a fugitive."

"I will be if I hang around you long enough."

"Masterson is a bit player." CJ waved at the luxury home. "All this is just luck. He was the right man with the right connections. In Iraq, he was running a couple of units like ours. But as Tratfors grew, they needed a British face with connections. Someone plugged into the old boy network who could get them into UK boardrooms and be a credible front for military and intelligence contacts. Someone they could trust to sell his own mother for the right price. They took one look at Masterson and said, 'That's our boy.'"

"You'll never get away with it. Turning up at this place and threatening him. You'll end up dead or in jail."

"No way. I'm going to do it by the book."

"What book?"

"The special forces playbook. Keep it simple. Stack advantages. And let the target dictate the weapon."

"So what's your weapon?"

"Look at the target." He nodded at the tablet where Enya was swiping through images of Masterson's country estate. "What does that tell you?"

"That he's probably got private security only a push button away and a shotgun or two locked in a gun cabinet."

CJ nodded. She was most likely right about all that, but none of it mattered.

"The weapon is fear. Look what he has to lose. Would you risk losing that—along with your trophy wife and daughter?"

"You're a bastard."

"You flatter me. Compared to him, I'm an amateur."

CJ left it there, stretching out on the sofa as Enya shut down the tablet. Minutes later they were snuggled up against each other, limbs entangled, fast asleep.

ELEVEN

Virginia Water it wasn't. Or maybe just in the wishful thinking of Philip Masterson. But it was close enough and still way upmarket, a neighborhood with estates big enough to have sidebar houses for the live-in staff and swimming pools and tennis courts. It was part of that swath of rolling green flecked with cute villages and quaint towns that hung off South London like a fancy scarf. Masterson's house was on its rural edge, where orderly roads and manicured hedgerows gave way to winding lanes edged with brambles, ditches and high walls. That was a gift. There was no neighborhood management with private security.

They pulled up onto a grassy verge and cut the engine.

"Recon." CJ waited for her to nod before getting out of the car. He stood a moment, scanning the wall and the trees above it. No cameras. The front gate was festooned with them and so was the house. But with so many trees and bushes, they'd be useless on the perimeter wall.

He jumped the ditch and cleared his way through the hedgerow. There was a gap between the hedges and the wall big enough to squeeze through. So he made his way along it, brushing aside branches that closed out the gap. He was looking for a way over the wall. It was ten feet high or better, and he wanted a leg up from one of the hedges at a spot where his entrance would be hidden by trees. But then he got lucky. A disused door. It must have been a side entrance a long time ago. It was boarded up, invisible from the street behind the hedgerow. He checked the boards. Rotten. And the nails were all rusted. He leaned against it, pinning his ear to its peeling paint and closing his eyes to concentrate on sound.

Cars on nearby streets. Birds, insects. A distant train. A jet biding its time waiting for a runway at Heathrow. He channeled them all, sifting. Then he had it. Muffled voices. Not far away. He focused tighter, closing out sound channels one by one. And as he did so, the voices got louder. Masterson and a child. A girl. Ophelia. The birthday girl. They were playing croquet. Ophelia was angry because the ball wasn't going where she wanted it to go. Masterson was calming her down.

Another voice.

A woman. Strident. Distant. On the terrace, perhaps, with the wings of the house gathering the sound up and projecting it out across the lawns. Mrs. Masterson was calling time. Ophelia had a cello lesson and her mother planned to drop her off on her way to the manicurist. Fifteen minutes. That was all they had left to play. There was mostly silence after that. Father and daughter. Happy days. The dull thud of wood on wood. And that special sound. A young girl's laughter. Warm and innocent. CJ was running the scene in his mind's eye, intercut with another movie. His movie. Iraq. The blood, the death. The stink of it. Enya was right. This was the flip side of his movie. The innocence of Ophelia. Private school. A gap year doing something worthy before heading to Oxford. A career? Take your pick. Then she'd meet someone called Piers or Sebastian who did something in the city and buy a house like this.

CJ charged back along the wall to the car. He jerked open the door and fell into the seat beside Enya.

"You look like shit," she said. "What happened?"

CJ wiped his face and dusted the leaves off his clothes.

"We're good." He took out his two phones. "I'm going to record a call—one side of it. And when I text you, you have to call Masterson and play it back to him. Got it?"

She nodded, and he set to work, staging the dialog with suitable pauses.

Relaxed, like it was a routine call.

"Hello, Phillip."

Tight and tense.

"You set me up."

Angry, vengeful.

"Sami was cut to pieces. Burned like a steak."

Loud, losing it.

"I know it was you, Phillip. You set me up just like you did in Iraq."

Cold and resolute.

"I'm going to find you. And peel your skin."

He gave Enya the phone.

"Note to self," she said as she took it. "Don't piss him off."

He opened the car door. "I need to get the jack

handle." He was halfway out when she said, "Run-flat tires. No spare. No jack handle."

He slumped back on the seat.

"Maybe this'll help?" She took a plastic bag from the pocket in the door and handed it to him. It was green, with the word Harrods written on it in gold letters, and it was furled around something heavy. He unrolled the bag and took out a cheap ballpoint, a scrap of paper, and a roughneck bar with a curved chisel on one end and a pointed hammer on the other. He looked at her, waiting for an explanation.

"In case I have an accident and need a pen and paper to note down the other driver's details."

"And this?" He hefted the roughneck bar.

"Other drivers can be disagreeable at such moments."

He nodded—not much else to say about that—and got out of the car.

"What's it for?" she called after him.

He closed the door and leaned on it, talking to her through the open window.

"It's for breaking and entering."

"So long as it's not for breaking his skull. It's got my prints and DNA all over it."

CJ reassured her with a nod and made his way back along the wall to the door, where he levered the rusty nails out with no difficulty. He jammed the point of the pry bar between the door and its frame and levered against it. He wasn't expecting it to be difficult, but it was even easier than he'd hoped. The door splintered around the lock. He stamped down the overgrowth of grass and forced the door open wide enough to squeeze through. He cleared a way through the shrubs beyond it and peered at the house, where Masterson's wife was walking on the terrace. She was holding the hand of Ophelia, whose blond hair bounced and trailed behind her as she hopped and skipped to keep up with her mother. They stopped at a set of French doors and turned back to Masterson. He was standing on the lawn with two croquet sticks held in one hand. The mother bent down and spoke to the girl, who waved to her father and blew him a kiss. Then they were gone.

CJ watched Masterson as he walked around the lawn, straightening croquet stumps, and he heard a car start and the clang of electric gates. Masterson disappeared into a white shed at the end of the lawn with the croquet sticks and ball and emerged empty-handed. CJ tracked his progress back to the house, working his way along the wall hidden by bushes and picking an ambush spot behind a utility shed next to the path. He sent Enya the text. Masterson stopped a few moments later and pulled a phone out of his pocket.

"CJ! … What? I did no such thing. … Oh my God, poor Sami. I saw something on the news, but… Steady on. You have no right to… Shit…"

He stood looking at the phone before setting off back to the house and stopping midstride.

CJ was standing right in front of him.

No words. No dear-old-chum stuff. Just a single hop and CJ's sidekick hit Masterson in the chest. He flew back, his phone skittering off into the rose garden and his foot catching on the curb lining the path. He tumbled, rolling back onto the lawn. CJ fetched the phone from the rose garden before attending to Masterson, who was on his back, his mouth opening and closing like a feeding fish.

CJ bent over him.

"Can't breathe, eh? Try thinking about something else."

CJ grabbed him by the ankles and dragged him across the lawn, scraping him over the curb so his head crunched on the path. That got him breathing again— a starter shriek followed by gasping and groaning.

CJ dragged him into the shed and slammed the door.

On one side, it was a gardener's world—mowers, clippers and blades, and cupboards stocked with herbicides and pesticides. On the other, it was a DIY shop with jars hanging underneath shelves full of screws and nails and carpentry tools arrayed on the wall above a workbench. CJ sat Masterson on a chair and tied his wrists to its arms with gardener's rope—thin plastic stuff with a braided metal core.

"Lovely workshop." CJ poked around. "Premium tools." He picked up a chisel and checked its edge. "German. Very nice." He set it aside, dragged a sawhorse in front of Masterson's chair, straddled it and pulled out his captive's phone. "PINs and passwords. You can't do anything these days without a bloody PIN." He grabbed Masterson's thumb, stuck it on the Start button and logged in. "I see you've got one of those encrypted messaging apps. Me too." He looked up. "But you really should put an expiration date on the messages. That way, incriminating stuff disappears. For example, this exchange between you and Kowalski after we had that chummy lunch by the river."

Masterson's chest was heaving, and pink foam was oozing out of his mouth. "It's not..." More chest heaving, still not ready for whole sentences.

"What it looks like?" CJ finished for him. "This bit, you mean? I told you to fix the bastard while he was out on his back."

"It was a trust fund. I was supposed to set it up for you. But I didn't. That's why I offered you the job."

CJ shook his head, incredulous. "If that's your best lie, you are way up the creek. So who did Sami?"

"God knows. That must have been some robbery gone wrong. The kids are all on drugs now. Crazies."

CJ went back to the phone, but he was locked out already.

"What's the PIN?"

"CJ, this has gone far enough. Cut these ropes. We'll shake hands. No real harm done. Nothing a glass of malt won't sort out."

"Come on, Phillip. This thumb stuff is a drag."

"Don't push your luck, CJ. I know you've got problems. But this situation is recoverable. I owe you that."

CJ stared at him. No more heaving chest. Now it was all puffed up with indignation, his red face shining with it. That was Phillip Masterson. He was tied in a chair with the shit kicked out of him, but he was still giving orders. CJ slid off the sawhorse and poked around the gardening tools.

"This takes me back." He picked up a chainsaw and yanked on the starter cord. The motor spun but didn't fire. He tried again. Nothing. "I saw a guy get his arm cut off with one of these." He shook it next to his ear to check for fuel. Then he pulled on the cord again, harder this time, and it fired. But as he eased it next to Masterson's arm, it stopped. "Damn." He put it on the bench and hunted in cupboards. "Say, Phillip, can you help a guy out here? I'm looking for some fuel."

"Screw it up your arse."

CJ turned back towards him. The conversation had

evidently moved on. Masterson had shifted gears. No more whining and cajoling, pleading and persuading. He'd done a racing change and zoomed up into threatening.

"I take it the spokesperson job is off the table?"

"You are so going to regret this."

CJ went back to the cupboards and pulled out a fuel container.

"Found it." He shook the can. "Not too much, though." He poured it into the chainsaw tank. "He was a friend of mine too. That guy whose arm they cut off. Columbian bastards." He yanked the starter, but it didn't fire. "We were in Florida. Some goddamn motel bathroom." He grabbed the cord again, then stopped. "No. Wait. That wasn't me. That was Scarface. I've never even been to Florida." Masterson looked up at him, terror draining his hubris, his puffed-up chest a thing of the past. "I must be getting better. Months ago I'd never have figured that out. It's one of my issues. Like inappropriate behavior." He pulled the cord and it fired. "The truth is that I have no personal experience of cutting off arms with a chainsaw. I'm just an amateur. But I watched that movie so many times, I feel like I'm fully trained."

He lowered the screaming chainsaw halfway down Masterson's upper arm and eased it closer, with Masterson skewing his head like a barn owl to track the action. Contact. But not too much. Blood sprayed in a fine mist and Masterson howled. Then the chainsaw stopped and so did the howling. CJ shook it again against his ear. There was plenty of fuel in it.

"Must be some kind of blockage." He tried again, but it wouldn't start. "I'm crap with machines. Alex was magic. The engine whisperer, we used to call him.

Anything that ate fuel loved that guy." He dropped the chainsaw back with the other gardening tools and searched a wall of blades and shears.

"You cut me." Masterson bawled it out, catching up on recent events in a single horrified moment. "Look at this blood."

"We could have done this nicely. I asked you for the PIN."

"You'd have done it anyway."

"You set us up in Iraq."

"I just passed on the damn message."

"Just following orders. The old Nuremberg defense. It didn't work for the Nazis and it's not going to work for you."

He pulled a curved blade from the top shelf. "Beautiful." He passed the kukri from one hand to the other, checking its balance. "Your average wanker would treat a blade like this as something special and mount it on the wall in his house. But in Nepal, these are just garden tools. So you keep it in the garden shed where it belongs. That's real classy."

He went back to Masterson and sat astride the sawhorse.

"Last chance saloon." He grabbed Masterson's hand, catching the thumb over the arm of the chair. "I need your PIN. Or your thumb."

"Enough damn theater. I get it. You're angry. A lot of bad things happened to you, and now Sami is dead. But think of it. That video. It's got to be MI6. Who else would have that?"

"I didn't mention the video."

"You did. You're getting mixed up again. Like that movie thing." CJ wondered about that. But no. His mind had glitches, certain cogs that wobbled and turned out random results. But simple recall wasn't an issue. He could remember every word that had passed between them, and none of them was video. In his desperation, Masterson had blundered. He'd confessed by implication, and explaining it away by blaming CJ's mental state was a weasel hole he was never going to escape through. "It wasn't me in Iraq. I was just running a few units. I never got down in the weeds on all that stuff. It was Kowalski and Preston. They made all the deals."

"PIN or thumb?" CJ lifted the kukri.

"CJ, I'm worried about you. I truly am. Just back off. We can sort this arm with a few stitches. No real harm done. But you need help, my friend."

"Isn't that just like old comrades? Your situation is not rosy. That chainsaw rip in your arm could get infected, and you're tied in a chair being terrorized by an individual of dubious sanity. But you're not worried about that. You don't give a damn about yourself. Your only thought is about me. Your old mate. That's real goose bumps stuff. And it's the same for me. Some of my brain scans break the machine, and I talk to the dead. But I don't give a damn about that. About myself. All I can think about is you, and how the hell you're going to play croquet with Ophelia with only one thumb."

It hung there. The image.

Then it dropped. The kukri.

And Phillip Masterson's thumb popped off and fell in his lap. He opened his mouth. But no scream came out. That was because he was sucking instead of blowing, and vocal cords don't work backwards. His eyes were getting it all wrong too. They were looking at CJ instead of the bizarrely inappropriate thumbs-up signal he was getting from his thumb which was caught in the ruck of his pants zipper.

"Two options." CJ leaned forward, getting in his face. "I walk out of here and your wife finds you like this. Not a happy moment. Or even worse, Ophelia comes looking for you. Now that's a thought that makes me sad. On the other hand, you could tell me the PIN. I'll cut you loose. You grab your thumb and stick it in your pocket, then scurry on back to the house. You call an ambulance on the landline. Better use your other hand for that. Thirty minutes from now, you're in hospital and surgeons are sewing your thumb back on. You get to tell your wife you're a klutz and you're never going to touch another gardening tool. Next summer you'll be back on the croquet lawn. Ophelia's hero."

"Eight-five-six-two."

CJ input the numbers. They worked. Only one thing left. Masterson. How to finish this?

CJ crouched in front of him.

"CJ, please…"

CJ pointed the kukri at him. "We were eyeball to eyeball. Alex and me. Right up to the end. You sent us into that. You knew. And now there's Sami. What are you guys protecting?"

"Rumbleby."

"Who's he?"

"I don't know. I swear." His head rolled and he wailed.

CJ watched him, his eyes tracking down from his tears to the stream of blood pooling on the floor.

"What should we do with him, Alex?" CJ called it back over his shoulder. Masterson snapped to attention, gawking down at the thumb in his lap, then back at CJ. "That's right, pal. Alex is here with us right now. He's always with me. He's deciding if you're going to live or die. I'm waiting to deliver the sentence. I know I said you could live. Have your thumb sewn back on. But I'm a goddamn liar. Ophelia can survive without croquet. And without a dad. I never had one, and look how well I turned out."

Masterson howled as CJ raised the kukri and slammed it down, slicing the rope and shaving the hairs from Masterson's wrist. The army man swallowed his howls with a gasp and snatched his thumb from his lap. CJ snipped the rope on the other side and was at the door when he turned around.

"Phillip…"

Masterson looked up. He was holding his injured hand under his chin and putting his thumb into his pocket with his other hand.

CJ hurled the kukri, its curved blade scything past Masterson as he dived for the floor. It nailed into the back of the chair and sent it rolling back to the wall.

"Tell Kowalski. We're coming."

TWELVE

"No blood." CJ held out the pry bar, but Enya ignored it. She was looking at his jacket, his face, his arms and his legs. There was plenty of blood there. He slipped the pry bar back in the Harrods bag.

"Is he dead?" She started the car as he buckled up.

"Only on the inside."

She glowered at him and took off, gunning the Mini through empty lanes. When they reached the main road, she eased back and they drove in silence, Enya drilling him with an impatient glare every time the car rolled to a halt in the Saturday-morning traffic.

"I got this." He pulled Masterson's phone out of his pocket.

"Great." She glanced at it. "Why don't you just send them a route map of where we're going?"

"I'll shut down the networking." He hit a few keys. "We're off the grid now."

"If you'd trusted me more, we could have done this a lot smarter. If you'd infected the phone with malware and left it with him, we could have spied on them. All you had to do was click a link on his phone. It's that easy."

He'd never thought of that. And why not? She'd fooled him easily enough. If it hadn't been for her blundering big mouth, he'd still be toting around the bug she'd put on his phone.

"What if I send Kowalski a message from Masterson phone? Would that work?"

"If he's dumb enough to click the link."

CJ thought about that. Masterson would be at the hospital already, or on his way there at least. But had he sent Tratfors a news bulletin after he'd called the paramedics? CJ was doubtful. That was not going to be an easy conversation. Masterson had failed three times. The night nurse, Sami, and now this. Setting him up for Sami's murder was the perfect solution, effectively fitting him up for a tight jacket in a high-security clinic. That would have made up for the night nurse fiasco. Masterson would be back on Tratfors' A-team. But none of that had happened. Three strikes. CJ had never seen a baseball game, but he'd hung out with Americans long enough to know the rules. And Masterson's strike three was particularly egregious. He'd been humiliated. He'd lost his phone. And his thumb. Not that Tratfors would be bothered about his lost appendage. If they found out he'd given up Kowalski and Rumbleby, he'd lose a lot more than that. CJ combed back through his memory, searching for the name Rumbleby, but he drew a blank. He was sure he'd remember. It was such an odd name.

"Pull over." CJ pointed to a supermarket and Enya swung off the road and parked in its lot.

They huddled over the phone and CJ typed in a reply to Kowalski's *fix him* message. *Does this guy look fixed or what?* Then he gave the phone to Enya and she typed in the booby-trapped link. She tapped it in without hesitation, pulling it out of her head like it was her birthdate. A short URL wired to malware that would turn Kowalski's phone into a pocket spy. CJ wondered about that. *What kind of person has stuff like that hanging off her fingertips?*

They sent the message, then switched off the phone's networking and eased back into the traffic.

"So if he clicks on it, what will that give us?" CJ said.

"It'll open a port to let me in. Firewalls block connections from the outside. But replies made to calls from inside out are permitted. It's the Trojan Horse thing. That's the basis of it. But I can't tell you what I can get to until I get inside."

CJ continued to check Masterson's messages.

"You were right," he said. "We were set up in Iraq. He admitted it. He killed Sami too. Or he was part of it. And I'm pretty sure he sent the night nurse."

"The who?"

"Never mind. We were set up to protect some guy called Rumbleby."

Enya turned into the entrance of her rental flat's underground parking and stopped. She pointed at the phone.

"Switching on airplane mode and even turning it off does not necessarily mean that the phone can't be tracked. It depends on how it was set up. We should stick it in the fridge when we get upstairs. I'll set up my computer. Then we can download it all and dump the phone somewhere."

The fridge?

He didn't even bother to ask.

The gate rolled up, and Enya drove down the ramp

and parked the car. They went up to the apartment and CJ washed off Masterson's blood in the shower, finding numerous cuts and bruises on his arms where he'd squeezed through the brush by the wall. He cleaned them up, then put on a fresh set of clothes. Back in the living room, Enya had already set up her laptop and was downloading data from the phone. She swung her chair around as he walked into the room, an ultimatum etched in frown lines on her face.

"Are you going to tell me or not?"

"What?"

"The blood. You killed him, didn't you?"

CJ relaxed. This he could handle. "Do you have a beer?"

"Is that supposed to be an answer?"

He fetched one from the fridge and settled on the sofa, looking up at her.

"I need to know," she said. "Or this is the end of the line for us. I will not be an accessory to murder."

"These bastards killed your brother. So what do you want me to do with them? I asked you before, but I got no answer."

"I want to hurt them. Expose them. Ruin their business. Their lives. Humiliate them. Look at that house. All that money. Status. I want to take it all away from them. That's the way to destroy them. Have their wives leave them and their brat kids mobbed on Facebook. That's the smart way. Not like a Neanderthal. Climbing walls and bashing heads in. I can't be a party to that."

"Are you finished?"

She turned away and stared out the window, but made no reply.

"Did you ever play games with your dad on a

Saturday morning?" he said. "Not croquet, of course. Maybe football."

She spun back towards him. "What the hell has that got to do with anything?"

"I was wondering what it must feel like to have a memory like that."

"Did you kill him? Yes or no."

CJ stood up, put his beer down and ran his hand through her hair, tilting her head up to look into his eyes. "I did not kill Masterson."

"You swear it."

"I didn't kill him." He let go of her head and picked up his beer. "That was the hardest part of it all."

He waited, sipping his beer and staring into her eyes.

She nodded. "Let's get some food."

He followed her into the kitchen, where they microwaved a ready-meal. A curry. Then they ate it in silence, lounging on the sofa, watching the news. Sami—so big in the morning—had already been swept off the front page by a mass shooting in the US. They watched the scene. Wall-to-wall coverage on all news channels.

"Did you ever go to California?" CJ said.

"I worked there."

"You know a place called Simi Valley?"

"I was more of a Silicon Valley type."

"Alex has family there."

"You plan to visit?"

CJ pulled himself up and sat on the edge of the couch.

"We had a geography book in school with a quote from some famous writer. "'The spring is beautiful in California'—that's how it started."

"*The Grapes of Wrath.*"

"It went on about flowers, grapes and old vines. And hills… *round and soft as breasts.* I was about thirteen at the time. So that was an image I could work with."

"I'm guessing your California dreaming is not just about literary nostalgia and family visits. Is Tratfors HQ on your sightseeing list?"

"I knew I'd end up in California as soon as I read that. *Hills like soft breasts.*"

"Point of information. California has the death penalty."

He nodded, his eyes following the aftermath of the mass shooting.

"So do I?" he said.

He left her and made tea in the kitchen, and when he walked back into the living room with two mugs of steaming brew, she was at the table, arms cradling the laptop, eyes inches from its screen.

"I'm decrypting it," she said. "The keys are on the phone. That way we can search it better."

"Find Rumbleby."

"I wouldn't hold out much hope. People say seriously weird things when their life's on the line."

"Like *Cat and Canary?*"

She looked up. Sharp. But not surprised.

"For what it's worth, I know you searched my cupboard and found that tape. You think I'd leave a strange man alone in my flat without a camera to keep an eye on him?"

CJ nodded. He should have guessed.

"So what did you expect to find on it?"

"If I knew that—why would I look for it? My brother said it before he died, according to you. I searched for *Cat and Canary* online, and that film was one of the few meaningful hits I got."

It was hardly an answer. But it was all he was going to get and he knew it.

"Sneaky bitch." He said it softly, more like a private musing than a personal insult.

She smiled like there was a buried compliment in there somewhere, but she didn't look up. "Don't knock it. If the sneaky bitch hadn't been around yesterday, you'd still be stuck in McDonald's. And I can help you tomorrow too."

"How?"

"I've got a contract in Paris. It was a last-minute thing and I couldn't get a flight, so I'm booked on the Eurostar. I leave in the morning. Why don't you come with me? We could amend the booking at the station. It's safer than the airport, and we could fly to California from Paris."

"If there's an arrest warrant for me, there'll be a Red Alert. It'll be all over Europe. Paris, London. Ports, stations, airports. It won't matter."

"You think there will be?"

He shook his head. "Not yet. Maybe never. These guys want me out of the way. That could mean dead. In a straitjacket. Hiding out in South America. They'd all work."

"I take it you already have a passport and a US visa waiver?"

"I don't need a visa waiver. I'm going to turn up at the Mexican border and fill in the forms there."

"You're booked already?"

"I'm heading to Schiphol. Early a.m. I get a connecting flight from there to Mexico City."

"Now who's the sneaky one." She stood up. "So that's it?"

"For us?" He shook his head. "I'll get a phone in the US and we'll fix up some way to keep in touch. And when you're in Paris, keep working on the phone data."

"I'm going to take a long bath," she said. "You better get some rest."

CJ stretched out on the couch as she disappeared down the hallway. He closed his eyes and was soon asleep. When he opened them, it was almost dark outside, and inside too with a single lamp angled over Enya's laptop. She was typing in spurts, muttering, her running commentary spliced with encouragement, admonishment and abuse.

Try that… no… idiot… that's better… what about?

He listened to her banter, smiling. He was lying on his side on the sofa, his head pointing directly at the table where she was working. She was facing him, wearing a burgundy silk kimono, her upper body and face partly hidden. He was looking straight ahead, watching her legs under the table. They were tracking her voiceover, her knees scissoring back and forth to record every triumph, her pale skin flashing white, ghostly against the dark cloth swishing in and around her thighs.

He closed his eyes.

He had never asked God. He didn't deserve it. He'd been told as much since he was a boy. Even during his years of captivity, pain, and torment. He'd never begged for salvation. He'd looked for something else. Something flowing inside him. Something bound up so tight to life that it was inseparable. He reached inside and touched it and made a wish. Then he was down by the river with Doctor Sam's voice frothing in his ears, seducing the entrails of his senses, tricking him into feeling once again.

His eyes opened.

Enya was looking down on him, her hand drawing its fingers across his cheek. He could feel her touch as her nails snagged each hair of his stubble. He took her hand and kissed her fingers. She watched as he separated each finger and kissed it, each touch a high-voltage jolt pulsing through him. She dropped the kimono to the floor and stood motionless while he studied her body. He reached up and she slid between his arms and unbuttoned his shirt and belt. When he was naked, she lowered herself onto him and they made love like that on the sofa.

In the bedroom later, she lit scented candles and they played with each other and poked fun at each other. They laughed and drank coffee. Then he took her again. Suddenly. A wall of uncertainty casting its cold shadow. How long had he got? The numbness would be back. Or some Tratfors hit man would get lucky. He had to love her like this was the last time. No salutary gestures. No perfunctory moves. A single loving to fill those years of empty nights and seize an endless future of joy that might never come to pass. He had to squeeze all that into now and play it out on the physical and emotional bridge between them.

It was still dark when Enya drove him to the airport. They were late. But the early a.m. traffic was light and they made up enough time to pull over by a dumpster and get rid of Masterson's phone. CJ turned it on to check for messages one last time.

"Did it work?" Enya said.

CJ shook his head as he read Kowalski's reply.

Hi, CJ, I hear you're on the way. Great. We've got plenty to catch up on. Sean.

"Damn," she said. "What do you think?"

CJ shrugged.

"I mean about the trip. They'll be waiting. We need to rethink this."

"What about justice? Turning them into paupers. Wives dumping them. Kids shunned on Facebook. What about all that?"

"That was yesterday. Today is something else. We're something else."

He turned off the phone and tossed it in the trash. He pulled her close and kissed her.

"Enjoy Paris. We'll talk when I'm in LA."

Part Two

LOS ANGELES

THIRTEEN

So this was California…

CJ surveyed the storied landscape. Not a grapevine in sight. As for flowers, there were a few. They were decorating the posters advertising two margaritas for the price of one and brightening up the graffiti on the construction barriers.

Hills like soft breasts, anyone?

Dream on.

He was at the San Ysidro Port of Entry, where twenty thousand people a day legged it over the border, and even on its best day, it was going to have a tough job living up to John Steinbeck's mellifluous prose. Besides, this day was far from its best. It was hot with no wind, and pollution lounged undisturbed, nestling comfortably on sidewalks and bridges. It was not CJ's best day either. He'd had a big night in Tijuana, and the aftertaste of tequila was dragging at his feet as he walked ever onward, his recently acquired baseball cap slung low. At least the entry had gone smoothly. He'd slipped a photo of him and Alex into his passport, a snapshot from the Iraq War. Both of them were in full battle gear. It slipped out of his passport as the granny-type border agent processed him, and she took a long look at it as CJ filled in the blanks, calling Alex a hero and telling her about his plans to visit his family to let them know how he died. She'd eyeballed the photo, shaking her head, almost tearing up. It went so well, he thought they might offer him a limo ride. But instead he got a bucketload of thanks and sound advice about how to take care of himself in the US.

Safely through, he ducked the taxis and ended up at the San Ysidro Transit Station standing at a ticket machine, the still center of a map of bodies on the move, everyone knowing exactly where to go and how to get there. All except CJ, his face inches from the ticket machine, his arm floating around above his head to block the sun as he read the instructions. When he finally got his ticket, he rode the tram to downtown San Diego, where he took a cab to the vacation rental in Santa Monica that Enya had fixed up, skimming a drive-thru en route to pick up a bean burrito, some beef tacos and a large black coffee.

CJ was all eyes as the driver slowed down to check the building numbers. Trees, lawns, and low-rise apartment buildings, all done in pastel tones lit by the orange light of the winter sun.

He picked up the key from the designated neighbor and let himself in. The apartment was on the second floor of a two-story building. It was small but comfy, its closets packed with a woman's clothes and its drawers stuffed with her boots and shoes. According to Enya, the owner was traveling in Asia and subsidizing her trip by renting out her home.

He was in the kitchen, cataloging the food supply

she'd left in the fridge, when a phone rang in the lounge. He ignored it, but it rang again, so he picked it up. It was Enya calling from Paris. After catching up, they talked about the Santa Monica apartment, which Enya had stayed in a year earlier.

"It's only a couple of blocks from the sea," she said. "There's a huge beach and a clifftop park. A pier. And Venice Beach is just down the road. They've got a boardwalk with street acts. I saw a guy juggling chainsaws there. That'd be right up your street."

"What about the phone data you downloaded?"

"Nothing going back that far. Just the incriminating messages you already found."

"No Rumbleby?"

"Zero hits."

"So nothing useful."

"For what it's worth, Masterson and Kowalski are both golf fanatics. They've got some sort of bet going on handicaps. Whatever that means."

"Where does Kowalski play?"

"He was crowing about getting a membership to some fancy country club."

That was a good hit. The perfect place to catch him with his guard down.

"Send the address," he said.

"Hold on. I've got another call. That's weird. It's the concierge at my Richmond place. I'll call you back."

And she was gone.

CJ continued to explore the apartment before zapping his coffee and tacos in the microwave and stashing his bean burrito in the fridge. He'd finished eating and was watching CNN News when Enya rang back.

"The police raided my flat."

"Looking for me?"

"Have you ever heard of the 1897 Police Property Act?"

"No."

"Well my lawyer has, and he's just told me—"

"What happened?"

"They took my computers. The entire rack. They were IT cops with screwdrivers and a warrant. There's just a bunch of cables in there now, according to the concierge."

CJ said nothing.

"What is it?" she said.

"Are you calling me on your mobile?"

"Damn. I'll get another phone."

"This is a landline. Even if they're not monitoring your calls, they'll be able to track the location from your phone record."

"How was I supposed to see this coming?"

It was a good point. But CJ wasn't into blame games anyway. The issue on his mind was the why behind the raid.

"Is there an arrest warrant for you?" he said.

"Me? There's not even one for you so far as I know. They didn't even mention you."

"You can't go back there."

"I have to. I live there. I'll get a new phone and post the new contact details and the address of that country club in the secure mailbox we agreed on. Then you can buy a burner cell and we can talk encrypted."

They signed off and CJ went outside. The apartment came with a car. A VW Golf. It was tucked in the shade down a ramp under the building. He left it there and strolled down to the shopping area around Main Street, where he meandered in and out of stores and gawked at Californians like a bona fide tourist. He bought two phones, some clothes, and a flashy multitool. He stopped off in a coffee shop with Wi-Fi and ate a sandwich while he unpacked one of the phones and set it up. He installed the encrypted app and he logged in to the secure mailbox to download the country club address. Enya had already purchased a new phone too, so he noted the details.

Chores done, he stuffed his new belongings into a bag, slung it over his shoulder and walked down to Ocean Avenue. The day was winding down and the clifftop park was buzzing between work and no work. Walkers, joggers, skaters. California's fitness interlude was playing out, with CJ Brink its idle spectator. He stood at the rail, looking down at the beach, and at the sun as it melted into the Pacific in a splotch of flaming colors.

He called Enya. Encrypted, safe.

"Any idea what they're looking for on those computers?" He wasn't expecting the truth. But it was worth a try. They were lovers now. That meant something. To him at least.

"Just our business. Technical stuff. And it's encrypted."

She was still hiding something. She didn't trust him. But the computers weren't the only issue. Their new status as lovers had other implications.

"Someone tried to kill me in the hospital and make it look like an accident. Then someone set me up for murder. Most probably the same someone. And that failed too. So I'm a target and you're my lover. That makes you a target too. That's one issue. And the second issue is jail. If you go back to the UK, the police will ask you for the passwords of those computers, and if you refuse, they'll get a court order. And if you refuse that, you'll go to jail until you change your mind. So why don't you skip London and fly from Paris to LA? I'll pick you up at the—"

"I'll message the ETA."

They closed out the call, and CJ waited for the sun to finish its business with the Pacific before walking back to the apartment through streets busy with hurry-home traffic.

The apartment was just as he'd left it. No issues. He booted up his laptop and set up a VPN session to ensure both his anonymity and his privacy. He opened a private browsing window and spent some time studying the country club site before moving on to the surrounding area with Google as his tour guide. It took him hours, flipping between satellite images and maps before drilling down on the detail in street view. The Sierra Mar Country Club was spread over rocky hills with views out over the ocean. Its entrance was at the end of a road bordered by the kind of houses you might expect in a neighborhood where a club membership cost several times the average US house price. The guard booth was on a center isle with a barrier gate for incoming traffic. The parking lot entrance was located behind the guard booth, so you had to pass through the barrier before you could make the turn to enter it. But the parking lot exit was before the guard post, so you could drive out without passing the guard booth a second time, although there was a driver-activated barrier to stop anyone from entering that way.

CJ studied all this, edging the street view avatar as close as he could to the guardhouse and the gates. The parking lot had to be the place. But there was no way to drive into it unless you were a club member or on a list of invitees, and no way to walk in off the road without being seen by the armed guard in the booth. So he turned his attention to the houses on the street that ran parallel with the parking lot, walking his avatar down the road checking each house. They all had neat lawns, no fences, and well-tended gardens. They all had discreet signs too. There were different names and logos on the signs, but always the same message. Armed response. Yes. These were people with something in common. They all had stuff worth protecting and neighbors who might make a call if they saw a strange Englishman wandering around the place.

Hours later, he had a shortlist. Three houses where the layout favored success. He was looking for a combination of factors—a lack of threatening signs, cameras that were nonexistent, poorly located, or fake-looking, and easy access to a backyard with plenty of trees to sneak around in. Satisfied with his plan, he stretched out on the sofa and ran it through his head over and over, visualizing the parking lot, the streets, the houses and running different scenarios late into the night, until he drifted into an uneasy sleep.

FOURTEEN

CJ woke early and walked to downtown Santa Monica, where he picked up some breakfast and found a mailbox center about to open. He bought packing materials and address labels, then headed back to the apartment, taking the long route via the clifftop park.

According to Enya, Kowalski had become a creature of habit, a sign that he was getting soft. Once upon a time, he'd been a US Army Ranger with a skill set fine-tuned for survival in conflict zones, where the cardinal rule was *change your routine and stay alive*. But that was there and then, and this was here and now. Sunny California. It was his home turf. And Sean Kowalski felt comfortable enough to run his life in well-worn grooves, one of which would deliver him at the Sierra Mar Country Club at ten thirty.

CJ put together some fake packages and made the trip with forty-five minutes to spare. He drove his VW along the now-familiar streets neither suspiciously slowly nor oddly fast. He was counting on the fact that in today's gig economy, the sight of a man in no special uniform driving no special vehicle turning up at the door of a house with a package was commonplace.

Reaching the first of his handpicked houses, he cruised on by. It was a blowout. Two cars in the driveway. The second was interesting. A prospect. He pulled up past the empty driveway, consulted his phone for the benefit of any nosy neighbors, then walked the package up to the front door. It had an old-fashioned peephole. No fancy technology. No hidden camera. No magic doorbell taking a mugshot and sending it to the homeowner. He rang the doorbell and smiled for the peephole as he held up the package. But the fictitious Holly Johnson wasn't at home. He waited, casually checking the street. Not much to see. It was all but invisible behind overgrown bushes. He left the box on the porch, slipped around the back and peeked through a window. The furniture was covered. The house was empty. Maybe it was for sale. The backyard had a footpath snaking around trees and shrubs that were losing the fight against an overgrowth of weeds. This was even better than he'd hoped—as close to a jungle as it gets in Southern California.

He made his way through the garden to the parking lot. No wall. Just a chain-link fence about six feet high. He peered through its green links. There were four rows of parking spots, but only two of them were shaded by awnings. The two center rows were open to the sun, except where they were shaded by trees that were scattered throughout the lot. CJ scrambled over the fence and walked along a line of parked cars before dodging behind an oak tree at the corner furthest away from the entrance.

In the next twenty minutes, four cars rolled up to the guardhouse, passed through and turned into the lot. CJ dismissed them one by one as he watched their drivers park and head up to the clubhouse or across the road to the tennis courts opposite the parking lot. Then he saw the Lincoln and he knew it was Kowalski. The barrier went up as soon as it rolled into view. No stopping. It didn't even slow down. But it didn't turn into the parking lot either. It drove straight past the entrance and continued up the road to the clubhouse. CJ groaned. His plan was in meltdown already. Kowalski had a chauffeur. All those scenarios he'd rehearsed—but none of them included a chauffeur. He'd planned for Kowalski the regular guy, a normal human being who would drive his own goddamn car. But what he got was Kowalski the big shot. What was it Masterson called him? Strategic director. Of course he had a driver. Tratfors was a billion-dollar company now.

A few minutes later, the Lincoln was back, turning into the parking lot and looking for a shady spot. There were plenty to choose from, but the driver was lazy. He just rolled it to a stop under the awning beyond the last parked car, gobbling up the best part of two slots. He got out and stretched. He was big. Six five or more, with muscles stuffed so tight under his jacket it looked two sizes too small. He opened the trunk and took something out of a sports bag. A tie. He folded it carefully, then stashed it in the glove box and got back in the car. But he left the door open, and a few minutes later, the rhythmic thud of hip-hop drifted across the concrete.

So Kowalski had a driver with a tie, big muscles and a taste for hip-hop. But not the kind of driver you get from a rent-a-chauffeur company. That kind of guy knows how to wear a suit. It happens every day. But this guy was clearly uncomfortable in his. He walked in it like a penguin. Even the few steps he took to the trunk were animated with weird stretches, his fat neck writhing like he was trying to crawl out of his jacket via the collar. Then there was that odd ritual with the tie, stashing it for availability so he wouldn't have to wear it unless it was absolutely necessary. Maybe Kowalski had a big lunch date after golf, so the poor guy had to dress up.

CJ waited ten minutes.

He couldn't see what the guy was doing through the tinted glass, and the shade of the awning made it doubly difficult. But he could guess. He was doing what everyone does when they've nothing else to do and what most people do even when they have something better to do. He was playing with his phone. Surfing the web. Checking his social media feeds. Playing some stupid game. The internet—that global seductress—was making out with one of her slaves and she had him in a trance.

CJ edged out from behind the oak tree. He slipped between the cars and the fence and worked his way towards the Lincoln. He'd always admired confidence. But where was the line between confident and cocky? This guy was getting that all wrong. He was huge. Muscles with muscles. A gun. And this was an empty parking lot in a secure location. R and R time. So why not kick back, listen to a few tunes and kill a few scumbags online playing your favorite game? He'd left the door open too, and that was a bonus. He couldn't see CJ approaching in the side-view mirror, and when he did see him, two blades of CJ's multitool were already pressing against his throat.

He dropped his phone on the floor.

"Hands on the dash." The big guy did as he was told. "It's a serrated blade and a wood saw," CJ said. "I know you were wondering."

A smear of blood oozed down the driver's throat, running in grooves of muscle. CJ reached under his jacket and pulled out a 9mm pistol. "Sig. Nice." He let the gun hang by his side and kept the blades under his chin. "Hands on thighs." He waited until the man had complied. "Out." The driver stepped out of the car in slow motion, CJ guiding his progress with the blades under his chin. "Hands on the car. You know the routine." CJ held the gun on him as he leaned on the car. He put the multitool on the ground and searched him. No backup gun, but a jackknife with an exotic wood handle and turquoise inlay. CJ slipped it in his pocket. "Now open the trunk."

The guy turned around and gave him a look like this was going to be a deal breaker. CJ was standing a few feet off. He lowered the gun, pointing it at the man's groin. "Please," he said.

Whether it was the gun, the target or the please, it worked. The driver trudged to the back of the Lincoln and opened its trunk.

"Drop the keys on the ground."

He did it.

"Now empty the trunk."

"There's nothing in it." It was the first time he'd said anything. CJ couldn't place the accent. American, obviously. But no Southern drawl or New York twang.

"Sure there is. The sports bag. Kick it under the car."

He did that too while CJ edged close enough to look into the trunk.

"The tools too. Under the car."

The guy hunted around and pulled out a tool kit rolled up in plastic and emergency medical supplies in a box with a white cross. He dropped it all on the ground and kicked it under the car. CJ was edging closer all the time. "Now get in," he said, and as the man turned to clamber into the trunk, CJ cracked him on the head with the gun butt. It was easy enough. He'd done it before. One thump and down they go. The big man groaned and his body jolted with the impact. Now all he had to do was keel over and collapse in the trunk.

But that didn't happen. Instead, his elbow slammed back into CJ's ribs and he spun around with an upright palm shooting out and smacking CJ in the face. The gun skidded off the concrete, and CJ tumbled back against a parked car. The driver glanced at the gun but he ignored it. He lurched at CJ's throat, arms outstretched. CJ was leaning back with his weight on the car so the crescent kick was easy, his leg sweeping the man's arms aside and clearing the way for his elbow. An oblique strike. Driving it down into the man's face, flattening his nose with a crunchy squelch like a truck tire rolling over a can of oil. The man staggered back, and CJ swept his trailing leg. The man teetered, then fell like a giant timber, his head cracking on asphalt. CJ stared at his spread-eagled form. The man's chest was cycling up and down, so he was alive at least. CJ picked up the Sig and stuck it in his belt. He dragged the man to the trunk, hauled him up and poked and prodded him inside it.

Son of a bitch.

CJ stared down at him in awe. He'd whacked his head like he was knocking home a six-inch nail, and the guy had shrugged it off. CJ took the tie from the glove box and tied his hands behind his back, still puzzling it over. Whacking people on the head with a gun butt and stuffing them in the trunk seemed so familiar. Routine, even. But the more he thought about it, the more he realized that he'd never actually done it. He slammed the trunk lid down and sat in the car. It must have been in some movie, but he couldn't even remember which one. This had all sounded so easy when he'd planned it the night before. But where was the contingency plan for a chauffeur-bodyguard with a pistol, a couple of black belts, and a head like a cement block? He picked the man's phone up off the floor. That was another problem. Kowalski was certain to call at the end of his game to summon his driver.

What then?

Fake an American accent? Try and talk like the big guy?

That was out of the question. One time in Iraq when they were waiting between jobs, CJ and Alex had passed the time by teaching each other accents. Alex had a gift for it, with an impressive repertoire of British accents. But CJ's best American was feeble, like an old-fashioned Southern gentleman with a speech impediment. He was never going to pass for the steroid penguin in the trunk. So hours later when the phone rang, CJ ignored it, letting it ring through to voicemail. It rang again a few minutes later, and that was followed by two text messages in prompt succession. CJ ignored them all. Sooner or later Kowalski would run out of patience. Then he'd have three options. Send a club employee to investigate, call the office and get them to send in a cavalry platoon, or come and investigate himself. CJ remembered Kowalski as self-assured to the point of arrogance. He was also bound to be armed. Besides, there could be an innocent explanation. The driver might have fallen asleep. Or something as simple as a flat battery in his phone.

CJ crawled under an SUV parked close by the Lincoln and waited.

Ten minutes later, he knew he'd called it right.

The boots. Expensive.

It had to be Kowalski. Some sort of reptile, Texas designer stuff. CJ let them disappear behind rows of tires before crawling out from under the SUV. He watched Kowalski slide between parked cars, drop into a crouch and pull a SIG 9mm from his sports bag. It was a P228 like the chauffeur's gun, which CJ poked in his head the moment Kowalski figured it was all clear and straightened up.

He raised both arms. No heroics.

CJ took his weapon and stuck it in his belt.

"Pick up the bag and head for the car," he said.

Kowalski snatched up the bag and walked with confident strides, like having a gun barrel stuck in his ear was all part of his plan. CJ had him drop the bag on the hood of the Lincoln, and he searched it. It didn't take long. A pair of fancy golf shoes and a phone. CJ pocketed the phone and waved the gun at the back door of the Lincoln.

"Get in," he said.

Kowalski didn't budge.

"Where's Grambo?" he said.

"Who's Grambo?"

"My driver. I can see you already met him." Kowalski smirked, nodding at CJ's face. CJ wiped at it. Blood. Congealed for the most part and now strewn in lumps across the back of his hand.

"He's in the trunk."

"The trunk?" Kowalski smirked again. "Not the

boot." He looked to the side, as though there was an imaginary audience to appreciate his humor. "You're a fast learner."

CJ sucked it all up. He didn't have much in the way of smart one-liners. But he did have two guns. He pulled the second Sig from his belt and stepped up to Kowalski, guns hanging loosely on either side. Daring him. Hoping. He leaned in close enough to smell the soap on Kowalski's face.

"I'm a trainee American," he said, his voice gravelly. "I've only been on the job three days, and already I own two guns. I'd call that a very fast learner."

The smirk fled. The applauding onlookers too. There was only CJ and Kowalski left. And only one way this was going to go. Kowalski got in the car.

There were two backseats separated by an amenities dashboard. CJ made him fold it out of the way and wriggle across to the far side. That proved to be something of a challenge. Kowalski was not the guy CJ remembered. He still had the broad shoulders and thick arms, but now he had a belly that looked oddly out of place. It was perfectly round, and it sat on his frame like a bolt-on extension, something he might have ordered online and been sent the wrong size.

CJ stuck one of the guns in his belt. He sat beside Kowalski, jammed the other gun against his extension belly and shut the door.

"Did you kill him?" Kowalski said.

"Grambo?"

He nodded.

"He'll be okay."

"Christopher." Kowalski intoned it, dragging out all the syllables like it was the opening line in a Shakespearean soliloquy. "There is no reason for any of this."

Ten years. That was how long it had been since he'd shared a conversation with Kowalski. That might be long enough to forget. But this wasn't forgetting. This was remembering. CJ hated that name. Regardless of whose mouth it came out of, the only voice he ever heard belonged to Mr. Philpot, the misanthropic psychopath who had run his high school. That was Kowalski's forte. He was a master goader. He always knew exactly where to poke that finger. And CJ couldn't fault him for trying. He was on the wrong end of two guns and his only play left was to put CJ off his stroke. And his plan was working too. CJ needed answers, but his thinking was clouding up already. Needs battling wants. And what he wanted most was to break Kowalski's ribs. But he had to fight that urge. Kowalski was the man. CJ was sure of it. He had Alex's blood all over him. But who else was part of the deal? CJ needed Kowalski alive and cooperative if he was ever going to get to the truth.

"Tell me why you set us up in Iraq and I'll be on my way."

"No one set you up."

"What about Rumbleby?"

Kowalski swept the question aside with a snort and a toss of his head.

"Your luck ran out that day. Face it and move on."

So that was it. Their chitchat was all done. And needs lost and wants won.

CJ shot him in the leg. No preamble. No threats. And not much of a shot either. But then it wasn't meant to be. It was an interlocutor shot. A go-between. A shot to communicate all the things that were getting lost in translation, draining away in the gap between

British and American English. CJ waited while Kowalski noted the new information with a lot of writhing and squeaking. But no screaming. CJ had to give him that. He was an ex-Ranger after all. A tough mother. But not that tough. The groaning went on and on.

"C'mon, Sean. Don't be a wimp. I just nicked the bone. The bullet went in the door there."

"You're crazy." Kowalski's face was pulsing red.

"I prefer cognitively challenged."

"Screw you, asshole."

"You're going to miss a few rounds of golf. No big deal. You'll be back in those cute golf shoes in weeks. But imagine if I'd caught your knee by mistake."

He left it there, the unspoken threat.

Imagine. No kneecap.

The squeaking and groaning stopped. For all his faults, Kowalski was a realist.

"Someone wanted to get rid of O'Brien. That's all I know."

"Why?"

"Ask Preston. He told me to set it up."

"Why not shoot him? Easy enough in Iraq. Stage some kind of accident."

"They wanted to get something out of him. Something he'd only talk about with his balls wired to a twelve-volt battery. But it all got cocked up."

"How was it supposed to go?"

"I made a deal with the militia. You all get grabbed at the ministry. Then they split you up and we get to work on O'Brien. When we're done, we stage a rescue and O'Brien gets tragically killed. You and Alex and the Boers get rescued. Problem solved."

"So what went wrong?"

"Iraq went wrong. Same as always. There was a complication. The militia had a rat. He went into business for himself. He wanted to trade your asses for some of his relatives held by Al-Qaeda."

"And Rumbleby? Masterson told me, so don't deny it."

"Forget that. We can still make this right."

"Not for Sami, we can't."

"That was Masterson's idea. But we can still do this my way. Just disappear. South America. Get lost."

"Why?"

"Because you lived. You're a witness. And now you're boning his sister. None of that's good. Then you start asking questions. And too many people with the power to say who lives and who dies don't like that."

CJ took Kowalski's phone out of his pocket, but he got stuck at the PIN prompt. He looked up at Kowalski.

"Did you hear about Phillip's gardening accident?"

There was a beat of silence while Kowalski considered his response, his eyes drifting down to his hands, each with a complete set of fingers.

"Three-nine-eight-seven," he said.

"Good man." CJ tucked the gun under his arm. He logged into the phone, opened a browser window, typed in a short URL, and clicked through a few screens, all as per Enya's instructions.

"Did you hear about CJ's blowtorch accident?" Kowalski was smirking again. Not a good sign.

CJ looked up from the phone.

There was a man leaning on the Lincoln's hood. He was wearing a blue baseball cap with the initials LA embroidered on it in a different color blue. But CJ wasn't looking at that. He was looking at the Benelli semiautomatic shotgun the man was pointing at him. Tratfors' cavalry had gotten lucky, sneaking up while CJ's hearing was still numb from the gunshot he'd let off in the enclosed space of the Lincoln's cabin.

Tap-tap.

CJ turned his head. There was a man at the side window. He didn't have a hat or shotgun. He had a 9mm pistol and he was using it as a drumstick to tap out a tune on the window. The door on the other side opened, and a third man, wearing a suit, helped Kowalski out of the car. CJ's door opened too, and the pistol man took the Sig from under CJ's arm and the other gun from his belt. He dragged him out of the car while the shotgun man covered him from close range. The suit man with Kowalski left him leaning against the Lincoln while he opened the trunk, and Grambo clambered out of it. His hands were still tied, but he'd managed to slip his legs between his arms so they were tied at the front. The man cut the tie off his wrist and Grambo walked over to CJ.

"See this?" He grabbed an amulet hanging from his neck, cowboy jewelry made out of silver with a turquoise gemstone. He clicked it open. It was full of electronics. CJ looked around. They all had one. "Technology. You dickhead dinosaur. An emergency transponder." He slammed his knee into CJ's groin and he folded up, protecting his chest and belly with one arm and his head and neck with the other. But Grambo wasn't fussy. He kicked and punched him all over while the shotgun and pistol were trained on him from a safe distance.

An SUV rolled up, fetched by the suit.

"Take him to the factory," Kowalski said as he hobbled to the SUV, his arm around the suit's

shoulders. "You can break stuff. But do not kill him."
The pistol man shouldered his gun and opened the
trunk. Grambo dragged CJ to the trunk and tossed him
inside it.

FIFTEEN

Jihadi Jill liked to tie CJ's hands behind his back and hoist him up over an open door, latching his arms over the top so his body would hang by the armpits. It was a poor man's crucifixion. Bloodless. Hours would pass with the pain growing and moans morphing into screams. But then, they too would pass.

Pain and breath.

So long as you had them, you were still alive. CJ was back in that space, following his breath. Pain everywhere. But muffled like the sound of a distant bomb blast from inside a shelter. He was more concerned with damage, maintaining a constant inventory. Head, neck, back, arms and legs. He was bloodied and bruised with humongous swelling. But nothing was fractured yet. And although the ribs had taken a beating, no bones had penetrated his pleural cavity, so his breathing was still good. He was sitting in a metal chair, his wrists bound to its arms with cable ties. The chair was set like a stage ringed by a wall of silent machines, a production line running in a U-shape under a roof of corrugated metal, surrounded by a yard littered with steel barrels. Grambo and the suit were standing at a nearby table. They were taking a break, drinking water from bottles and staring at CJ. The suit wiped his sweaty hands on his white shirt. His collar was open and his tie loose, his jacket flung across the table and topped by a pistol in a shoulder rig.

"What do you think?" he said.

"I think it's the last time he puts me in a trunk."

Grambo put down the bottle and went back to CJ, bending forward to get in his face.

"Welcome to America, *mate*."

He lifted CJ's chin off his chest and looked for a spark in his glazed eyes. The suit edged around to his side.

"Did we overdo it?"

"Screw that." Grambo dropped his head and stepped back.

"Thanks," CJ said, coming back to life with a jerk.

Grambo glanced at the suit and they shared a laugh.

"Don't sweat it, tough guy. We're just warming you up for Kowalski."

"I owe you guys." CJ shook his head as if in wonder. "They tried drugs, surgery. You name it. But it turns out that all I needed to help me remember was a good old-fashioned beating."

"Glad to be of service," Grambo said.

"I say 'good,' but that's just a manner of speaking. The truth is, you guys are shit at this. You wouldn't even make Al-Qaeda's B team."

Grambo lurched at him, but the suit grabbed his shoulder. "I'm going to finish this guy." Grambo shrugged off his hand and towered over CJ, jaw set, fists balled. "You know where this place is, tough guy?"

CJ's eyes roamed around the conveyor belts stacked with red and yellow barrels. The air was acrid, viscous and noxious, like breathing sandpaper.

"Hell?"

"Now you're talking. Welcome to Wilmington. It's a real choice neighborhood. You got the port, chemical plants, oil refineries and hundreds of oil wells. This is Pollution City, and guess where it goes to the toilet? Right here. Hell is soft-soaping it. This is West Coast Drum. It's hell's shit can. An abandoned toxic waste barrel recycling plant. So once upon a time—before California got green—there'd be a bunch of wetbacks loading that belt with empty barrels. I say empty, but there'd still be shit in them. Leftovers. Chemicals, pesticides, *whatevercides*. World-class carcinogens. So these greasers—walking stiffs who'd end up with lumps the size of footballs—they'd send these barrels banging along this line, where they'd get steam cleaned in that unit there." He pointed it out. "But we still got plenty of dirty ones, and that's where you're going to end up. You just get one last choice. Red or yellow. Yes, sir. You get to choose which color barrel you end up in. Then we'll stuff you in it, bang on the lid and drill a few holes in it to make sure you can breathe. We'll stick it out there in the yard, so you'll get plenty of sun. You'll cook in that barrel, eyes on those pinpricks of light feeding you air. You'll sweat to death. Dehydration. You'll be delirious. That's when I'm going to stand on the barrel and piss on it. You'll be thankful, licking up the piss that drips through the holes. The last thing you'll hear is me laughing as you drink my piss."

He stood back, hands on hips, clearly impressed with his oratory.

CJ followed it all with his eyes—the barrels, the production line, the cleaning unit bristling with pipes and tanks.

"I like barrels," he said.

Grambo turned to the suit as if looking for a translation, but he just shrugged and said, "He's one of a kind. I'll give him that."

"Me and barrels go way back," CJ explained. "I have an affinity for barrels."

"He has an *affinity*." Grambo tossed out the word with a campy British accent.

CJ ignored him, lost in his thoughts. "It's all coming back. The barrels. The beating. I'm connecting the dots. Remembering. And the truth is, there's no way I could have done what I did in Iraq without barrels."

"He's losing it," the suit said. "We need to leave something for Kowalski."

CJ looked up at them.

"I learned real old-school karate, and they started me with hand conditioning. Barrel after barrel. The first one was filled with sand. I had to stab my hand into it like a knife blade. Over and over. Months later, they switched me to dried peas. More months. Then I graduated to iron filings. That was a real son of a bitch. Three barrels. That's how I turned my hands into blades."

Grambo frowned and glanced back at the suit, but neither of them spoke.

"I remember now. Jahil had Alex's head in one hand and a knife dripping with his blood in the other. I drove this hand"—he nodded at his bound right arm—"into his belly and scooped out a handful of his guts. I held them above his head, and as he looked up at them, I bit his throat out."

They stared at him, wrong-footed, a sea change underway. Everything was the same on the surface. Grambo and the suit were still in charge, and CJ was still beaten and bound. But all that was cosmetic. They were going to die, and their fate was written on Grambo's face, his eyes shading with fear.

CJ stared into those eyes, hunting down the other man's fear and goading it into terror. "And although I appreciate your letting me choose my color barrel, I don't plan to extend to you the same generosity. So I'm going to stick the suit over there in a red barrel. But for you, Grambo, it has to be yellow."

Grambo stiffened, his face twisting. "I'm going to get the bat," he said, his voice tinny, edging on squeaky. "And shut this bitch up for good."

The suit went to protest, but Grambo shouted him down. "This is going to be noisy," he said, walking to the production line breaker box and scanning the instructions before throwing a switch. There was a jolt. Metal on metal. Then the clunk of gears and cogs engaging as the conveyor belt jerked into motion, barrels rattling as they crawled towards the cleaning unit, the dead air coming alive with discordant harmonies and an angry hiss of steam.

There was an office building separating the factory area from the delivery yard inside the front gate. Grambo was walking towards it when he pulled a vibrating phone out of his pocket and checked the screen. He held it to one ear and stuck his finger in the other. He swung around to face the suit, and walking backwards towards the office, he mouthed the words hospital and Sean. The suit nodded and drank more water as Grambo disappeared into the office and shut the door behind him.

CJ stared at the cable ties binding his wrists to the chair. They were extra-heavy-duty and metal-reinforced. But they were still just cable ties. As restraints, they worked on the pain principle. If the captive struggled, the ties would cut into his flesh. So their effectiveness hinged on how much pain he could take. To CJ, they were more of an insult than a restraint. He checked on the suit. He was standing at the table, his back to CJ, glugging water.

CJ twisted his right forearm to catch the tie with his bony outer wrist and watched his blood drip onto the floor as he levered his arm up and the tie cut him to the bone. When it snapped, he stood up and folded the metal-framed chair flat, transforming it into a handy club. As he was doing this, the suit was fitting his gun rig back across his shoulders and slipping into his jacket. He was halfway through it all when he turned back towards CJ and the chair cracked him on the jaw. He spun to one side, catching his fall on the table and reaching for his gun. He was fast. And the gun was already out of the holster when the chair smashed into his arm and sent it spinning across the floor. The next blow was under the chin. The suit stumbled back against the conveyor belt, his arm lurching out and getting jammed between barrels. He struggled to pull it free, his eyes on the cleaning unit hissing putrid steam as the belt fed it barrels through a curtain of rubber slats.

CJ scooped up the gun and covered the office door. No sign of Grambo.

The suit had a tough choice. Get gobbled up by the steel teeth and scorching breath of the toxic monster, or break free and get shot by CJ. He grabbed the conveyor belt rail and pushed, trying to free his trapped arm. But his balance was skewed and his hand slipped under the belt and into its driving cogs. His body arched as he wrenched it free and pointed it up at the corrugated steel sky. There was only a stub of it left. No fingers, no thumb. And his other arm was still trapped between barrels. He lost his footing and his legs scraped on the floor as the belt dragged him.

Closer, closer.

One last whimper, and one last look at CJ, his eyes begging for mercy. He didn't deserve it. But he got it anyway. CJ shot him in the head.

The suit hit the gateway a moment later. There was a momentary pause—flesh and bone jamming the works—with a cascade of steel on steel crashing down the line until the flesh and bone yielded and the barrels rolled onward with a swish of rubber curtains and a sigh of steam. The suit crumpled in a pile, the stump of his shoulder trailing blood down the machinery all the way to the floor. CJ retrieved his multitool and slit the bag tie still holding his other wrist. Then he tucked in behind the cleaning unit, his gun braced against its steel frame and trained on the office door.

Grambo emerged from the office with his jacket in one hand and his phone in the other. He was reading from the phone, but he stopped. Some sixth sense. And looked up. It wasn't a Hollywood shot. That neat hole in the forehead that TV and movie heroes pull off every time. CJ's bullet hit him in the middle of his face. Just about the right spot to blast through his head and blow out his brain stem. Grambo hit the floor without even another heartbeat. CJ searched his pockets and retrieved his phone. They hadn't pressed him for the PIN—most likely waiting for Kowalski—but they'd know the number and that made it useless. But for now, he'd have to stick with it as he needed it to contact Enya.

He went into the office building and cleared it room by room. Reception, offices, bathrooms and a grubby kitchen-dining area. CJ used a bathroom to clean himself up as best he could, staring into the mirror at his busted and bruised face. His options were simple. There was a Tratfors SUV sitting in the loading yard. He could take it and withdraw to fight another day. Or he could cut the power to the production line, hide out and get the jump on Kowalski when he showed up back from the hospital.

But what then?

He was in no shape for another confrontation, and ambushing Kowalski with a kill shot would deliver nothing in terms of information. Besides, he had to pick up Freckles at the airport. She was counting on him. And he was counting on her. He went back out to the factory and cut the breakers. The conveyor belt ground to a halt. He slipped on the suit's shoulder rig and holstered his gun. Then he found Grambo's gun and stuck it under his belt at the small of his back.

Nearly done. But something was missing.

A message.

He had to message Kowalski. Something cryptic and meaningful. He rolled two barrels to the middle of the factory and stuffed Grambo into one of them headfirst. It was a yellow one, just like he'd promised. He needed something to write with, so he fetched the suit's tie and daubed it in the bloodied flesh where his arm had been plucked from his torso, and he wrote on the barrel, graffiti style. His artwork done, he dumped the suit into the red barrel feet first, so his head poked out and his eyes stared in a manic greeting. His staging complete, he tested it by walking into the factory from the office, so he'd see it just the way Kowalski would. The message wasn't original. But then again, this was a recycling plant, and his tried-and-tested graffiti looked very much at home.

CJ—was here.

SIXTEEN

CJ dragged back the heavy gates at the factory entrance and drove Tratfors' Cadillac SUV out onto a street lined by run-down buildings and yards with chain-link fences shored up with sheets of metal. There were a few parked cars, but no sign of life other than a distant tower trailing a hazy blanket of smoke around the sun. The buildings were either empty or little used, and the yards were all gated and padlocked. There was a vehicle recycler next door with cars teetering in piles, but that too was locked up.

He drove off, following some instinctual sense of direction.

LAX.

It was an airport and not an attitude. He'd already figured that much out, and now he had to find it. CJ considered the built-in satnav, then rejected it in favor of the maps in his head and the hours he'd invested in crawling around Google Earth. Los Angeles was a big place. But compared to a rat's nest like London, it was not so difficult to get around. It had pronounced features, mountains one way and an ocean the other, and freeways pumping traffic north or south, or east or west. It had broad avenues that stretched endlessly and were conveniently gridded with numbered crossroads. CJ soon found himself on East Sepulveda, and he was heading towards the Harbor Freeway when his phone chirped a message. He pulled off the road and parked in the shade of a FedEx truck and read the message.

Still at CDG Paris! French air traffic controllers strike AGAIN. Passengers storming the Bastille. Message you when we're done.

CJ eased back in the seat. No rush now. He wanted to see Enya for a host of reasons, but he had to admit to a sense of relief. He was a mess. At least he'd have time to clean up properly. His eyes flicked up at the rearview mirror, picking out a red Prius in front of a Starbucks on the other side of the parking lot. He wondered if it was the same red car he'd seen when he was sneaking out of Wilmington's empty streets. He let it go and drove out of the lot, his plan shifting gears now that he had time to spare. He found an on-ramp to the Harbor Freeway, then cut off onto the 405 heading north. Around Inglewood, he got snarled in traffic and had plenty of time to bookmark LAX as he passed it. The red Prius was nowhere to be found in his rearview mirrors, but he couldn't get it out of his head. He told himself it was paranoia. It couldn't be Tratfors already. Besides, the Prius was a tree hugger's car, definitely not Tratfors' style. They were more save-your-own-ass than save-the-planet. He turned off at Exit 52 on a whim and drove east on Venice, heading downtown instead of back to Santa Monica.

It was just an impulse and he followed it. He'd been getting a lot of moments like that lately. No indecision.

No self-doubt. Somehow he always knew the right way to go, like there were footprints laid out in front of him marked *CJ walks here*. Only this time it was *CJ drives here*, and that turned out to be a few blocks before he looped back through side streets, so he could cross Venice and head back along it the other way without making an illegal U-turn. There was traffic everywhere. And on this day, it looked like half of the cars were red. He backed into an empty slot by the curb outside a burger restaurant located on the corner of some side street. He did it quickly, no shunting back and forth. But it still kicked off trumpeting horns and finger-work signage from the drivers stuck behind him. CJ grinned and waved to them. It was his first day on the job in LA, and he'd already shot his former boss, killed two lowlifes and had the crap beaten out of him. So pissing off local drivers was a cup-runneth-over moment of biblical proportions.

He locked the SUV and ducked down the side street and into a body shop across from the eatery. A few minutes later, the red Prius cruised by. He noticed the woman in the passenger seat first, black hair flashing as she checked out the Cadillac. The driver was a man, older than the woman with a lot less hair. The car idled as it passed the Caddy, but a blast of horns soon moved it on, and it turned into CJ's side street, where it slowed to a stop as it passed the restaurant. The man and the woman checked out its diners and the line of cars at the drive-thru. There was a quick exchange between them. Then the woman jumped out and the man drove off. She checked something in her bag, then walked past the cars in the drive-thru and went into the parking lot in front of the restaurant. The lot was cut off from the avenue by a hedge and a strip of grass with scruffy plants in gardens. The woman picked a spot behind the hedge close to CJ's Cadillac. She pulled out her phone and was soon updating her driver as to where she was located.

CJ didn't need his cat's ears to eavesdrop on that conversation. He'd sneaked up behind her and he was standing just feet away. He waited for her to ring off, then said, "Shall we grab a coffee?"

She stumbled away, catching herself against a parked car, her hands diving into her bag.

"I've got a gun."

"So have I. Are we going to need them?"

"Are you going to work for Tratfors again?"

"So you know who I am. How about returning the favor?"

"What happened to your face?"

"I had a job interview, and…" CJ paused, rummaging for the right word in his growing American lexicon. "I flunked it."

The Prius pulled into the parking lot, and the man was halfway out of it when the woman held up her hand to stop him. He stayed on the safe side of its open door, one hand perched on top of it, his arm raised to give easy access to the bulge under his armpit.

"Coffee?" CJ pointed at the door with his thumb, but he kept his eyes on the man. "I really need one."

She went over to the man and they spoke. Then the man slid back into the driver's seat and she headed for the restaurant, beckoning CJ to follow. She picked a table by the window with a view of the parking lot, where her driver was standing by the car, looking in at them. CJ fetched two black coffees and sat opposite her. They both sipped their coffees, glaring at each other like an estranged couple with so much bad history that neither could be bothered to make nice.

"My name's Christopher James. My friends call me CJ."

"What the hell happened in there?"

"Why were you following me?"

More silence. Someone had to stop asking and start answering, and in the end it was the woman.

"We weren't following you."

"So you were watching Tratfors?" CJ nodded at the man pacing around the car. "Ex-cop, right? So what does that make you, a private eye?"

"My name is Leila Rose. I'm a journalist. So now we've done the introductions. Why are you in America?"

"I came to visit with the family of an old war buddy."

"Bullshit."

"Seriously."

"Okay. I'll buy it. Alex Solo. Now give me the rest. Why else?" She reached into her bag. "I need to record this."

"Why do I get the feeling I'm on *60 Minutes*?" CJ stood up but left one hand on the table.

She dropped the phone back in her bag. "Off the record."

CJ slid back into the booth.

"How come you know so much about me?"

"I covered the Middle East for ten years."

"Iranian?"

"I was born in Texas."

"But you speak Farsi?"

She nodded.

"And Arabic?"

She nodded again.

"Why were you watching Tratfors?"

"West Coast Drum is their Gitmo. People arrive in cars and leave in barrels."

"You know that for sure?"

"You think I'd be talking to you if I had it on tape?"

"So your buddy here was watching the place?"

"From the empty office across the street. And you magically appeared from inside—a person leaving a place that he never was seen to arrive at. A person who looked like he'd been auditioning for a zombie movie."

CJ pulled a paper napkin out of a dispenser and wiped blood off his face.

"That better?"

"Not much."

He gave up and drank more coffee instead. That was a big help. It was clearing his head, reviving him.

"You must be an encyclopedia of the Shia militia," he said.

She stopped midsip, the coffee cup pasted to her lips, her eyes widening. She set the cup down, an easy smile curling her mouth. "I know why you're here. May 17, 2007. A hundred militia show up like they've been waiting all week for you. So you have a couple of questions about that for the guys who sent you there. Only it looks like they wrote their answers on your face. Am I getting close?"

CJ said nothing. He just tapped on the window.

"Why all the drama? That guy's not a journalist."

"Does the name Phil Jenkins mean anything on your side of the pond?"

"Famous news anchor."

"That's Phil. Inside stories like cruise missiles."

"I thought he died."

"He did. Suspiciously. He was my colleague and we

were working the same story."

"Tratfors?"

"And associates."

CJ looked out the window at her bald bodyguard. He was leaning back against the Prius, talking on the phone.

"Is he good?"

"He's expensive. Why? You looking for a job?"

As CJ leaned back to think about that one, he noticed a spot of blood he'd dripped on the table. He rubbed it off with another napkin.

"I really need to take care of this." He brought both hands up to frame his face.

"How about we do a deal, you and me?" she said. "We're both looking for answers. How about it? Una mano lava la otra." She mimed it for him, one hand washing the other.

"Why not? Have you got some encrypted messaging app?"

She took his bloodied napkin and scribbled on it, then passed it back to him along with the pen. She'd written the name of two messaging systems, one keyed to her phone number and endorsed by a celebrity whistleblower, the other based on a username. CJ was familiar with both. He scribbled his username, ripped the napkin in two and pushed it back across the table.

He stood up to go.

"Wait." She slid out of the booth and stood so close to him that their bodies were almost touching. "You can clean up at my place if you want. It's just a few blocks away. I'm a certified hypochondriac. I've got a medicine cabinet that looks like an ER storeroom."

CJ weighed the options, looking out the window at the detective. The big man had finished his call and was reading something on his phone, holding it with both hands down below his belly like he had a vision problem.

"He's done for the day. And I'm thinking, if we can move this forward right now, why not do it?"

"You trust fast."

"I play hunches. Follow my gut. Besides"—she shifted her body closer, blocking anyone's view as her hand emerged from her bag with a hammerless .38 Special, its snub nose inches from his groin; she looked up at him and waited until he caught her eyes—"I can take care of myself."

CJ's phone intruded. Enya's ringtone popping the tension like a bodkin in a bag of balloons.

She slipped her gun back in the side-pocket holster of her bag as CJ pulled out his phone, but the ringing stopped before he could answer.

Leila Rose was still waiting.

"I play hunches too," he said. "And my gut tells me we have things to do together. But not today." He tapped his phone. "I've got things to take care of."

She waited some more, looking him over like no was an answer that she just didn't process.

"Twenty-four hours," she said finally. "Or I'll make you the star of my show whether you like it or not. And judging by your face, a lot of your old colleagues would not look favorably on that."

She watched him spinning it all out in his head for a beat, then headed for the door.

SEVENTEEN

Enya rang again, and CJ answered it as he watched Leila exchange words with her ex-cop partner before driving off. Enya updated him with the latest travel news, lacing it with sidebar editorials. The air traffic controllers were not on strike. It was a slowdown designed to embarrass the government by stacking planes in perpetual circles above the city and simmering thousands of angry passengers in bottlenecked departure lounges. CJ listened in silence as he studied the menus written above the service counter. So many combinations. He was torn between the ready meals and à la carte, and he got so distracted by it he almost missed her bottom line.

I'm about to board now.

He noted it all down in his head. Flight times and numbers. Then they traded lovers' words and rang off.

Plenty of protein was the order of the day—food to rebuild damaged tissue. So he went to the service counter, and five minutes later, he was tucking into a Four-by-Four, a selection lavishly described as four burgers in one bun, decorated with squirts of mustard and succulent lettuce and tomatoes. No fries. But the extra pickles and onions made up his all-important five portions of veggies a day. CJ washed it all down with another jumbo coffee.

Suitably nourished, he left the restaurant, crossed Venice Boulevard and found a drugstore and a pharmacy, where he stocked up on antiseptics, salves and first-aid dressings. He headed back to Santa Monica after that, parking the Cadillac opposite his apartment. That was risky. But he had no intention of leaving it there for long. He was planning to clean up his wounds, then dump the car downtown on the sort of street where no one in their right mind would leave a Cadillac. From there, he could get a cab to the country club neighborhood, pick up the VW and drive it to the airport to pick up Enya.

He stood under a hot shower for twenty minutes, soaking and cleaning his wounds. He could feel the water as it bounced off his skin, but the sensation, like the pain of his wounds, was remote. Bloodying the towel as he dried off, he inspected each trauma site, giving each its due, a summary dismissal, a smear of antiseptic or a surgical dressing. When he was done with that, he put on a fresh set of clothes and was watching the news when the doorbell rang.

Only it wasn't like that.

The doorbell was ringing. That was for sure. The front door downstairs. But not then. Not right after he'd cleaned up. Way later. It was dark already.

Not even that.

It was getting light already. He'd fallen asleep watching TV and now it was the next day. He staggered up off the couch, disoriented. He'd pushed himself too hard. His adrenaline batteries must have run flat. The fight with Grambo, the beating, his escape and the confrontation with Leila. The cost of it all was exhaustion. And then came the coup de grâce. That fat-laden Four-by-Four. He felt more like he'd been hit by one rather than eaten its namesake sandwich.

Knock, knock.

Now his visitors were banging on the apartment door, having bypassed the front door security. Not a good sign. But at least they were knocking on the door. Not knocking it down.

He struggled to catch up, his head murky, crawling out of dreams. All the usual suspects had shown up there. Enya and Alex, of course. And Leila too. He scrambled around and found the napkin she'd scribbled on. She was real. Not just a dream. That was her writing. And his blood. He slipped one of his guns under a newspaper lying on the table by a bowl of fruit and held the other one at the ready as he checked the peephole.

Ashford and Colby.

Not unexpected. Enya had sent them a virtual wish-you-were-here postcard when she'd dialed the apartment's landline. He opened the door and stepped back, giving them plenty of room to see the gun hanging at his side.

"May we come in?" Ashford, the gentleman. So British. Colby said nothing, but her body language was a world away from that, eyes unblinking and focused on the gun.

"Please." CJ waved them in, and they walked into the living room, where Colby spun a pirouette.

"You're not going to need that." She was holding a small frame 9mm and pointing it at CJ. Nice move.

Ashford had shifted his body as they entered the room long enough to block CJ's view of her.

"Put it away," Ashford said. "He knows we're just here for a chat. Don't you, CJ?"

"Sure. I wasn't expecting visitors, so I got nervous. America's a dangerous place. I thought it was probably a home invasion." He hefted the gun. "I found this in a drawer." He went to the kitchen counter and stuck the gun in the shoulder holster and left it there next to the coffeemaker. He sat at the table and waved them towards the couch. Ashford sat down, but Colby was still standing there holding her gun.

"Alicia, please." Ashford patted the sofa at his side. It took her a while. She had a point to make first. But then she slipped her gun back under her arm and joined him.

"You should have called," CJ said. "I could have organized some catering like the last time, or—"

"Cut the bull," Colby said. "There's an arrest warrant out for you."

"So where are the cops?"

"She's talking about the UK."

CJ thought about that. He didn't believe it. But who knew?

"Extradition takes forever," he said. "The British Embassy has to serve papers on the secretary of state, then—"

"You want to see how fast that can happen?" Colby was bunching up on the edge of the couch.

Ashford touched her arm. "Take it easy, Alicia. CJ's a smart chap. I can see he's been looking into his options. I'm sure he'll do what's in his best interests."

"I didn't kill Sami."

"Like hell." Colby lurched forward, jerking to a stop

when Ashford grabbed her shoulder. "You tortured him. You held his face on a hot plate and sizzled it like a steak. You found the video on his computer. Then you lost it. A hundred and eighty stab wounds. That's not personal. That's psychotic. The sort of thing an ex-secret agent on Mars might pull."

CJ winced. Another ouch moment.

Total Recall was a movie from his favorites catalog in Iraq. Someone in the hospice had been mouthing off.

"She's right, CJ. The police got your medical records. It doesn't look good. There's nothing about your recovery that suggests psychological stability."

"I'm the perfect fit. Of course I am. It was a murder made to measure."

Ashford pulled himself forward.

"Nobody wants to see you in court."

"She does."

"Alicia was a military police officer. She has certain trained reflexes. But like all of us, she can see the big picture. You served with distinction in our armed forces. And as for what happened that day in Iraq, maybe you're right. Maybe there was a leak somewhere, and maybe you didn't kill Sami. But there's enough evidence for a warrant and maybe even a charge. Of course, you could plead out of it. Diminished responsibility. Mental disorder. I'm not a lawyer. But I'm sure they can spin your medical reports into one hell of a defense. You know the rest. You'll be sectioned. Detained at Her Majesty's pleasure. They'll throw away the key. But who wins in that scenario? The tabloids will have a field day. Brit Wolverine. That's what they were calling you when you came out of that coma. You won't end up in the dock. The doctors will. The system will be on trial. They'll drag out the Iraq War again. It'll be a circus."

"What he's trying to tell you, Brink—in his roundabout way—is back off. This vendetta has gone far enough."

"Nicely put, Alicia. So give him our recommendation."

"Get lost. Just head on south back over the border."

"Why do you care about all this? About me. About Sami. About Enya O'Brien's computers."

They shared a quizzical look.

Colby sat back like she was giving up—on talking, at least—her arms crossed under her breasts, her right hand under her jacket.

Ashford leaned forward as if to share a confidence.

"You want justice, right? At least that's what you think. But to me, it looks like something else. Alex Solo. Declan O'Brien. You had their backs and now they're dead. You failed. It's time to understand these things. Vigilantes never die well. Do yourself a favor. Stop remembering and start forgetting."

CJ ran his sermon back and forth in his head. There was some truth in it, but not enough to camouflage the pile of lies underneath it.

"We could even help you financially," Ashford said. "You're an orphan. That makes it easy. We all love a Dickens story, and it turns out you have great expectations thanks to a distant cousin who made a name for himself in the mining business in Australia. Poor chap just passed away. No kids. So you've got a tidy sum on the way."

"That's very generous," CJ said. "Is that memory card really worth that much?" Ashford glanced over at Colby, but she kept her eyes on CJ and her hand tucked into her jacket. "Why else would a cash-strapped British government write me a check and deal me a get-out-of-jail-free card?"

"You know what we're up against," Ashford said. "You've experienced it firsthand. Inhuman brutality. We don't fight in the gutter. That's their turf. We have a rulebook. But it has too many pages. And sometimes, we have to skip a few. Whatever happened—it was not what was meant to be. You still have options. I'm here to help you make the right choice."

CJ stared back at him, all out of conversation. "You want a coffee?" he said standing up and making a move towards the coffeemaker and the gun sitting next to it.

"Sit down." Colby's gun was out and she was on her feet. CJ froze—hands up—a nice show of compliance. She collected the holstered pistol from the kitchen counter as he eased himself back in his chair, noting the time on his wrist. It was half past Enya already. She'd arrived hours ago.

So why hadn't she called?

He had to get rid of Ashford and Colby. They weren't here to help him. They were working damage control, part of a coverup. Why else would they want him out of the way? As for sending him back over the border, that set off sirens in his head. He could just see the headlines. *Britain's Bionic Man Gunned Down in Mexican Drugs Deal.* How easy would that be to arrange?

Colby lifted his pistol up to her face and sniffed the barrel poking out of the holster.

She glanced at Ashford. "He's fired it."

"Okay, I agree," CJ said. "I'll head south."

His quick gear shift had them wobbling. But Colby's cop reflexes were still driving the conversation.

"Who did you shoot with it?" She raised her gun.

That was an interesting question. It told CJ that they didn't yet know about the bodies at West Coast Drum.

"Sean Kowalski. He was beating the crap out of me. He pulled a gun. We struggled and it went off. The bullet clipped his leg. He's in hospital. You can check it out if you don't already know it."

"Why would we know it?" Ashford said.

"Because they work for you. Or else you work for them. I haven't got that part figured."

"We haven't used Tratfors for years. Too much bad press. And looking at your face, I'm sure you can guess why. I'm assuming you didn't pick up that minced beef complexion at the local mall."

"I met with them, and it didn't go as well as I'd hoped. So California is not going to be the best place in the world for me to hang out. That's why I'll take your offer."

Colby passed the holstered gun to Ashford, and as her eyes slid away from CJ, he spun out of his chair, grabbed the other Sig from under the newspaper and closed the gap on Colby. She jerked up her pistol, but he snatched it out of her hand. She yelped and held her hand up to her face, her index finger hanging weirdly to one side.

"Toss it." CJ nodded at Ashford, and he threw the holstered Sig at his feet. "Now stand up and take your jacket off." He made Ashford spin on the spot. No guns. "Now fix her finger."

Ashford reached out tentatively towards his colleague's dislocated finger, but she was having none of it. She swerved away from him, nursing it with her good hand. So CJ did it instead. He stuck her gun under his arm, grabbed her hand and snapped the finger back in one fluid move. She grunted and stared down at it.

Ashford glanced at the holstered gun on the floor, but made no move to go for it.

CJ's phone was vibrating on the table.

"Sit down, both of you," he said, shuffling backwards and snatching up the phone and reading the message.

Never keep a lady waiting. Luckily, we were on hand to take care of her. We're all having a blast. But she can't take much more of this. I'd give her two hours before she gets stuffed in a barrel. See U. Sean.

It hit him with a jolt, anger ripping through him and flattening everything he needed to get her out of there. Stuff like rational thinking and a clear head. He could see it all getting blown off the edge of his horizon. Freckles, the temperature-controlled wine cabinet girl with the Manhattan-skyline-cosmetics dresser was a guest at the CJ-was-here toxic factory.

"Give me your car keys." CJ reached out his hand, but Colby didn't react. Not at first. She was probably about to. Maybe she was thinking about it. His first bullet hit a cushion between them on the couch. That got their attention. And the second bullet closed the deal, burying itself in the seat between Colby's thighs.

She tossed him a key fob and he put it in his pocket.

"I don't want any more trouble with you guys," he said. "So I'm going to leave your gun and keys outside. Do not follow me. Just make sure I can see both of you standing at that window from downstairs. That way you'll see where I hide your stuff, and also I can make sure you're not following me."

CJ walked backwards out of the room. That was important. He had to keep his eyes on Ashford and Colby and not let them wander to the side, where they might notice other things. Like the keys to Tratfors'

Cadillac on the coffee table. They were hidden from where CJ had been sitting, but they were right in front of Ashford and Colby on the couch. They had to have seen them. Now CJ was forgetting them. It had to look convincing.

He dashed downstairs and ran across the street to the Cadillac, one hand in his pocket, searching for keys. He stopped and looked up at them at the window. He idled a moment, feigning confusion before pulling out Colby's remote and clicking it. A Chevy SUV parked two doors down called out a hello. CJ took out Colby's gun, held it up for them to see, then slid it under the Tratfors' Caddy.

They disappeared from the window. But CJ was long gone by the time they hit the street, and so was Colby's Chevy.

EIGHTEEN

CJ drove south on the 405, juggling certainties and unknowns. The Chevy SUV he was driving was a certainty. It was a rental, so it was bound to have a tracking device. But Ashford and Colby were spooks. They didn't have the law enforcement creds to strong-arm a rental company into coughing up that info. Ironically, that was a pity. CJ wanted the car to be tracked. His plan didn't depend on it, but having Ashford and Colby hot on his trail gave it a real boost. Could they still track him? That was the first unknown. His guess was yes. He'd been standing right in front of them when he'd received a message from Kowalski, an isolated data connection at an exact time and location. The spooks might not have local law enforcement clout, but they had the signals networks in their pockets. They could ID his phone, track it, then follow him.

Did they know about West Coast Drum?

Were they still in league with Tratfors?

The answers were on the way.

Ashford had protested mightily when CJ had accused them of being in cahoots with his erstwhile employers, and there had certainly been issues. After the Iraq War, Tratfors had won contracts worth billions from allied intelligence and defense agencies. But during CJ's hibernation, a rogue Tratfors crew had been caught on camera murdering Iraqi civilians. That video had taken political and military scalps and put an end to the fat cat days of contracts with strings of zeros. But alliances written in blood often survived bumps in the road and they didn't always need to get signed off with government ink.

CJ drove past West Coast Drum, scouting the street and noting the junkyard next door, with its chain-link fence and locked gates. He skirted the block, finding an auto paint shop that backed onto both West Coast Drum and its neighboring junkyard. The paint shop gates were open and a couple of guys were working at the side of the yard in the shade of a metal roof. CJ parked and slipped in through the gates, concealing himself behind a shed. The painters across the way were standing with their backs to him, looking down at a handsome hog in the midst of a makeover. CJ's side of the yard was littered with bikes and work sheds. It was limited cover, but enough. He made his way to the back of the yard and picked a spot on the fence behind a parked van where he could work unseen. He was directly behind West Coast Drum, although that didn't help much since his view was limited by a stack of barrels inside the fence. He listened. Strange acoustics. Walls of barrels bouncing sound, filtering and distorting it. Sean Kowalski. He could hear his voice. And four or five men. And Enya, the voice apart, a voice in pain.

He used his multitool to cut a hole in the fence big enough to crawl through. It took more time than he wanted to spend, but hoping that Enya was in good enough shape to scale the fence was a risk too far. Sneaking back out onto the road, he ordered a taxi to pick them up at the paint shop in sixty minutes. That was a contingency plan. His first choice was to bushwhack the painters and steal their handsome hog.

With all that in place, he dialed 911 and faked his best American accent.

Some guy just smashed his car through a wall. He's gotta be DUI. There's blood everywhere.

He told them the street name and rang off.

How long would the cops take? That was the hit-and-miss part, but having reported the accident, he now had to stage it. He drove back to the factory, and as he turned the corner at the end of the block, he saw Ashford and Colby cruising towards him. The big Caddy was two blocks off. Only it wasn't cruising anymore. The moment he saw them, they saw him and their SUV lurched forward like a sprinter coming out of the blocks.

CJ toed down and made it to West Coast Drum before they had turned into the street. He spun the wheel and crashed into the factory gates. There was a chain looped around hooks on the other side of the gates. The chain held, but the gates didn't, buckling half-open with the hooks twisted and broken. CJ jumped out and ran up the street, scooting over the neighboring junkyard's chain-link fence and dodging through piles of wrecked cars. He was looking for somewhere to perch unseen, where he could stage-manage the drama about to unfold, invisible to any cop car cameras. He ended up in a junked Toyota, balanced on a stack of wrecks, concealing himself as Colby skidded the Tratfors tank to a halt by the wrecked Chevy. She jumped out of the car as a posse of Tratfors goons came running out from the yard, brandishing weapons. CJ wondered if Leila's private eye was watching from across the street. If so, he was in for hell of a show.

CJ heard the black-and-white when it was several blocks off. No siren, but the hurried pace of its V-8 was a standout from the background buzz of city sounds. It turned into the street and slowed down as the patrol officers scoped out the scene. Assessments, decisions. It was all done in a blink, with all their attention on the armed citizens milling around the two vehicles blocking the road. Then the black-and-white burst into sound and light and screeched forward as CJ let off two quick shots. The first took out a headlight. The second ripped a hole in the hood. The patrol car zigzagged to a halt, with both officers taking cover behind open doors, guns drawn and aimed at Ashford and Colby and the Tratfors crew.

CJ was already out of the Toyota and scrambling over the chain-link fence into the factory by the time cop voices boomed out ultimatums. He dropped into a narrow corridor between the fence and a wall of stacked barrels. He'd heard four or five voices, but there had to be more. Kowalski was trained for this stuff. He was out of shape, but he wasn't out of his mind. And he wasn't stupid enough to believe that an unknown SUV crashing through the gates, the simultaneous return of their stolen Caddy delivered by spooks, and the arrival of a police car were a coincidence. He'd see it for what it was. A diversion. But that wouldn't stop it working. There was no way to ignore that Chevy parked on the wreckage of their entrance, or the spooks driving their stolen vehicle. As for the pissed-off cops pointing shotguns, explanations were due.

CJ was expecting to find one man guarding Enya, so he was flattered to find two. Closest was the blue baseball cap. The man with the shotgun from the parking lot. The second guy was new. He was wearing a shiny bomber jacket and standing on the other side of the yard. They both had Enya in eyeshot, and they both had their weapons out. But they were distracted, one on each side of the office peeking around the corner to check out the commotion in the street. The factory floor was just as he'd left it, his Halloween-themed conceptual artwork untouched. The broken chair-dash-bludgeon was still on the floor by the table. Grambo was still deep-diving his barrel, and the suit's head was still poking up, his eyes bright with surprise like a jack-in-the-box. But now there was a new addition. Enya was slumped on a barrel set between them, head lolling, face bloodied, blouse patched in red. Her hands were tied behind her back and her legs were strapped around the barrel. Between her legs was a heart daubed in her blood with CJ scrawled inside it.

He pulled himself back behind the barrels, rage swooning, fingers clawing the chain-link fence. He wanted to shoot both of the goons. But that would bring the cavalry, and he'd have no time to cut her free. He stuck his pistol in his belt and worked through the barrels until he was as close as he could get to Baseball Cap. The din from the street was settling. Cooperation, explanations, hands up and plenty of yes-sir, no-sir. It was all working.

He left the cover of the barrels and took two long

steps before catching Baseball Cap as he spun around and leveled his gun. CJ got one hand on the gun, jamming the slide, and slammed his other hand into the man's face, driving him backwards and smashing his head against the wall. He slid to the floor, his head trailing a smear of blood, his baseball cap rolling to one side. CJ plucked the gun from his fingers, then picked up the baseball cap and slipped it on. An engine fired up. The Chevy. Something was happening out on the street, and Shiny Jacket across the way wanted to find out what. He edged around the corner of the office, where he could check out the front gate and keep his eye on Enya at the same time.

He was snapping his head back and forth between them, too fast and too focused to catch sight of CJ peeking out from the other corner. But Enya saw him. She looked from CJ to Shiny. CJ wanted her to do nothing and leave it to him. But he knew that was never going to happen. Now that she'd seen him, she'd be right on it. Some plan. What? He didn't know. He just had to hope it worked. She started to sway her upper body from side to side. CJ eased back behind the bricks.

Distraction.

That was the plan. She was going to create a commotion and get the full attention of Shiny. The ever-resourceful Ms. O'Brien was about to gift him the edge he needed. The empty barrel beneath her wobbled on each swing of her body. Shiny looked back.

"Bitch."

He ran at her, wielding his gun like a club, but her barrel toppled over before he got to her. It crashed into Grambo's and knocked it over, and she ended up sprawling between Grambo's legs. Shiny kicked her, then holstered his gun. He was bending to grab her hair, when CJ tackled him, bowling him over Grambo's barrel. He went for his gun as he fell, but CJ was on him already, lacing his arms around his neck. A dull crack bounced off the barrels and faded into Enya's muffled gasp as Shiny and his floppy head fell to the ground, and CJ reared up over him, covering both sides of the office with his gun.

No one. Not yet.

He pulled Enya up off the floor, flicked open his knife and cut the tape binding her to the barrel. He grabbed her bound wrists, and they took cover behind the steam cleaning unit. They were just feet away from the stack of barrels and its labyrinth of pathways to freedom. CJ checked. Still no one. He cut the tape around her wrists and she peeled it off.

"This way." He turned and ran towards the wall of red and yellow, but Enya went the other way. CJ whirled around. She was crouched over Shiny, rifling through his pockets.

Hurried footsteps.

CJ aimed his gun towards them as Enya sprinted back towards him and they dashed for the barrels.

Hollering. Shots.

They made it to the fence with the sound of running feet too close. They were never going to make it. They had to stop them. CJ ducked down between the fence and the barrel wall. Enya didn't need a manual to figure out his plan. She dropped to the floor beside him, and they both put their backs to the barrels and pushed off the fence with their legs. It was chancy. The barrels at the top might come crashing down on them. But with Tratfors guns just feet away and no guaranteed pickup on the other side of the fence, they had to take the risk.

They pushed. Combined weight, about three-twenty pounds. Theoretically not enough to shift those heavy barrels. But the goons with guns were a big help. The wall teetered, threatening to crush them both, before it tumbled over. One stack into the next. Barrel on barrel. Rolling and crashing. A psychedelic symphony syncopated with screams.

CJ hopped through the hole in the fence and covered Enya as she scrambled through. They were in the clear behind the parked van in the paint shop yard. The barrel-rolling stunt was a masterstroke, but it came with a downside. That amount of noise was sure to alert the guys painting the hog. But CJ was beyond caring. He'd saved Enya. Priority one was accomplished. And he certainly wasn't going to let a couple of guys with fancy paint guns stop him. On the other hand, a couple of guys with pump shotguns was another story. And that was what the painters were holding.

"Drop it, fella." The one with the headband spoke first. There was one standing at each end of the van. CJ looked from one to the other. No way out. He dropped the gun. "Now step away." He took a pace away from the gun, and Headband scooped it up. The other one had a leather waistcoat in place of a shirt and arms festooned with ink. He nodded at them to start walking, blue eyes sparking over ruddy cheeks, reminding CJ of a kid in school they all used to call Porky.

As they stepped out from behind the van and headed towards the workshop, Porky glanced at Headband and said, "Mr. Kowalski is going to owe us big-time."

NINETEEN

"They ain't going anywheres." Headband was on the phone. "Yes, sir. Quaid's got the Mossberg aimed right at his belly."

And so he did. He was standing about six feet away, inked arms—elbows out, shotgun shouldered, porky eyes trained along its sights at CJ and Enya, who were sitting in wood-and-canvas folding chairs like Hollywood bigshots presiding over a movie scene gone badly wrong.

Ten minutes. That was CJ's guess. That's how long they had. Even if the cops kept the Tratfors crew bogged down longer, Kowalski would make a phone call and someone else would storm through the paint shop gates and it would all be over. And this time there would be no fooling around. It would be a bullet in the head and a body in the barrel. At least for CJ. As for Enya—with no training—she'd soon break. And tell them what? Everything she hadn't told them already. Everything she hadn't told him. Like why she'd risked everything to get something from a dead man's jacket.

"I got it, sir." Headband rang off. "Keep a close eye on this one." He pointed at CJ. "He's super special."

Porky flicked his eyes in acknowledgment as Headband disappeared into a caged-off area and emerged carrying a nest of cables. "We don't got no rope strong enough, but this'll work." He stepped behind CJ, a length of cable stretched between his hands as a car roared into the yard kicking up a cloud of dust.

Tratfors? Already?

In a black Jag?

Headband stopped, his eyes on the car emerging from the cloud of dust. No alarm bells. No concern. So Porky checked it out too. A glance. Just a second. But a long one. CJ leapt out of the chair, his hands on the shotgun. Porky jerked it around and it went off, punching up dirt. CJ stomped Porky's knee catching the joint at the side. Enya threw herself on the ground and hid under her hands. Headband was racing for the cage, reaching for something. Porky was screaming, rolling around and holding his knee. Headband reared up with the other shotgun as CJ fired, knocking him backwards, his body crashing into a table of paints. In a screech of tires and a slipstream of dust, CJ's late-but-welcome luxury ride skidded out of the yard and roared off on another adventure. CJ looked down at the screeching Porky and leveled his gun. The screeching stopped and the porkiness drained from his face. He lifted his hand like a shield and pleaded for his life in a monosyllabic nasal whine. CJ whipped the gun around and clubbed him into silence with its butt.

Enya was pulling herself up, her eyes stuck on Headband. He was slewed against a wall in a shambles of busted paint cans, blues, greens and whites dribbling into the blood-red mash of his chest and face.

"Come on." CJ leapt on the Harley and fired it up. Enya vaulted astride it as an SUV skidded into the yard. They flashed past it as they swerved out the gate in clouds of gravel and dust. There was a flourish of spinning heads in the SUV and a brandishing of guns, but that was already way too late.

Outside in the street, CJ swung the bike in a circle. He cocked and aimed his pistol, and when the SUV roared out through the gates, he fired six shots in groups of two. The SUV buried itself in a tangle of chain-link fence and metal poles opposite the paint shop. CJ gunned the motor and they sped off. Three blocks away, he hauled the Harley back to a modest urban speed. Even so, they had to dump it fast. They needed a discreet getaway vehicle, and a partly painted hog, its hollow pipes booming, was a howl for attention. Besides, they had no helmets. A peccadillo—given the destruction left in their wake—but many a big crime has tripped on a minor infraction, and CJ had no plans to feather the hat of some eagle-eyed officer on traffic patrol.

With Wilmington's grime fading in the rearview mirror, they were soon navigating the smart streets around the country club, where they swapped the Harley for the VW and faded into the flow of traffic. CJ drove inland over surface streets, following a route map in his head, destination unknown. It wasn't important. Not yet. Putting miles between them and the bodies in Wilmington was the priority. There were errands to take care of too. Enya confirmed that she did not need hospitalization, but CJ wasn't convinced, and he kept up a barrage of side-glance inspections. Her brave face cracked at times with bouts of sobs and sniffles as she mopped her cuts and bruises with bloodied tissues.

He pulled into the parking lot of a shopping plaza, where she finally convinced him that she did not need a doctor. So he bought up the local drugstore instead, and not just first-aid supplies, but a poor man's survival kit of energy drinks, protein bars, vitamins, painkillers and brandy. They continued to drive inland after that, towns thinning into an arid dusty landscape, their eyes skimming signs and billboards as they cruised by. The destination might be unknown, but the goal was clear.

Anonymity.

They needed a place to stay off the grid. No ID and no credit cards. But CJ had never checked into an American hotel. He didn't know the routine. Most places in Europe, you need a passport to use a public toilet, never mind a hotel. But how did it work in the land of the free? If it was a movie, they could check in as Mr. and Mrs. Smith and pay cash. Enya had stayed in countless hotels in America, but he didn't want to ask her. She was shell-shocked and in need of rest, not more anxiety. CJ pulled into a scruffy motel, a place with not much going for it except a lot more rooms than cars in the parking lot. He had a story to tell, and this was just the kind of place to tell it.

We've been robbed and beaten up.

That was the gist of it. They certainly looked the part. Foreigners. Bloodied and bruised. Welcome to America. He'd rehearsed it all, and he had two hundred dollars ready to facilitate the negotiation. But in the end, none of it was necessary. He'd barely gotten the first line out of his mouth when Enya picked up the story and ran with it. The honeymoon from hell. Her version began with the air traffic controllers strike in

Paris and ended with how CJ had fought like a lion to protect her from the muggers. The desk clerk was spellbound.

"Thank God my husband had some emergency money in his boot," she said as CJ slid some cash across the desk in exchange for a room key. "Otherwise, we'd be on the street."

So there they were. Safe and off the grid. Upgraded even. They got the Honeymoon Suite at the regular rate. Although suite was more spin than reality, it turned out to be a regular room with an electric bed and a whirlpool jet in the bathtub.

After washing down painkillers with an energy drink, Enya was wallowing in hot water, massaging aching muscles in the jets and sipping brandy. The bathroom door was open, but CJ left her in peace. He was lying on the bed, his head cupped in his hands. He was worried about Enya.

Internal bleeding? Fractures?

Injuries like that were not always obvious. He was irritated with her too. He kept running it all back and forth, but he always ended up at the same spot.

What was it?

The precious thing that she had gone back for.

Something so important she'd risk everything.

She was still holding out, and that had to end. He pulled himself up off the bed. One obvious shortcut to the truth was to grab her by the throat and dunk her in the suds. But that was never going to happen. He peeked around the bathroom door and looked at her—a battered head floating on bubbles, a face with a feeble smile.

"Any better?" he said.

"Getting there."

He looked around.

The precious thing?

It came to him in a rush. It had to be. He'd grabbed it over a coffee at the hospice when he'd asked her if she had a boyfriend, and she'd knocked his hand away. She always wore it. But now it was gone. He remembered it hanging from her neck as she'd slid out of her clothes and clambered astride him on the sofa. The locket. She had gone back for it, and now she'd hidden it. He looked around the bathroom. Her tattered clothes were discarded all over, draped over a stool, hung from a hook behind the door and dumped in a pile by the wall.

In some pocket, maybe?

He coasted his eyes over the washstand, trying to be casual. He didn't want a confrontation, not with her in this state.

"Are you okay?" she said.

"Sure. I'll get some ice for those bruises."

She nodded, and he left her in the suds and stepped outside with an empty ice bucket. But halfway to the ice machine, he took a detour. He settled behind the wheel of the VW and patched an encrypted call through to Leila.

No reply.

He tried again before fetching the ice and heading back to their room. Enya was done with the suds. She was sitting on the bed in a pink bathrobe emblazoned with the word HERS. The color was back in her cheeks, and a skin closure had taped up her split lip. But she still looked like a model in a domestic violence hotline commercial. He splashed a shot of brandy over an ice cube and sat next to her.

"You need more pills?" he said.

"I'm good. They're working."

"When I was with Kowalski, I got into his phone and set up that hack you gave me. Did it work?"

"Let's find out."

He gave her his remaining unsullied phone, and she checked the motel's Wi-Fi instructions and set up a VPN connection.

"The information I can get is limited. Some of his messaging is encrypted, so I can't get into that. But there should be something. If I can find a log, a trail of IP addresses, I can do a geolocation lookup."

CJ waited in silence, watching her.

It took her twenty minutes.

"Do you want to know where he is? Or where he's going?"

"Both."

"He's somewhere east of San Bernardino. He's not on a Wi-Fi network, so he's probably on the road."

"Where to?"

"He's just used his weather app. Somewhere sunny. No surprises there. Las Vegas usually is."

CJ stood up and eased the phone out of her hands. "We'll check again tomorrow. You need rest."

"I'm too hyped up. My nerves are rattling so loud I'm going deaf."

"You want to watch some TV?"

She picked up the remote, switched on the TV and flicked through channels.

"Either that," he said, "or you could tell me about your locket."

"Tell you what?" She frowned, overacting.

"Tell me what's on the memory card inside it."

It was as if he'd freeze-dried her. No reaction. She just stared at him with the same fake frown. So he stared back. No way out. And she knew it. She flung the remote at the floor, bursting it in a scatter of batteries and plastic, then buried her face in her hands. He left her to it, waiting until her shamed face slid from behind its shield.

"I didn't lie to you about that," she said.

"You didn't tell me the truth either."

"I didn't know if I could trust you. You were a British soldier—"

"Marine."

"Whatever. You pledged allegiance to Queen Elizabeth, not Queen Enya. You've got HM Government Property written all over you. I'm Irish. We've got twenty-twenty vision for signage like that."

"And now?"

"Now I feel like shit. It makes me look insincere about us. And that's not true."

"So what's on the card?"

"A key."

"To what?"

"A digital vault."

"And inside the vault?"

She clenched her jaw. "If I tell you the truth, you'll think I'm lying anyway."

"Try starting at the beginning."

"We don't have time. Besides, it's the punchline that counts."

She got some brandy and ice, then sat in the chair by the dresser, facing him.

"My brother started the Iraq War." She waited for his riposte—a smirk, a peal of laughter, a theatrical groan. But none of that happened. CJ waited in silence. This was a story he'd waited a long time to hear.

"You remember Curveball?" she said.

CJ nodded. "The Iraqi chemical engineer. One of the Allies' so-called credible witnesses to their WMD weapons program."

"He was the foundation stone they built the case on. He wanted asylum in Germany, but his pregnant wife was stuck overseas and effectively a hostage. So he went to the BND, the German intelligence, and spun them a yarn that was a perfect match for item number one on Dubya's Christmas list. *Reasons to go to war with Saddam Hussein.*"

"I remember. Curveball made those fantasy sketches of bioweaponized trucks, and no one asked too many questions."

"Nobody asked any questions. It fitted the narrative. So why would they? All it took was a few bad CIA operatives—career-before-country types with a sharp eye for an opportunity like a president who wants war. But Curveball wasn't enough. Not for war. So they had to complete the picture. And for that, they needed someone outside the intelligence community. Someone to create a fake trail to fool their own organization as well as the NSA and GCHQ. An unethical contractor with a digital black box of dirty tricks."

"I remember Colin Powell's speech. There was a lot of stuff—emails, recorded phone calls, photos."

"The photos were bullshit. Like Rorschach inkblots. Look hard enough and you can see whatever you want. It was the emails and the recordings that nailed Saddam's arse to the gallows. And they were all fake."

"Declan?"

"The emails were simple. Script kiddie stuff. Spearfish key government and military personnel and a few insurgents. Infect their computers with malware and set up incriminating email conversations."

"About what?"

"Tenders for specialized equipment or supplies with the exact keywords needed to trigger the NSA's snooping algorithms. Something like aluminum tubing with the precise specifications you need in a centrifuge to enrich uranium. Or maybe some chemical precursor for Sarin or VX or some other nerve agent. Or a lab kit that rings alarm bells because it's just what you need to rustle up a batch of anthrax or botulin."

"What about the phone calls?"

"Voice matching. Hollywood does it all the time. Two actors. Voice biometric authentication has come a long way since then, so it wouldn't be so simple now. But back then it was easy. Declan had voiceprints of the military officers they were impersonating and hours of recordings. So they rehearsed until the voiceprints matched. All he had to do then was get access to the telecoms network and route the call so it looked natural enough to get snooped on."

"Who at the CIA?"

"I don't know any of that, and neither did Declan?"

"So who's Rumbleby in this?"

"Sorry about that. It's not a who. It's a what. The operation codename. The rumble was the Iraq War, and the bee was the buzz they needed to kick it off."

CJ went back to the garden shed and Masterson's howling confession. He must have said… *to protect Rumble Bee.* And CJ had heard it as one word and made an assumption.

"So join up the dots for me," he said. "Where does the memory card come into this?"

"It was Declan's insurance policy. He did what they

asked and it worked like a dream. These days, faking internet data is an industry. And if the Russians could swing the US election and the Brexit vote, imagine how easy it was to fake a few emails and phone calls back in the day when nobody would even suspect a fake. Just fool the NSA and it ends up in a report that might as well have been engraved on a slab of stone by Moses. All Declan had to do was play God and dictate the message. He was the granddaddy of cyberespionage as disinformation and the Iraq War was his firstborn."

"If he was so useful, why did they want him dead?"

"Because he grew a conscience. You've got to understand the process he went through. It wasn't like one day Tratfors called him and said, 'We understand you're good with computers so we'd like you to help us start a war.' They got his confidence with small jobs and big money. They told him that the Iraqis had WMDs, but that they were clever at hiding them, and way too smart to be talking about them in emails and phone calls. So if only he could fake a few. And it worked. And when Saddam's statue came tumbling down and Iraqis danced in the streets, he felt good about it."

"But then?"

"Torture, murder, rape. It ground away at his spirit. Drip, drip. It was driving him crazy. Turning him into some kind of Lady Macbeth, always trying to get the blood out. There were so many recriminations and he knew so much. He was afraid for his life."

"So he made the card. His insurance policy. Some kind of record pointing the finger."

"There was way too much to stick on a card. So he downloaded it from Tratfors' servers to his own computers."

"In the flat? That the cops took?"

"It's okay. There's a mirror in the cloud."

"So the card is a decryption key?"

"You've heard of two-step authentication."

"Like a password plus a code they send to your phone."

"It's similar. To unlock the vault, you need the key on the memory card. But the card itself is password-encrypted."

"How did you get your copy of the card?"

"Declan sent it to me from Afghanistan before he flew to Baghdad. He was supposed to call me from Iraq and give me the password, but…"

CJ sipped his brandy, the blurred landscape of his life these past years drifting into focus.

No password.

Enya had a copy of the key but no password to decrypt it. Now it all made sense. Her patience and persistence through all those years he was lying comatose. Her fascination with those final moments. Ordering that black-and-white Cat and Canary tape all the way from Hollywood. Declan was for real after all. He'd been telling the truth. He'd traded the password for his life. But then, all the players had died. All except CJ. And now that password existed in only one place—buried under piles of dross in his own head. The disinformation bomb he'd dropped on Ashford and Colby turned out to be the opposite. He'd inadvertently told them the truth, albeit an embroidered version. No wonder it got a reaction.

"You said he grew a conscience, but that's hardly something he would share with Tratfors."

"Of course not. He wasn't stupid."

"So what made them pull the trigger?"

She looked into her drink and swirled the ice cubes and brandy around like it was some mystical divination technique.

"He talked about blowing the whistle more than once. He had an idea that if it was public, Tratfors would be finished. They'd all be running scared and he'd be safe. I told him it was a pipe dream. The dawn of the whistleblower was still on the horizon back then. There was no WikiLeaks. No Snowden or Manning. My guess is, he reached out and they got wind of it."

"So you need the password. But what then?"

"I follow through. The world's a different place now. If I blow the whistle, I won't bring him back. But at least I'll destroy his killers."

"I know people who'd pay you a fortune for that data."

"I know even more who'd cut my throat for it. And on that topic, I'm hoping I didn't make a mistake about you."

"So it's revenge—as simple as that?"

"I never hid that."

"And us? Is that what keeps us together?"

"Who knows? Holy vows sworn in the church of payback may work as good as any other."

"You don't believe that. You're not so cynical."

"You want the same thing I do. So we ended up in the same bed. All sorts of things grow out of beds, but never anything you can plan for."

She got up off the chair and put down her glass. "I'm woozy. Brandy and pills." She picked up the bottle and checked the label. "And not exactly Cordon Bleu."

CJ patted the pillow. "Get some rest."

She was crawling back on the bed when CJ's phone

vibrated on the nightstand. It was a message from Leila.

In Vegas. Just arrived. Call tomorrow AM.

"And that is?" Enya said as soon as he put down the phone.

"Tomorrow's plan," he said, tucking the sheet around her neck. "We'll go through it all in the morning."

"Tell me now."

He went to put his fingertip on her lips, but she was already asleep.

It was dark when CJ woke up. There was some sound. Or was it a dream? He checked Enya—sleeping soundly—and eased his head back on the pillow. It was just the sound of a wheel knocking. A wheel inside his head. He spun it around, over and over. He had the truth at last. But not all of it. He rolled his head to the side to look at Enya, her face little more than an outline in the glow of some LED.

Had she told him everything?

He worked through it all logically, then summed his conclusions and his gut instincts onto a single bottom line. She'd left something out. He was sure of it. But not something big enough to matter. He tried to get back to sleep but failed. Another wheel was squeaking, and this one had to be fixed. The scale of what was going on now was all wrong. Iraq was old news. There had to be something else. Bush and Blair were yesterday's men. Colin Powell had done his mea culpa. History had already written it off as the world's biggest-ever intelligence cock-up. So what if a few overzealous patriots had faked bits of it? Who would care enough about it to stick Sami with a knife, then barbecue his face on a stove? Or send the night nurse with his fatal shot? Or snatch Enya at the airport and beat who knew what out of her? Or fly Ashford and Colby halfway around the planet?

Enya murmured and rolled over. He stroked her hair. No texture. No real feeling in his fingertips. Just enough to let him know he'd made contact. He shut his eyes and wandered inside his head, looking for the levers of his mind. He'd been doing self-hypnosis so consistently that the results were less variable now. Not guaranteed, but getting close. He no longer had to walk by the river and go through the forest. He just had to find the oak tree with the door, and as he walked down the spiral staircase inside it, his mind shifted gears. So when he got to the bottom and sat in the chair, he was ready for his pill. He worked through his routine a few times, then drifted off, and when he woke up it was still dark. But there was light from the bathroom, and he could hear Enya cleaning her teeth. She turned towards him when he stood in the open doorway.

"I couldn't sleep," she said. "The painkillers wore off."

"I'll get you some more pills."

"No." She spat in the sink and rinsed her mouth. "That thing you do to get your feeling back… does it work the other way around?"

"I think it only works if you're halfway crazy."

"Then I'm well qualified."

He reached out and ran his hand through her hair, feeling every strand.

"I answered all your questions," she said. "So now it's my turn to ask."

"Shoot."

"Quick ones. Just two."

She untied her belt and let her robe fall to the floor.

She stepped closer and pressed her naked body against his, scraping her breasts back and forth across his chest.

"Can you feel this?"

He answered her with a kiss.

"Second question," she said, breaking away. "I know you can be rough. But can you be gentle?"

He picked her up and carried her back into the bedroom, cradling her in his arms. He stood by the bed, looking at her in the half-light before laying her down tenderly like a lily on a lover's grave.

Part Three

LAS VEGAS

TWENTY

After a long silence, Enya said, "That's very odd."

"What?"

"The whole thing. The way you met her."

CJ cleaned the last of his pancakes off his plate and nodded to the waitress offering him another cup of coffee from her bottomless pot. His plan was simple.

Las Vegas.

But Enya had other ideas. They both wanted payback. But after her brutal interrogation at West Coast Drum, Enya's priority was survival. And not just hers. The words us and we were working their way into the conversation at every turn. They'd moved on. And now she'd told him the truth, they could both focus on recovering the password, a task they could work on anywhere. They had money and resources. They could bide their time and finish the job the smart way by exposing Tratfors and its crimes.

All these points were duly noted by CJ. But none of them made any difference. In his mind, payback and survival were inseparable. The vault was a digital neutron bomb, and he'd already lit the fuse. Powerful people were intent on stopping that bomb's detonation, and unless they could get to another planet they were never going to survive if they ran. Outing Tratfors by sharing the vault's explosive contents with bloggers and journalists was the one thing they did agree on. But they split on the how of that too. To CJ, it was one more reason to get to Vegas. Leila Rose was a professional journalist with a reputation for breaking big stories. She was a valuable ally. If Enya really wanted to destroy Tratfors, then Leila had to be a part of it. He waited until the waitress had moved on to the next table before getting back to their conversation.

"There's no reason to be suspicious," he said. "They were following me, and I got the drop on them. It's not like they were planning to contact me."

"Maybe that was part of her plan too. Women like that can be devious."

"Enya… please, we've got to go there."

"And she's got a gun."

"That was just bravado. In case I tried something."

"Like what? Steal her burger?" He ignored that and peeled off some bills for the breakfast. "And why didn't she call you back?" He ignored that too, sipping his coffee.

The waitress took his notes and gave him a sly wink.

He looked at Enya and shrugged.

"So?"

Enya stood up. "Alright." She tossed her napkin on the table. "But I'm telling you—it's a mistake."

CJ was driving the VW on the I-15 freeway north, with Enya's silence an unfamiliar load dragging along beside them, when his phone buzzed.

Enya leaned across as he held it up to check the

caller.

"Talk of the devil, and here she comes," she said.

CJ pinned the phone to his ear. "What are you doing in Vegas?"

"Hunting." Leila's voice was echoey, with a background meld of sounds like she was in a quiet corner of a hotel lobby. "There's an oil industry convention here, so the old boys' club is staging a few sideshows. Preston's in town. And so is Nazar, the boss of OneOil. He lives in Monaco behind a wall of lawyers, and the place must have caught fire for him to break cover. What's up your end?"

"I need to drop off the grid. With a friend."

"Who?"

"Enya O'Brien."

"Why?"

"Tratfors snatched her at the airport. They were entertaining her at West Coast Drum when I dropped by and picked her up."

She said nothing. So he left her to her thoughts until a while stretched into way too long.

"Leila?"

"I'm here. I'm checking the newsfeed. What did you pick her up with… a B-52? Cops shot at. Bodies getting trucked out of there. The FBI has a statement pending. I don't know, CJ. I'm not even comfortable with this call. I'll push things to the limit to get a story, but you've got no idea where the limit lives."

"What if I told you that Enya has an encrypted hard drive with a log of Tratfors' digital black ops? Wouldn't you like to know how they faked the intel that got us into the Iraq War?"

Silence phase two.

He could all but hear the scales rocking back and

forth in her head. Stacked on one side was not just her reputation, but her career. CJ was potentially as toxic as the barrels at West Coast Drum. But balanced against that was a scoop to die for. And something else. He'd sensed it at that first meeting. Something that churned her up inside. Something beyond career ambition and payback for a murdered colleague. Something personal. Leila wanted heads on sticks. Preston, Nazar. Maybe others. They were all candidates for her trophy cabinet. He'd never heard of Nazar. But he knew OneOil. He'd escorted their engineers to fix sabotaged pipelines on more than one occasion. Maybe Nazar was the key to that, some personal issue with him. Another Iranian. Some family business back in Iran pumping her with venom. Whatever it was—CJ was counting on it. He needed her. He was a stranger in a strange land with few resources and an impressive inventory of powerful enemies.

"Okay," she said. "I'll get a place. Call me in a few hours before you get to Vegas."

He rang off and put his attention back on the road, leaving Enya to simmer in a silence that lasted all the way to the San Bernardino Mountains. But as the urban sprawl faded behind them and the deserts opened up ahead, she came back to life.

"Point of information," she said. "Where are we keeping that hard drive you mentioned?"

"I had to spice things up. She was playing hard to get. I didn't have time to explain all that vault stuff. Anyway, we can download it by the time we meet her. You've got the address in the cloud, right?"

His own words echoed back on him and gave him a jolt. UK cops had seized Enya's computers. So what if they'd gotten to the backup?

"Where are those cloud servers based?"

"They're buried under a mile of granite in a Swiss Fort Knox. Retina scans, electromagnetic blastproofing. They've got the works—and ice-cold glacier water to keep them cool."

That was comforting. It wasn't stashed in a five-eyes country. Switzerland wasn't even in the fourteen-eyes intelligence-sharing club that included most of Europe. Any lawful request to access would involve the Swiss police and judiciary, and they'd ask too many questions.

"Did you check it?"

"I hadn't checked it for years. I set it up while Declan was in Afghanistan, and I uploaded the files from our own servers at his request. The service gets paid from our offshore company account and automatically renewed. So I had no reason to log in there again. And after everything that happened, I got suspicious that I was under surveillance and I didn't want to lead anyone to it."

"But when the cops took your computers?"

"I checked it from Paris using a VPN and Tor. I logged in to the server okay and verified the encrypted folder was there. More or less."

That was an odd way of putting it, and she made it worse by screwing her face in a lopsided frown.

"More or less?"

"I had very little time. I could have made a mistake. It's just that the folder is much bigger than I remember it."

"Maybe he added something."

"There wasn't much time for that. After I set it up, he logged in and signed off on the hardening I'd done on the server. Then he sent me the key card and hopped on the plane to Iraq."

"Any ideas?"

"There might be some housekeeping process logging endless petty faults and exceptions. I didn't have time to check it out."

"We have to download it."

"For sure. We need to stop off somewhere and buy a drive, then find a Wi-Fi network. But we've still got no password."

"We can work on that."

"How? I had a cracker running on a GPU cluster pumping out half a million passwords a second."

"Based on what?"

"Everything. Brute force at first. But when that failed, I tried dictionary and mask attacks built around the way he thinks."

"What if I gave you every word of that exchange between him and Hussein?"

"More of that cat and canary malarkey. I think we can skip all that."

"I couldn't remember because I was blocking it subconsciously. Now I want to remember. We can do this."

She didn't look convinced, but she said nothing. So he left it there.

An hour from Vegas, they pulled over and CJ called Leila.

"Turn off the I-15 before Vegas," she said. "Take the exit for Henderson. It's a quiet place. Pull over there and call me back. I'm in the middle of something, so you may have to wait a bit. Find some mall and get yourselves something to eat."

He rang off and updated Enya.

"Henderson?" She repeated it several times with a different intonation, like a drama school student practicing a new line.

CJ gave her his phone, and she researched the town's retail options and directed him to an electronics store.

"Good news and bad," she said as they pulled into its parking lot. "On the happy side, Henderson is the second-safest town in America. Although updates on that are pending in view of your recent arrival. They also have a few halfway decent stores. Suburban chic from the look of it. But at least I won't have to look like a bag lady anymore. Just a woman with appalling dress sense. In the sad column, Nevada is the second-most-dangerous state in America, and the smart money is on it becoming number one sometime soon."

"It doesn't have to be like that. If we can figure out the password, Leila will have that story global in hours. Tratfors will disintegrate, and Kowalski and company will all be on flights to some jungle."

"And that's it? You'll let it go there?"

"That's what you want, isn't it?"

"What does my want have to do with it?" She waited for an answer, but CJ said nothing. "Catherine O'Brien—my mother, by the way—did not have a child stupid enough to believe that Christopher James Brink is going to let that man Kowalski live. You're a steel-souled bastard. I know that. And Kowalski is a dead man." She pulled down the vanity mirror and inspected her face, touching each bruise and abrasion with a fingertip as she shifted her head from side to side. "I might have had a problem with that back when I was a girl. But now I'm all grown up. So do it. Do it for Declan and Alex." She turned towards him. "And if you're not going to do it for them, then kill him for me."

He took her hand, easing it away from her battered face. He held it up to his lips and went to kiss it. But she pulled it away and kissed him full on the mouth. He had avoided kissing her mouth when they'd made love in the motel out of deference to her split lip. But pain be damned, here she was burying her mouth in his, all soft bruised skin and sharp-edged plastic closures.

They bought a high-end laptop and a sleek portable storage drive in the electronics store, then drove to a mall, where they split up. CJ picked up some clothes and toiletries before finding a sporting goods store, where he bought four magazines for his collection of Sigs as well as the day's special offer—a bucket of 350 bullets to fit in them. He was back with Enya eating a sandwich when Leila called. She was still on the Strip, her voice excited, skimming off traffic noise. They finished their meal, loaded up the VW and met her outside in the parking lot, where they followed her Range Rover out onto quiet suburban streets.

The traffic petered out as they drove through neighborhoods with single-story homes set on lots with no fences and plenty of space between them. They ended up on a street like a broad ribbon on the edge of the town, bordered with the same tidy homes. Beyond it was the desert. Endless space. It was a commodity available everywhere in America and the locals didn't even notice it. But CJ was a Brit, reared on an island where only people were endless and horizons were limited except for the beaches and the promise beyond their seas. Despite that, this land felt like home to him. Not his orphan-boy homeland. But the home he'd chosen. The horizon beyond its seas. It wasn't Iraq either. But the desert was close enough. He felt free here. Confident. At the end of a circle. And he knew with a certainty that the oath he'd sworn in blood in a faraway desert land was about to be redeemed in this one.

They pulled into a driveway and stopped in front of a garage door wide enough for three cars. There were introductions. Short and sweet. Handshakes and pleasantries. Leila's driver was called Jerry. He was her cameraman. Fifties. But working hard on looking younger, with a Mohawk hairdo and hieroglyphs tattooed on the sides of his head. The famous hard drive CJ had touted on the phone didn't come up. He figured that Leila wanted to get Jerry out of the way before that issue was discussed. Besides, she'd had an adventure, an encounter with Preston and she was eager to see the video. Enya tucked herself under a desk in the office and went to work on her new laptop and Leila and CJ settled on a couch in the lounge while Jerry wired his tablet to the TV.

"Preston and Nazar. I ambushed them," Leila said. "As they were coming out of a restaurant. I nailed them both in that crack in security before the car rolls up. And did he ever squeal."

"What's Nazar in this?"

"You must know OneOil."

CJ nodded.

"They provide industrial solutions to the energy sector, according to their website. But that's pretty much a sideline. I got onto them doing a story about money laundering and bribery. FCPA ring a bell?"

He shook his head.

"Foreign Corrupt Practices Act."

"*Baksheesh*. Kickbacks."

"You got it. Greasing the wheels. The US calls it bribery. But in the Middle East it's a way of life. Thousands of years of cultural programing doesn't get wiped out because Washington passes a law. And OneOil is the perfect vehicle. It's a nest of offshore companies with subsidiaries all over the world. People, equipment, services—all shuffling from this jurisdiction to that. Who's to know if thirty or forty million dollars here or there is actually delivered in services? And what about all those containers of equipment and chemicals? Do they all really get checked?"

"So a client pays OneOil for a Service X—that never gets delivered—and that money ends up in the pocket of some politician or bureaucrat who green-lights their client's deal."

"Exactly. So that was my angle at first. But then I met Phil. He'd been investigating Tratfors' links to political corruption and election rigging, and that led him from Tratfors to OneOil. So he met me going the other way and we pooled resources."

"But Tratfors isn't a OneOil client. It's the opposite. OneOil is a client of theirs."

"Not just a client. An appendage. They're two legs of the same monster. Tratfors can't have any direct dealings with the Russians because of their links to Western intelligence. But OneOil is a major player in Russia and Central Asia. Nazar has the Kremlin and a string of Russian oligarchs on speed dial. And he couldn't operate in Russia without buy-in from Russian intelligence. As for Tratfors, their black book is an index of corrupt politicians, spooks, and shady companies in the West."

She left it there and turned to the TV as Jerry used the remote to pull up a menu and switch the source to his tablet.

"Let's see what we got," he said.

The backdrop was a regal-looking entrance to a classy restaurant with plate-glass doors and a lush interior decorated with flowers and *objets d'art*. A man in a tuxedo was standing under an awning shaking hands with two men. A maître d' sucking up to VIP customers. The men were a study in contrast. One short and round, his coiffured mustache a black wax smudge at odds with his fashionably gray stubble. The other was at least a head taller and oozing military from his close-cropped head, broad shoulders and lean body right down to his polished Oxfords. The sort of guy who'd run three miles and do fifty press-ups before breakfast every day until he dropped.

Same old Preston.

CJ's recollection was dated but still good. He remembered Preston turning up in Iraq to rally the troops wearing a desert brush combat outfit fresh out of the laundry. Clean. That was how CJ remembered him, his face all sharp lines and angles like it was carved out of wood. And here he was ten years later. A fresh outfit, but otherwise the same. It was hard not to draw lifelines and add up the scores. Preston, CJ, Alex. No parallel lines of fortune here. Preston was the out-and-out winner.

There was a heavyweight minder close by. CJ recognized the tie from his run-in with Grambo, some sort of uniform. He was talking to a valet, dismissing him. Not needed. The limo was on the way. It pulled up and the minder walked to the car as Preston led Nazar out from under the awning between walls of potted plants. And there she was—zooming into frame—Leila, sticking her furry mic right in Nazar's face. The camera was so close that Jerry had to be right on her back. They must have been hiding in bushes by the entrance.

"Is the UK's SFO investigation into OneOil killing your business?"

Nazar's *no comment* was barely audible as he faded away behind Preston, who reared up filling the screen.

"Please, if you could just…" Preston swept his arm as if to make a way past her, but it was more like a shove.

The camera jumped and Jerry yelped from off mic. He looked back at them. "Knuckle in the ribs," he said, making a one-knuckle fist. He tapped his chest and winked at CJ. "Martial arts vest. Been there. Done that."

The camera was bouncing and Preston's hand lurched up to grab it, but Leila pushed it aside as she thrust her mic in his face.

"The incident at West Coast Drum yesterday. How is that linked to Iraq?" Preston stopped—no more shoving and evading—even an old warhorse has to blink when the ground explodes under his feet. "And why was a warrant issued in London for a former Tratfors employee? Brink was a war hero. What was he doing there?"

The camera skewed off to the side, and the screen blanked out before settling on a close-up of the red and yellow stripes of the awning. More jostling. Bodies in motion. Then a hand covered the lens. Scuffling and shouts.

When the picture resumed, it was from way back, a few yards off the awning. The security detail was center screen, two guys big enough to fill up most of it. Preston and Nazar were back under the awning conferring. Preston was bent over, whispering, his hand on the other man's shoulder. Secrets done. He strode out onto the sidewalk towards the camera as Nazar bolted for the limo. Preston spoke to the security detail, and the men stepped aside but kept their arms outstretched to make sure no one got any closer than Preston wanted.

"Hijacking businessmen on the sidewalk." Preston pointed at Leila. "You call this professionalism? I call it cheap soundbite crap, typical of your fake news network. You want answers? Try the truth. Tomorrow. Eight a.m. My suite. You know where. I'll give you fifteen minutes on camera. But don't expect an easy ride."

The security detail blocked the screen after that, smirking like their team had hit a home run. The camera backed off and caught the limo as it peeled off into traffic.

Jerry poked his trackpad and the picture froze.

"What do you think?" he said.

"We got him mad at least," Leila said. "But mad enough to drop the ball? I don't know."

"That warrant question," Jerry said. "It was like you shoved the mic up his ass."

CJ was thinking the same thing and wondering how smart it was. If the flipside of hanging out with Leila was being a stick to poke at Tratfors, he might need a new partner.

They left Jerry packing up his kit and joined Enya in the office. She was sitting behind a laptop screen with a download bar showing ten percent, but she wasn't looking at that. She wasn't looking at anything.

She was slumped forward, lying across the desktop, her head resting on folded arms. CJ touched her shoulders with his fingertips. Her eyelids were still, her breath a slow cycle. Forty-eight hours from Paris to Las Vegas via the bumpy route. The bill had finally arrived, and it had hit her like a strip of Ambien tabs.

"I guess the rest will have to wait," Leila said.

They both stared at the storage drive wired to the laptop. It was blinking frantically as bits and bytes streamed through its innards.

"The download has to complete anyway," CJ said. "Why don't you come by tomorrow after your interview with Preston?" She turned to go, but he caught her shoulder and eased her back around. "Now you've told Preston that we're in touch with each other, you'd better use plenty of street savvy on your way back here tomorrow."

That hit her with a jolt. He was telling her that she'd been dumb, too greedy to get a soundbite.

She nodded. "I'll be careful."

CJ steered her out of the room and they collected Jerry, and he walked them both to the car. When they were gone, he checked the house—every room, every closet and drawer, every door and lock. Then he took the range bucket out of the Honda's trunk, checked his pistols and loaded the spare magazines. He made a pot of coffee and took it into the office with two cups. But one was wasted. Enya was out for the count. He carried her upstairs, stripped off her pants and shirt and tucked her under a sheet. Back in the office, he drank the coffee and settled back on the couch with his phone and studied maps and satellite photos of the surrounding streets and deserts and the mountains beyond. It was after midnight when he signed off on that and stepped out into the garden. It was the low-maintenance type, a sea of pebbles with islands of cactus and desert blooms. Their colors were bright and their forms soft in the warm light from the house. But as he walked away from the house and down to the end of the yard, their colors faded into black and white in the cold light of the moon. He stood by the wall and let his eyes adjust to it until the landscape was floodlit all the way to the mountains and his ears had fine-tuned into an empty desert teeming with the sound of life.

TWENTY-ONE

Dawn was peeking through the blinds.

Somewhere out there, the sun was oozing over a mountain ridge and the night chorus of desert life was taking a bow and leaving the stage. CJ rolled onto his side. Enya was facing the other way, curled into a ball. He reached out and touched her hair. Feeling. No need to pop the magic pill. It had lasted a whole day and night. The more he worked on it, the better it got as neural pathways opened up and learned new habits. He soaked in it like a weary body in a hot bath, stroking her head with all the tenderness he could muster.

Don't wake. Not yet.

But she did, with a sigh that wrapped itself around his touch. She rolled over and he folded himself around her and held her, feeling the warmth of her belly against his, her nipples hard up against his ribs. He slid her on top to protect her bruised body from his weight and they made love. But before it was done, she stopped and reared up, looking down into his eyes, her face lighting up as if she'd found something special there, as if something she'd been waiting for a long time had finally showed up.

After loving, Enya took a shower and he lay back, listening to her sing Edith Piaf with a smile on his face. She might not have the chops to make it in music, but she did have world-class hacking skills, and that brought him to the day's main event.

The password.

Somehow he had to find the *Forgotten Password* link buried in his head. He had to find a way to play it all back, everything that Declan had said that day, including the Arabic. With luck, they'd hit the jackpot before Leila showed up, and if not, she could help. It was going to be tough, but he did have an ace card.

Self-hypnosis.

It had worked for his sense of touch, his rewired brain proving to be uniquely receptive to autosuggestion. If the technique could work for that, then why not his memory too? If they could get that password and access the vault, the plan would write itself. Leila belonged to some international consortium of investigative journalists. As soon as she plugged the data into that network, it was game over for Tratfors. It was a great plan. And with luck it was doable. But CJ was wary. It was all too easy. Las Vegas was the home of Mike Tyson, and fittingly his oft-quoted wisdom was echoing in CJ's head. "Everyone has a plan until they get punched in the face." That was the problem. There was a punch coming. It was winding up right now, somewhere out there beyond those blinds.

Enya finished up in the shower and went down to the office to check on the download while CJ cleaned up in the bathroom before joining her.

"The download is done," she said as he stepped

through the door. "But look at the size of it! It's huge."

He left her, muttering about logs and processes, and went to the kitchen, where he made coffee and eggs and toast. He brought it all back on a crowded tray and they ate in front of the computer, with Enya pointing at the screen and making technical points.

After they'd cleared away breakfast, CJ found a notepad and a pencil and he gave them to Enya.

"What's this?" she said. "You're the one who's got to remember."

"I'm going to put myself in a trance." He wanted it to sound like a breakthrough idea, but Enya looked far from convinced. She frowned, lopsided, bent out of shape by a fresh set of Band-Aids. "It's like I have switches in my head," he said. "Don't ask me how it works. Something to do with my cross-wired brain and how it processes information."

"That sounds like all hope is lost to me."

"It'll work. All you have to do is write it down." He checked his watch. "Leila will be here soon. So let's do it. Make two columns. English on one side. Arabic on the other."

"I can't write Arabic."

"Just write down how it sounds in English letters. Leila speaks Arabic. If there's something there, maybe she can find it."

"It won't be anything in Arabic. We used password conventions. The usual stuff. Upper and lowercase. Alphanumeric and special characters. At least twenty. But it wouldn't be random. That would make it impossible to remember. He hated password safes, so all his passwords were memorable—based on a thing, a place, an object, a something—and jazzed up with numbers and special characters."

"Just write it down. We'll figure all that out later."

He closed his eyes and ran the script he'd prepared in his head, soundtracking it with Doctor Sam's voice. The minutes on either side of Alex's death had been the most intense of his life, his world playing out frame by frame in Technicolor with stereophonic sound. The detail might be buried, but it had to be inside him somewhere, and if anything could dig it out, it was Doctor Sam's sudsy voice dragging him back through time and into the darkness inside him.

Deep breaths.

He hit the Play button and the virtual video flooded his inner screen. Declan screaming. Hussein pleading. Jahil lusting for blood.

CJ was shaking, veins bulging and blood trickling from his nose. Enya went to stop him, to shake him. But as she reached out, he jerked back, hands all knuckles crushing the armrests. Inside his head, the focus was tightening on Declan and his broken stream of verbiage. CJ barked it out, a staccato stream, and Enya scribbled it down. It was all English at first. Declan's promises. Discrediting the government. Shaming the CIA with a truth big enough to turn the entire world against America. He had the password and offered a simple trade. Jahil ignored him. Declan was screeching, calling out to Hussein and switching to pidgin Arabic mixed with English.

CJ sat motionless when he was done, staring at the wall. Enya wiped the blood dribbling from his nose with a tissue, and his eyes flashed up at her.

"Thank God," she said. "I thought you'd gone catatonic on me again."

She left him the tissue and fetched more coffee, and by the time she got back, CJ was studying her notes.

She put two cups on the desk and pulled her chair up next to his. CJ was shaking his head in a slow denial, unable to accept what his eyes were telling him.

"This is useless," he said.

"You did your best."

Enya squeezed her head into the frame and they checked it together. She pointed at cat and canary.

"I felt so stupid writing this down again."

CJ shrugged. "That's what I heard."

They continued to study the list.

"You said that Declan never used random characters because it had to be memorable."

She nodded. "It was always something you could remember, or tell someone. Like he planned to tell me."

"For example?"

"The Battle of Waterloo. That's a word with numbers attached. It happened on June 18, 1815. So that would give us Waterloo18061815. But that would be guessable. So we always added our own string of special characters."

"Like question marks?"

"We called it our family sauce, and we had a few recipes."

"So the password isn't here explicitly. It's described here. Something on this list is like a password hint."

"That'd be my guess. He planned to tell it me in a phone call. So it had to be something he could say once and I'd remember without having to write it down. But it wouldn't be something simple like the battle of Waterloo. It would be something super clever. And immensely difficult to crack."

Their eyes went back to the notes, but there was still nothing jumping out at them.

"Let's eliminate the unlikely," CJ suggested. "This stuff at the beginning. The sales pitch to Jahil. It's got to be here in this end part with Hussein."

CJ underlined the Arablish—the Arabic mashed up in the English alphabet—and started making a new list.

"What are you doing?"

"Certain words he repeated over and over. That's why I remember them so clearly. I'm making a list of them. Plus the Arabic words. They have to be special. How well did he speak it?"

"That depends. I doubt he could discuss philosophy. But computer science, that's another thing."

CJ's shortlist had eight lines. Three English and five Arabic.

salmon
cat and canary
GPS
mushfira
moussadaka
kalamah alsiru
tassy fon
muhadila

Enya read it, then closed her eyes. But it didn't look like she was thinking. It looked like she was giving up.

"Hey…" He slipped his arm around her waist and hugged her. "We can do this. Let's drink some more coffee and get our heads into it."

She bucked up and took a slug of coffee.

"The only thing that gives me hope here is GPS," she said. "But GPS coordinates is too simple and obvious. Plus, I used GPS in rule-based attacks on the password and got nowhere. As for this Arabic, who are we kidding? This is an Irishman's Arabic transliterated by a brain-damaged Englishman, then written down by a nonspeaker in an alien alphabet."

"Leila speaks Arabic. And by the way, my brain is properly described as reconditioned, not damaged."

They shared a smile before going back to work. Enya set up the password cracker and tuned it with scripts and rulesets. CJ let her get on with it. He didn't have much faith in the cracker. The key here was not so much brute force as blinding inspiration. But they'd gotten no closer either way when he heard the distinctive growl of Leila's diesel a block away. He slipped a Sig in his belt and went outside, checking the street as she pulled into the driveway.

"I was careful," she said as she stepped out of the car. "Besides, they were all gone. That asshole was messing with me. They checked out overnight."

That didn't sound right. Preston's take on messing with people was more like burying them in concrete than standing them up for an interview. He checked the empty street again before breaking the rest of the day's bad news to her.

No password.

Leila grabbed his arm and jerked him around.

"You're kidding me?" A hangdog face was all the answer CJ could muster. "That's all you've got for me? Password Sudoku?"

"Enya's an expert. She's got special tools. And you can help with the Arabic. The biggest jackpot Vegas ever saw is right here in this house. We just need to roll the right dice."

He was pretty pleased with that Vegas metaphor, but Leila was inconsolable. Her day had gone wrong from the get-go. Pumped up and ready to rip into Preston, she was still in attack mode and CJ was a handy new target. He steered her into the kitchen and made her coffee while she thrashed away at him. Half a cup later, her pressure valves vented, he told her about Rumble Bee, and as the bonanza lying in wait on the far side of twenty-odd characters came into focus, her eyes lit up and CJ knew they had a new recruit on their team.

"Do I have to do this myself?" Enya said, sticking her head through the kitchen doorway.

They followed her back into the office, where they settled down, each with a copy of the shortlist, which Enya had transcribed into the laptop and printed out. CJ started by giving Leila the background, describing the scene that day and its players and how they'd drilled it all down to this list. Enya talked technical and security, helping her understand Declan's approach to passwords and what she'd already tested and tried.

"Tell us about the Arabic," CJ said as Leila studied the list.

"I suppose you both know that Arabic has its own alphabet. So when you write it in the Latin alphabet, it has as many possibilities as there are people with ears. Also, they usually omit vowels when they transliterate. So this is something else yet again. It's phonetic and——"

"I know. I know," Enya said. "But let's skip the obvious and take this forward. Can you see anything meaningful? I need to make a mask and a set of rules to crack this."

CJ looked from Enya to Leila. Nothing to add. That was right on song. Enya started to drum her fingers.

Leila took the hint and put her eyes back on the list.

"As a matter of fact, they do. I speak Arabic, but I don't read or write it." She glanced up before getting back to the list. Enya eased up on the drumming. "So I think in phonetic terms. And since we know the topic is computers, some of this jumps off the page. *Mushfira*, for example, means encrypted. But you know that had to be part of the conversation already."

"And the rest?" CJ said.

"The same computer words he said in English repeated in Arabic. This one"—she pointed at *muhadila*—"is something like recipe or formula, and *kalamah alsiru* means password."

"What about *tassy fon?*"

"No idea." She continued to study the list. "These English words are so weird." Leila pointed them out. "Salmon, cat, canary? Are you sure that's salmon and not Salman, or Suleiman? They're common names."

CJ thought about it. He wasn't sure at all. He wasn't sure of any of it. Salman? Yes, it could easily be. And it was not only a common first name but also a place name.

"We went to a town called Salman. Alex and me. We took some journalist there. Alex knew it well. He went there during the war. It was supposed to be a major bioterrorism center, but all that was a load of bull."

"Salman Pak," Leila said. "Saddam's counterterrorist training camp for special forces. No WMDs, of course."

"That's the place. South of Baghdad." CJ turned to Enya. "Try the GPS."

But she was already on it. "It'll take me a few minutes. There's not just one GPS format. I can guess which one he would use, but I'll program them all anyway."

CJ opened his phone as Enya keyed in strokes at warp speed. He pulled up Wikipedia, found Salman Pak and read the listing out loud. "'The city overlaps with the ancient metropolis of Al-Mada'in, which includes the ruins of ancient...' Wait." He shared the screen with Leila. "How would you pronounce that town?" He picked out the word Ctesiphon with his finger.

She said nothing, staring. Then she grabbed the shortlist.

"That's it. *Tassy fon*. That's how I'd say it. I don't think it's a military site. There's some sort of monument there."

CJ was finding his way from Ctesiphon to another Wikipedia page, dedicated to Taq Kasra, its famous monument. "It's an archway." He stopped and turned to Enya. "Forget the GPS for Salman Pak." He went back to the page. "'The arch is the largest vault in the world.'" He looked up again. "And you can forget cat and canary too." His eyes went back on the page. "We can write that mistake down to Declan's Irish accent. It's a C-A-T-E-N-A-R-Y arch."

"What the hell is catenary?" Leila said.

CJ shrugged.

Enya was shaking her head. "That's my brother for you. Always the smart arse. Catenary is a mathematical equation. If you hang a chain between two points, it's the way gravity makes it hang. And if you swing those same dimensions the other way, you create a self-supporting arch."

"So it's the GPS of Ctesiphon," Leila said.

"That's too short and too obvious," Enya said.

CJ was searching online. "But it must be a part of

it," he said. "Maybe he was saying, 'The password is the GPS of Ctesiphon near Salman Pak, plus…'"—he held his phone in front of Enya—"'the catenary equation of its famous arch.'" She had already typed the GPS coordinates of Ctesiphon into her ruleset, and now she added the catenary formula.

They all stared at the result.

33537N443451Ey=a.cosh(x/a)

"That first part doesn't look like GPS," Leila said, leaning in closer. "What about the degree symbol?"

"It's not on a standard keyboard. And neither are the prime or double prime characters. They're the minute and second markers that look like quotation marks. He'd only use typable characters. Special characters like that are system dependent. He'd keep it simple. Same with the equation. No fancy symbols. Besides, even with the spaces removed, it's still twenty-six characters. That's plenty of password entropy. It would take billions of years to crack. Typical Declan."

"So that's it?" CJ said.

"More or less. These are the building blocks," she said. "Now I need to create a mask and finish the ruleset. I'll code it to check GPS coordinates in every possible format and test different equations used in catenary calculations. Then I'll stir in some family sauce, and we'll give it a go."

CJ and Leila waited as Enya's fingers whirred over the keys, driving a blinking cursor that was trailing lines of code.

"Ready?" she said, twenty minutes later, as her hands left the keyboard and hovered above the Enter key. "If we're on the right track, we should know in less than a minute." There was one big breath shared between the three of them, and Enya hit the key.

"We're in."

It was that fast. Not a minute. Not even half. Just a few seconds of cascading characters and the screen burst into scrolling lines of files.

"All those goddamn years," Enya said.

They crowded around her, bodies hanging over the screen, dwarfing the laptop.

"But look at these dates." Enya stopped the rolling screen and scrolled back. "What the hell. 2017. Shit." Enya flipped screens. "This is the connection log. There've been daily connections right up until a few months ago."

Leila was lost looking from one to the other. "What does it mean?"

"There's only one explanation," Enya said. "Declan left his ghost in the machine. He buried malware so deep in Tratfors' network that it's been pumping out files ever since. That explains this massive amount of data."

It explained a lot more than that to CJ. The night nurse and Sami's barbecue, for starters. The scale of what was happening had never seemed right. It had to be more than Rumble Bee. The Iraq War was a history lesson now. But the names flashing up on the screen were right out of today's headline news. Whatever the cost, whatever it took, these people had to be protected. With all the players dead, or in CJ's case, the next best thing, Rumble Bee was a closed file. But when he'd come back from the dead, someone had opened it. Maybe that had triggered a security audit led by a new generation of geeks, guys smart enough to sniff out Declan's ghost.

"How come they didn't find the leak sooner?" CJ said.

"He hid it too well. They have a global network. They'll do backups like any company. Databases replicating. Certain files getting archived. And somehow he found a way to bury his code so it went unnoticed and dripped secrets into the cloud for all these years." She looked up at CJ. "It's not just your friend Alex who came back from the grave. My brother Declan has been living in their network ever since he died, and he's been crying for help. I'm his twin. Somehow I heard him even though I didn't know it."

Leila was staring down at the laptop, mesmerized. She jerked her head at the screen. "Let's dig in and find out what we've got."

Enya shuffled through folders and files.

"Stop. What's that?" Leila jammed her finger at a fleeting file name. "Bortnik. That's Yakov Bortnik. Check that folder. He's linked with Nazar."

"There are gigabytes of files here," Enya said. "We don't have time to trawl through them all one by one."

"He was the top cybercrime guru at the FSB—that's Russia's Homeland Security. He got arrested last year by Russian military Intelligence—the GRU—along with the hackers behind that Democratic Party email hack. Some sort of turf wars between Russian intelligence agencies."

CJ and Enya shared a look like the ground was opening up underneath them.

"I've got a pen drive," Leila said. She grabbed her bag and searched inside it. "If you can just copy that one for me now."

Enya continued to scroll through the files until CJ grabbed her shoulder. He pointed to another file but said nothing.

"Isn't that the guy"—she looked up at him— "who

got poisoned?"

CJ nodded, his eyes still on the screen.

"Here it is." Leila whipped something out of her bag and stopped, her face breaking into a slow-motion frown. It looked like a memory stick. Only it wasn't.

CJ snatched it and looked at it closely. Then he stuck it in the doorjamb and levered the door closed. The plastic cracked open, and a tiny battery fell out and rolled around on the floor at his feet.

Leila was ashen, her hand in front of her open mouth.

CJ pulled out his gun and stepped over to the window. The street was deserted, exactly as it had been when Leila had arrived, the same cars in the same driveways.

"Did someone bump into you at Preston's hotel?" he said.

"No, I swear. No one. I waited for him. We both did. Me and Jerry. No one touched me, I…" She stopped, her body slumping under the weight of realization. "The bathroom. Some woman. She fell. She said she was diabetic. Hypoglycemic. I helped her sit down on a chair. That's all."

CJ checked through the window again. The street was a snapshot of picture postcard, peaceful suburbia. His mind was racing, shifting gears and sorting plans. There were two freeways and a beltway within reach. That's a lot of options. If they could only sneak out of the neighborhood, they were home free. It all came down to the next ten minutes. He snatched Leila's keys from the table as Enya slammed the lid on her laptop and tossed it into her satchel. Sixty seconds later, the Range Rover lurched out of the driveway and skidded off down the road.

TWENTY-TWO

PACE

CJ's reflexes were clicking through his planning acronym a lot faster than he'd hoped. P stood for the Primary plan. But that was history. So they were working on A for Alternate.

Run.

With an orderly withdrawal the preferred option. Not that preference counted for much. The choice was down to luck, notoriously available in only one of two flavors, and theirs depended on the location of Tratfors' start line. When CJ had crushed the bug, the signal had dropped and the starting gun had fired. But where was the Tratfors team listening on the other end located? In a downtown hotel room? Or a surveillance van a block away? That was the difference between A for Alternate, and skipping C for Contingency and proceeding directly to E for Emergency, a shoot-out with all the wrong odds, asymmetry in spades. They'd be outmanned and outgunned by a team of ex-military killers.

Preston had outmaneuvered them. Leila was a great reporter, but a lousy covert operative. She'd forgotten the obvious. Every question gives an answer. Every question tells your adversary what you know. She wanted to rattle Preston, and she'd succeeded. The shoot-out at the toxic factory was all over the news. But none of those reports mentioned CJ Brink. Preston was an old war dog. Seasoned. So used to thinking on his feet he could do it lying on his back. She'd knocked him down alright, but he'd landed a killer counterpunch on the way. He'd heard what she'd said. And what he'd heard was, *Follow me and I'll take you to him*. All the rest was a setup.

Three blocks from the house with no sign of pursuit, the hairs on the backs of their necks were starting to soften up. There was no surveillance van down the block or they'd know about it already. So it looked like the Tratfors crew would be starting from some downtown hotel. That made sense. Bugging Leila had been a last-minute thing, a split-second decision. They were bound to have a suitcase full of spycraft junk in the trunk of a car. But a surveillance wagon? Not even Preston traveled that heavy.

CJ cut the speed to respectable levels, cruising streets that had never looked so good. Quiet. Sublimely suburban with a refreshing absence of automatic gunfire. They picked up the I-15 heading south back to LA. They'd escaped—albeit with a nagging doubt that it was all too easy. He glanced at Enya. She was sitting in the passenger seat with both arms cradling her laptop satchel against her chest like a mother nursing a baby. She was stony-faced, her eyes on the road ahead. She'd been expecting Rumble Bee, not this. The scale of it all had to be terrifying. He squeezed her thigh and smiled. She nodded an I'm okay—a lover's message. Then her eyes went back on the road and her face went back into stone.

"We need to get that stuff out there," Leila said. "Once we do that, we'll be safe. I have contacts in Germany. If I can get this to them, whatever's in it will go global."

She'd wanted to use her phone as soon as they'd left the house. But it would certainly be tracked, so she'd agreed to turn it off.

"What about your exclusive?" CJ said.

"It's not important anymore. My new priority is survival. There's so much there anyway. It'll take teams of journalists to figure it out. But as soon as it gets out there, Tratfors will implode. The ones that get caught will make deals and turn on the others. And the ones that escape will burrow into the ground and never be seen again."

"I can live with that," Enya said.

They rolled on down the road. Three minds, one topic. Survival.

CJ ducked his head and looked up at the sky.

"What's up?" Enya said.

He didn't answer, his head snapping back and forth between the road and the sky.

He glanced at Leila in the rearview mirror.

"When you were waiting for Preston, where were you parked?"

"I left the car with the hotel valet. Why?"

"See the skydivers?" He nodded beyond a concrete block of a hotel rearing out of the desert on the other side of the freeway. "There's some kind of airstrip up ahead. So plenty of planes. But that Cessna"—he pointed with a finger back over his left shoulder—"has been flying back and forth since we hit the freeway."

An upcoming off-ramp was marked with a green sign. Exit 12. CJ swung the wheel and they left the freeway. There was a gas station on the right. He pulled into the forecourt and parked under its canopy by a pump.

"Does anyone have a mirror?" he said.

They both shook their heads.

CJ considered ripping out the vanity mirror before stepping out of the vehicle and wriggling under the SUV at the back. That was all it took. He crawled out a minute later with a transponder concealed in his hand. He walked by a van gassing up at the next pump. The van had California plates. CJ crouched and tied his laces as he sneaked it underneath, listening for the click of its magnet as it grabbed onto the metal. The van driver finished up and pulled out of the gas station and headed back towards the I-15. CJ watched as the van turned into the on-ramp bearing south, picking up their route where they'd left it.

The gap between pulling off the freeway and sheltering out of sight on the gas station forecourt was a few minutes. The spotters in the plane might have caught it. But it was making a detour at the time to avoid the skydivers. So most likely, they'd missed it. Especially since they had no reason to fret about losing a white import glowing in the sun with a transponder pumping out find-me signals.

CJ gassed the Range Rover and bought coffees, and everyone used the restrooms. They checked the skies were empty before pulling out of the gas station and heading on down the road away from the freeway. The spotters would take a while to figure out what was going on, but not forever.

"So what's the plan?" Leila said.

C was for Contingency, and this was it.

"Find somewhere down the road here with covered parking and hide."

Leila pointed through the windshield at the deserts and mountains swallowing the road ahead.

"You call that somewhere?"

"Goodsprings. It's a town. I saw the sign. Here." He gave Enya his phone. "Check it out."

Enya was silent as she thumbed through pages. Then she looked up and said, "Oops."

"C'mon," CJ said. "This is Nevada. There's got to be something. A bar. A casino. A brothel. We could all do with some R and R." He winked at her, trying to lighten the mood. But that was never going to fly, and she admonished him with a flash of green eyes.

"No brothels in Las Vegas County," Leila said.

Enya smirked at him before going back to the phone. "At the last census, there were two hundred and twenty-three people there."

"We should have ducked under the freeway," Leila said, "and gone the other way. There's a big hotel."

"That's the first place they'll look." CJ said. "And that'll take them forever."

"No casino," Enya said. "But they do have a bar. A famous one. The oldest bar in Nevada. It's got a bullet hole in the wall where some guy was shot dead in a gunfight a hundred years ago." She looked up, thoughtful. "One measly bullet hole and they're still making a living out of it. That's typical Nevada. They'd roll out the red carpet if only they knew who was about to breeze into their town." She offered him the phone. "You could set these guys up for millennia. I hear they're already doing Toxic Showdown tours in

Wilmington."

He growled at her and snatched it back.

"Is that it?" Leila said.

"No," Enya said. "There's another place called Sandy Valley down the road on the other side of those hills." She pointed ahead. "It's called a community. That's an American word for a bunch of houses that no one in their right mind would call a town. I checked the photos. It's a garden spot for people who like to shoot at cactus in the desert. And as for hiding out there—please—will you take a look at the three of us? We don't exactly blend in around here. We need a lot more concrete and a lot less rock."

CJ flicked through a few pages, double-checking her report. It was spot-on. Aside from these communities, the road would peter out into a labyrinth of county roads and trails, a maze squeezed in and around deserts and mountains. There might be some way to pick your way through them into California and back onto the I-15, but they'd never make it even if they were kitted out with enough supplies. The landscape was empty. No cover, no traffic. And the sky was clear blue. Even the most inattentive and myopic spotter would have no difficulty picking them out from a plane. They'd be better off taking their chances back on the freeway or mingling in the traffic in Vegas. But it was too late for second-guessing. They'd already arrived at the outskirts of Goodsprings. The rocky landscape was dotted with isolated buildings that soon gave way to homes on generous plots sprinkled with trucks in various states of disrepair. Enya was right. Nowhere to hide. They slowed down by the celebrity saloon, rubbernecking like tourists, taking in its tin-roof awning and shaded boardwalk. It was right out of a movie set. But cowboys didn't drive cars. And there was no covered parking anywhere. Then it was gone. And so was the town. More or less. CJ cut back and switched left and right through a few streets before ending up back on the road to Sandy Valley, the blacktop ahead rising gently to meet bare conical hills. But as the hills got closer, CJ pulled over. This was the road to nowhere. He did a broken U-turn and headed back towards Goodsprings.

"We'll go to that big hotel," he said, "then split up. Enya, you book a room with your credit card, but take a taxi back to Las Vegas. Go to the Irish Consulate and tell them you've lost your passport and your credit cards and ask for help. Take the laptop. But give the hard drive to Leila."

"I don't have the files on the laptop. Only the drive."

"But you know the cloud server address and login. You can download it again." He glanced back at Leila. "You need to call your network from a public phone at the hotel and get them to order an air taxi to take you back to LA."

"And what are you going to do?" Leila said.

"Me and deserts go way back. I'm going to take these guys for a detour."

"No way," Enya said, "I'm not going to do it and you can't make me. I'm not giving that hard drive to anyone until I know for sure that it will end up spread like the plague on TV, online, everywhere."

"I don't know the password anyway," Leila said.

"No," Enya said. "And you're not getting it either." She turned to Leila. "It's not that I don't trust you. Don't think that." She turned back to CJ. "As for you, I'm never going to leave you. So forget it. We can check into the hotel, barricade ourselves in the room, then use their Wi-Fi to start posting this stuff online. We'll blast it out like a shotgun all over social media. That's how the web works. Once the virus is out, you can never get it back."

CJ was quiet, wondering how to get everyone back on the same team. But he didn't have to wonder long. The road ahead had gentle curves winding downhill to a plain. It was empty except for a cloud of dust oozing out of the landscape and creeping towards them. That was a clue. But it wasn't the clincher. That was the sound. The roar of big-bore V-8s screaming, upstaging the Rover's discreet supercharged gurgling.

He slammed his foot on the brakes, skidding off the blacktop onto its shoulder. This time the U-turn was not broken. He just spun a loop in the gravel on either side of the road and they were heading back towards the hills at speed as their pursuers emerged from the cloud. Enya and Leila looked from each other to CJ but said nothing. The new reality was obvious enough. They must have been spotted when they'd turned off the freeway, or back at the gas station. Leila twisted around and posted watch out the rear window, holding on with both hands as CJ flung the SUV around snaking bends.

"There's two," she said. "A big truck and an SUV. They're still a ways behind yet."

CJ's eyes were dancing back and forth in the mirrors, and he caught them taking a bend back down the hill. Maybe a thousand yards. Maybe less.

"Still got that thirty-eight?" he said.

"You bet," Leila said.

"Can you shoot a nine-mil?"

"I can shoot a Kalashnikov."

"Pity I don't have one. An RPG would be handy too." He pulled out one of his 9mm pistols and passed it to her. "Give the thirty-eight to Enya."

She hesitated. But then she took the revolver out of her purse and handed it over. Enya took it like it was a wet fish, and one that didn't smell too good.

"I had the trigger smithed," Leila said. "It's got an eight-pound pull on double action, but only four on single. Smooth as butter. So take it easy."

Enya looked down at it laid flat across her palms.

"I've never even touched a gun," she said, her face floating up towards CJ.

"Put it in your satchel. Only use it if you're real close. Just point it at the middle of their body and squeeze the trigger."

"Amen," she said, sliding the gun into the satchel next to the laptop.

"Can we outrun them in this?" Leila said.

"We'll never get the chance. In these hills we're protected by all these bends. They can't get a shot off. Besides, they're too far back. Even with M4s or Kalashnikovs, they'd be out of range."

CJ took another bend before he broke the bad news.

"But this is the A-team. They'll have sniper rifles and people who know how to use them. When we make it over these hills, we'll be heading down into a valley. The fastest vehicle will continue the pursuit. The other one will pull over and set up. Elevated position. Perfect visibility. Little or no wind. That's not too hard. And even if they miss and we escape the pursuit vehicle, it won't be for long. They'll send a chopper and pick us off from the sky."

That was the talking done. Its aftermath was silence.

Enya nursed her satchel. Leila checked the pistol. CJ looked for a venue. It was official. This was Plan E for Emergency. It was all down to a shoot-out. The only choice left was to pick the place. The road was still going up, but steeper, its shoulders gone, the hills squeezing up to the edge of the road. CJ was looking for an exit. They passed a trail heading off into the scrub on the right, but he let it go. The hills were too low on that side with no twists and turns. No place to hide. He needed a bolthole, a trail that snaked in and out of rocks and bluffs as soon as it left the road. And he found it. Just after the pass. A trail on the left.

He slewed the Range Rover off the road, its tires scrabbling stones and dirt. The trail was narrow and well worn, its route decorated with abandoned telephone poles that were now just spikes of wood, their wires long gone. CJ spun the wheel, cutting left and right around interlocking fingers of rock, and the road was soon lost from sight. When the V-8s were close—almost at the turnoff—CJ cut the engine and closed his eyes, following the sound as they roared on by. No pause. No second thoughts. The howl of their engines bounced off the rock walls of the trail and faded in waves as they twisted on down the road. They'd soon realize their mistake. The road would straighten out—no more twists and turns—and they'd get a clear line of sight across the valley. There'd be a few cars on the road, but no white Range Rover. CJ started the engine, a big decision looming. Life was all about choices. Good and bad. And in CJ's world, the way they added up was called living or dying.

So which way?

Option one was the hotel. In minutes, they could be back on the road heading towards it. They might make it, too. But the odds were not good. They'd be out in the open for too long. And what if Tratfors had deployed a second team? They could be waiting down the road already. They'd end up in a shoot-out in the wrong place, outnumbered by trained killers. They'd be outgunned too. The Tratfors team would have long guns. Most likely full auto. The first rule of tactics is that the weapon dictates the movement, and in open country, their long guns and superior forces gave them control. Heading into wide-open spaces was playing to their strength. It was running in fear with the hounds at their heels. That was rarely the best choice. Ask any rabbit.

Option two was more snake than rabbit. Sneak down a hole and lie in wait. The Tratfors vehicles weren't armored. Leila knew how to shoot, and they had hundreds of rounds. Close quarters. If they could only find cover and catch them in the open. With the range cut back to fifty yards, the odds would switch. That was a lot of ifs. But the goal had shifted. Escape was grand. But survival was essential. And squeezed in between these hills down the trail, there might be an ambush point.

CJ shuffled his deck of priorities, CPD reflexes kicking in hard. Close protection detail was a day at the office for him, a way of life he'd lived for years in the world's most hostile environment. Getting ambushed was a constant risk and a frequent occurrence. Kalashnikovs, RPGs, IEDs and grenades. Name it. If the insurgents used it for killing, he'd been in its sights. But he'd survived. And so had all of his clients. At least, all except Declan O'Brien, and he'd already paid over the odds for that mistake. Outing Tratfors and going public with the data was a laudable goal, but CJ could make do with dreaming it. The same with Kowalski. CJ wasn't going to trade vengeance for the lives of Enya and Leila. He had to save them, and that meant heading further into the hills. He'd read the writing on the trail, and those splintered telephone poles were a history book, signposts of a bygone era, frontier days when this trail had led somewhere worth going. He'd heard about Nevada ghost towns. Once-thriving communities, built around mines that had never fulfilled their promise. Either that or they'd gotten swept aside by the vagaries of economics and social change.

"What's that?" He'd heard something. Not the V-8s. Something different. Super high revs. He checked the mirrors, but all he could see was dust.

"I got it," Leila said, her face pushed up against the side window. "It's a drone."

"Oh God," Enya said peering into the side-view mirror. "It's a drone on steroids."

CJ couldn't see it, but he could hear it. There were two distinct frequencies. One high. One low.

"It's a quadcopter," he said. "Two engines. The blades are electric. Battery-powered. But they get charged by a fuel engine. Gasoline or hydrogen. Hours of flight time."

"It's getting closer," Leila said, spotting it out the back window. "It's carrying something… grocery bags. Those single-use plastic bags they banned in California. There's a bunch of them hanging underneath."

CJ saw it too. It was feet away from the rear window, a freak wasp with chainsaw wings, an escapee from an insectivore Jurassic Park with howling rotors and screeching motors.

And shopping bags.

CJ was slapping the Range Rover around the bends, scraping the rocks. A hard target. But the predator wasp was hanging in there, following every swing of its tail like it was tied to it with a tow rope. CJ had his eyes on it, keeping the trail ahead in his peripheral vision. He was studying the bags swinging underneath it. They were thin white plastic. Almost see-through. And so close he could make out the contents.

What was it Leila called them?

Single-use.

You betcha.

"Get ready."

For what. He didn't say, and Enya and Leila didn't ask. They grabbed belts and handles and hunkered down as CJ coiled his body around the wheel. There was a sudden burst of revs, a crescendo that cut through them like a sound sword. Then the copter pounced. here.

TWENTY-THREE

In 2004, US Special Forces in Afghanistan used a drone called a Tarantula Hawk to drop grenades on the Taliban. That was a first. But good ideas make good travelers. And ten years later, ISIS were already making their own version. Improvisation. The insurgents were masters at it, and a canny student of conflict like Kowalski was never going to pass up a good trick. He'd even updated it with a quadcopter that wouldn't be out of place in a new science magazine. But the bombs underneath were another story. They were cut and pasted right out of the insurgent's make-and-mend playbook. Mason jars. The home accessory for preserving jam now had a new line of work. The important bit was to get the right size so that it kept a tight squeeze on the grenade's lever after you pulled the pin and slid it into the jar.

CJ hit the brakes, spun the wheel and stamped on the gas all in the same second. No plan. No applicable page in the training manual. Just a roll of the dice. Sounds and images. Floods of terror. And all three of them got washed away with it, including CJ. But he had questions too. Not articulated. Not laid out neatly in a logical thinking process, but popping up like sparks amid the mayhem.

What type of grenades? Time-fuse or impact?

That's a big issue when glass is shattering and levers popping. And hanging off those important unknowns were a bunch of more trivial concerns about their vehicle. With an old-fashioned rear-wheel drive, CJ could have controlled the skid, stopping the vehicle's forward motion and sliding it off the trail and up the bank to one side. But this was a modern four-wheeler with a computer doing its own line of thinking and shifting power and traction according to a set of rules which certainly didn't include *evasive maneuvering when attacked by drone on rocky mountain trail.*

Whatever he did, it was brave-new-world stuff.

The Rover hit a fist of rock as it spun up the bank, and a two-part explosion shattered a window and dinged holes in the roof. Leila yelped and keeled over, grabbing her face. Another sound. Tympanic. A jar bouncing on the roof. CJ watched it tumble down the windshield onto the hood and slide off the edge.

That was it. They were on solid rock. It was over.

But the flimsy plastic caught on the wipers, one of its handles snagging on a blade. They were perched at a precipitous angle at the side of the trail, pointing down, wedged up against that fist of rock.

The drone?

It was still there. He could hear it but not see it.

"Leila," CJ's voice barked out, cutting through shell-shocked ears.

She cried out. Not a word. That universal sound. Pain. Just enough to tell them she was still with the living.

CJ unbuckled his belt and tried to get out, but he couldn't open his door. He slammed his shoulder against it and the Range Rover jolted, bouncing on its springs. All eyes went to the plastic bag hooked on the wiper.

How thick was that recyclable plastic?

CJ swung his legs up and laid them across Enya's lap so they could reach the passenger door. He put his hands on the driver's door and pushed by straightening his legs like a horizontal squat. The door burst open, and he ducked out, using the SUV for cover. The drone was about seventy to eighty yards away. He was about to reach for the plastic bag and secure it. But he stopped. The drone had to be relaying video. The Rover was pointing away from it. Maybe they hadn't seen the bag snagged on the wiper. It wouldn't be so easy in so much dust and smoke. The grenades had been dropped in front of them. They had time fuses with a four-to-five-second delay. So all they had to do was drop them from the right height and the right distance in front of the vehicle. They didn't even have to guess its speed. They tracked it. That was why the drone was hanging off their tail. It wasn't rocket science. But it wasn't an exact science either, not with the split-second calculations involved.

CJ had his pistol out and targeted on the drone when they made him. The copter swooped to one side before turning tail and heading back up the trail gaining height. CJ's arms were braced on top of the Range Rover. A tough shot. But the Sig Sauer was an intimate friend, and a drone is vulnerable. Even a feeble 9mm round exhausted at the end of a long trajectory has enough juice to damage it.

One hundred yards.
Two hundred and rising fast.
Bullet drop? Windage?
No time for arithmetic.
What did Alex call this?
Arkansas elevation and Kentucky windage.

In other words, pants it. And CJ did just that. He laid it down. The whole clip. Even though bullet number twelve did the job, catching one of the pods and knocking out its rotor. The drone lurched to one side, then swooped down skimming a rocky outcrop like a bird of prey on the hunt for game before shattering in splinters of metal and swirling blades. Silence. Then a hot wire found some leaking gas and flame trailed black smoke with a twirling finger up towards a blue sky.

CJ unhooked the bag hanging from the wiper blade and squeezed his way past the buckled door into the driver's seat. He could hear the V-8s. They were back on the trail already. Enya was kneeling on her seat, leaning back over it to nurse Leila.

"She's been hurt," she said. "She's got glass in her face." Enya grabbed a handful of Leila's hair to hold her head steady as she plucked a shard of glass from her cheek.

CJ reached into the bag and pulled out the Mason jar. Sitting inside it was a M67 fragmentation grenade with its spoon jammed up against the glass. That thick glass and solid metal lid, along with the angle of the Rover's roof and its motion, had saved their lives. Like a stunt man rolling out of a fall, the force of the impact had been dissipated when it ricocheted off the roof and tumbled down the windshield. Not just a stroke of luck, but a seismic shift in fortune. A jackpot with a five-star bonus. Not only had they lived through a potentially lethal attack, but they now had a grenade.

"Are we good?" He checked Leila in the mirror.

"Good." She was holding a bloody tissue against her cheek, her voice little more than a squeak. Enya turned around and fell into her seat as CJ backed off their savior rock and they slewed down the bank onto the trail in a scramble of wheels and stones. They headed deeper into the hills, snaking between banks of gravel and gnarls of chiseled rock.

"Can't we just call the cops?" Leila was grabbing at straws, but when you've been on the wrong end of a grenade, that'll happen.

CJ pulled out his phone and passed it to Enya. She checked the screen. "No signal. Maybe if we sit on top of one of these hills, a 911 call might go through. But I still vote no. Assuming we're not already dead by the time they get here, these guys would kill the cops like they're wiping their noses. And even if they didn't and we all survived—two big and unlikely ifs—we'd have to explain things. CJ would get arrested. The hard drive would end up in an evidence locker and get sucked into a black hole. And all this assumes that Tratfors don't have a local law enforcement officer in their pocket. In which case, Nevada's finest will shoot us by mistake." She offered Leila the phone, but Leila shook her head. So she turned it off and dropped it in her satchel. "Like it or not," she said, "our world has been simplified. Survival. It's all we have left to worry about. So cheer up. We've got the world record holder sitting right here at the wheel."

They rounded a bend, and CJ swerved to avoid a concrete block sticking up out of the ground. They skidded to a halt in a clearing. The trailhead. An arena the size of a schoolyard cut out of the base of three mountains. CJ drove to the end of the clearing, then banged his way out through the Rover's buckled door and scanned the lie of the land. It didn't take long. This was the perfect spot for an ambush. That concrete block they'd almost crashed into was one of many by the entrance to the clearing, foundation stones of some structure built to house something heavy like a generator. At the other end of the clearing, there was a derelict building, a pile of wood bristling with blades of corrugated metal, the remains of its roof. A timber headframe arched over the debris, trailing broken cables onto a pulley system once used for hauling out ore on rails. Beyond the headframe was the main entrance to a mine, an adit, not a vertical shaft, but a horizontal tunnel burrowing into the mountain. Higher up the slope, all but hidden in a cluster of rocks, he caught the black wink of another adit. There was a third entrance too on the northern mountain halfway back towards the concrete blocks. It had two strands of barbed wire stretched between poles in front of it, and there was a sign clipped between them, announcing in red and black:

DANGER
UNSAFE MINE
KEEP OUT
KEEP ALIVE

It was a somber message, rendered all the more dramatic by its punctuation with bullet holes. There was a platform close to this adit, a rusted steel grid mounted on two timbers laid flat on the ground, a staging point for loading ore.

CJ was sizing it all up. Three adits and extensive infrastructure meant that it had once been a big mine. An easy place to get lost in. An easy place to lose someone. Successful in its day, but dangerous. With lots of ways to die even in its prime. Add to that decades of decrepitude and a pack of heavily armed killers, and dangerous turned into insane. But compared to the open country, it was the right choice. The open country was suicidal. Insane versus Suicidal. There was only one way to call it.

CJ banged the roof of the car, and Enya and Leila hopped out as he fetched the ammo bucket from the trunk. The pitch and fall of Tratfors' V-8s as they whipped around bends along the trail were getting ever closer. Enya and Leila followed CJ towards the main adit, clawing their way through the matchstick pile of debris. All the wood was rotten, and all the metal was rusted. Nothing to stop a bullet. CJ tossed aside some beams and kicked open a broken door sealing off the adit. Beyond it, the tunnel was big enough to stand up in and braced with heavy timbers and crossbeams. It was inclined, rising gently, just enough for water to drain out. CJ filled his pockets with bullets and gave Leila the range bucket.

"Head down the tunnel," he said. "They're going to blow the hell out of this entrance"—he waved his arm back at the woodpile—"so you need to be a good way down. But don't get lost. I need to find you when I get back."

"What if you don't?" Enya blurted it out. "Come back, I mean."

"I'll be okay," he said. "We were lucky back there on the trail. You never know. Maybe we've got someone special looking after us."

Enya's face fell. "That sounds like *Cry God for Harry, England, and Saint George?* When Brits start calling on their patron saint, you know you're up shit creek."

He pulled her close and kissed her lips.

"Take it easy. My saint's a US Marine Corps sniper."

She mouthed another protest, but he was already gone.

He grabbed the grenade from inside the Range Rover and ran back towards the trail, rehearsing Kowalski's arrival in his head. The first thing he'd see was the Rover parked near the headframe and that was as far as they'd go. They'd take cover behind the concrete blocks and pound the whole arena with lead before taking a closer look.

CJ stood by the trailhead figuring it all out. Orchestrating the battlefield is half the victory. One grenade. An M67 with an injury radius of fifteen meters and a fatality radius of five. He secreted it in a creosote bush on the slope behind the concrete blocks. Then he dashed to the steel platform by the boarded-up adit on the northern slope and crawled underneath it. It was a tight fit with not much more than a foot of clearance, but enough for him to raise his head and target a pistol over the thick timbers it was mounted on.

The Tratfors lead truck made the same emergency maneuver he'd made, taking the bend too fast, seeing the concrete blocks at the last minute and skidding to a halt. But those concrete blocks were the last of their problems. CJ took out the guy in the front passenger seat with a head shot and picked off the driver of the SUV behind it as he swerved to avoid the truck and crashed into a rock. Two down. Kowalski and the rest of them were out of their vehicles, taking cover and laying down fire in his direction, with two guys sneaking behind the concrete blocks. Intense fire. Full auto. Sheets of it all around him. CJ was grateful for the foot-thick timber between him and the bullets and the narrow slit under the steel grid he was shooting through. The automatic fire was good news too. Seamless sound. Just what he needed. If they heard the Mason jar breaking, they'd do the math like a supercomputer and take cover before the explosion.

He took his shot and saw the grenade roll out of the bush and tumble down the slope towards the shooters behind the concrete blocks. He ducked down and crawled under the steel grid the other way with one of two scenarios about to unfold. The worst case was tits up. They'd see the grenade and take cover. No fatalities and barely a pause in the storm of lead raining down on him. In that case, he'd dive into the barb-wired adit nearby and hope it connected with the main adit where Enya and Leila were waiting. The best case was that the shooters got caught in the explosion and their numbers diminished. He'd killed two already. He'd counted eight. So if he could kill a few more and interrupt their firestorm long enough to get back to the woodpile, then the odds would switch in their favor.

He rolled out from under the platform as the grenade blew and sprinted across the clearing. It worked. Even the Tratfors crew who escaped the blast were shocked and disoriented, and he was already scurrying through the wood and debris around the headframe when their first wild shots rang out. He made it into the main adit and was soon out of range, the sound of their gunfire ever fainter as he went deeper into the mountain. He made quick progress at first with the light from the entrance to guide him, but as that faded to dark he had to slow down. Forty to fifty yards from the entrance, there was evidence of a cave-in. The tunnel wasn't blocked, but there was a pile of rocks big enough to force him down on all fours to clamber over it. The light was even dimmer beyond it, barely a glimmer.

"Enya," he called out. This was a perfect place for them to hide. Even full-auto bursts directly into the mouth of the tunnel wouldn't get past these rocks.

He listened. Tuning out the torrent of muffled sound from outside as the Tratfors survivors demolished what was left of the headframe.

"Enya."

He called it out once more before heading into the darkness.

TWENTY-FOUR

Enya had the phone, and she'd obviously used its light to go deep inside the mine. But where? There should be a glow up ahead, but there was nothing but blackness. CJ continued, finding his way with his feet, his ears tracking scurrying rats and the fluttering wings of bats as they swerved to avoid this unexpected obstacle. The risk was holes, cave-outs where the floor had collapsed through to another tunnel or a water channel. One wrong step and he could end up at the bottom of a hole, nursing a broken neck and looking back on the good old days when he was an Al-Qaeda hostage. As he got deeper into the adit, the gunfire eased off. The survivors of the ambush would be taking a closer look. They'd find the entrance and they wouldn't stumble through it blind like CJ. They'd have flashlights or night vision. They'd soon make up for lost time. There could only be three or four of them left, and Kowalski was sure to split them up. Two outside. A spotter and a shooter. Then one or two to search the adit and flush them out.

"Enya," he shouted.

Still nothing.

He pushed onward and found a stick with his probing foot. He picked it up and used it like an ant's feelers to scrape the dirt in front of him so he could make better progress.

At last, he picked up a light. Faint. More of a shift in the tone of blackness. He heard something too. Not voices, but sibilance. Distant words bouncing off rocks and trickling around bends in the tunnel. He hurried towards its source, finding a pool of light with an island of rocks shimmering at its center. The rocks were studded with cracked wood and rusted wheels, bits of a broken cart that had once ferried ore out of the adit. He looked up towards the source of the light. There was a vertical shaft above the rocks, a passage heading up from the roof of the adit.

"CJ?" Enya's voice was hushed, urgent.

"Are you okay?" he called out.

"There's a ladder," she said. "Climb on the rocks and you can reach it."

He scrambled up the rock pile and reached into the shaft.

"Be careful," she said. "Some of the rungs are missing and we broke some more. It was scary. But we both made it."

He nodded, although there was no one to see it. More of an acknowledgment to himself. A rotten wood ladder. It had survived Enya and Leila. But neither of them weighed over one-forty. CJ tipped the scales at two hundred, and that was before he'd flown west and discovered burritos and all-you-can-eat diners.

He pulled himself up into the shaft and used his arms to haul his body from rung to rung. When his feet finally reached a rung, he tested it with one foot before committing any weight to it. From there, he worked his way up with extreme caution. The trick was to make sure his entire weight was never placed on a single rung, but always spread over at least three. That meant moving one limb at a time. Slow progress. But the image of his body broken on a pile of rocks waiting for his executioners was a powerful incentive. Enya grabbed his arms as he reached the top, and Leila held the light as he clambered out.

"We voted to explore and use our initiative instead of waiting for you," Enya said. "Since we had the light."

"You did good," he said, taking it all in. They were in a chamber with passages leading off. Most of them were small—just big enough for a miner to crawl into on all fours—all except one that was roomy enough for even CJ to stand erect. That had to be the adit they'd seen in the rocks up the hill above the main entrance. The chamber was littered with rusted metal objects, fossils of ancient tools, empty cans and lamps whose flames had long ago died like the miners whose labors had cut this mausoleum out of the rock. Next to the top of the shaft he'd come up through, there was a crude bin held together by wooden stakes. It was piled with rocks waiting to get shipped outside and processed. Copper, zinc, silver whatever they were mining, they must have found another seam up here, and digging a shaft between the two finds was the easiest way to get the ore out. They could lower it down the shaft in buckets, then use a cart to haul it out of the main adit. CJ checked the bin. The wood was rotten and the rocks inside it were threatening to burst its walls. He picked up a rock and dropped it down the shaft. It bounced off the ladder onto the wall, then hit the rock pile below.

"In fact, you did great," he said.

"Why don't we use these rocks to break the ladder?" Leila said. "Then they can't follow us."

"They'd climb up the mountain and get to us via the upper adit," CJ said, still checking the wood of the bin, testing its soundness. "We got lucky. This could have gone at any moment."

"So we dump it on them instead," Enya said.

"That's the idea. They're down to just three or four men. They can't check all the tunnels. And they can't wait us out. We're not so far off the beaten track here. Four-wheelers. Hikers. Recreational users. Someone will turn up soon. Maybe in the morning. They'll want to clean this all up before dawn. They know I disappeared into the main tunnel, so that's where they'll go looking. They won't know about this connecting shaft. They'll send in one or two guys to flush us out."

He looked around, finding a stout stick. He jammed it into the bin between the rocks and the wall of boards and levered it back and forth, and several rocks spilled off the top and fell into the shaft. Then he set it aside and hid behind the bin.

"Can you see me from the top of the shaft?"

Enya shuffled back and forth and stood on tiptoe.

"No," she said. "But what about us? Where do we hide?"

"You head back along this big tunnel," he said, pulling himself back up on his feet. "But don't go anywhere near the entrance. They'll have a sniper covering all the adits."

Enya and Leila left him, Enya lighting the way with

her phone and Leila scanning the tunnel ahead with her Sig. CJ used the last of its light to take cover behind the rock bin. He made himself comfortable, still figuring out his plan. Dumping the rocks as soon as he heard someone below was like a random shot in the dark. It had to be more subtle than that. If there was more than one down there, he had to nail them both. Otherwise he'd be giving away his location and losing the element of surprise. When he was satisfied with his plan, he made himself comfortable and let the darkness take him back to Iraq. He'd spent years in blindfolds, so darkness was like an old acquaintance he'd never really taken to, but finally learned to live with. Alex had been his lifeline back then. They'd lain side by side—blindfolded, shackled and gagged—feeding each other's spirits simply by their presence.

The stillness was broken by the sound of slow-motion steps. There were two men and they were good. Not a word. Hand signals. Or well-drilled teamwork. A light flickered shadows on the roof above him. CJ waited, poised, transforming the soundtrack he was getting into a video. One was staying below holding a flashlight while the other was making the climb. CJ could see his shadow projected on the roof of the chamber as he navigated the latticework of ladders. The climber switched on his own light when he reached the chamber, its beam probing the tunnels leading off it and various objects strewn about the floor.

Then he spoke.

Quiet. No hollering down the shaft. Using some off-the-grid, ad hoc Wi-Fi system.

"Room up here with passages. Tracks in the dust. They're up here somewhere. Come on up."

CJ followed the man's movements with his ears as he clambered out of the shaft. He had to wait to make sure that the other man was already on his way up before making a move. But not too long. The first man was sure to check the bin. And that was what he was doing, gun in one hand, flashlight in the other, when CJ shot him in the head. He keeled over and disappeared down the shaft.

Clatter and bounce. Ladders and walls. Yelps and groans.

CJ was already at the rowing station pulling on the timber he'd jammed into the bin wall. He braced his feet on a ridge of rock and heaved it like an oar. The bin stakes cowed under the strain, and rocks rumbled. One more stroke and a stake gave way, snapping in a spray of splinters. It was like a dam busting in a flood. Once breached, it was all over, rocks sweeping aside rotten boards and cascading down the shaft. There was a scream, short-lived and lost in a thunderous crash. CJ picked the flashlight off the floor and checked the shaft. No more ladders. No more men. Just a pile of rocks at the bottom with a leg sticking out of it.

He found Enya and Leila waiting down the tunnel. Enya was holding her satchel at her chest like a breastplate, the phone stuck in a side pocket so its flashlight was peeking out the top. The .38 was in her other hand, its barrel roaming wildly. Leila was in full combat mode, braced against the opposite wall, both hands on her gun. They'd heard the gunfire, the screams and the crash of rocks. Now someone large was looming out of the darkness, heading towards them, and everything they had was aimed at him. The blue-on-blue disaster was averted at the last moment when CJ called out.

After a brief update, they continued on towards the entrance with CJ lighting the way with his newly acquired flashlight. With some way to go, they pulled over to the rock walls and CJ edged forward alone. He could tell by the light from the approaching entrance that the sun was almost gone. That was an event that triggered a timer. He had to use what little light was left. After nightfall, the odds would shift back to the team with night vision. He had to find out where Kowalski was holed up. He was out there somewhere with telescopic sights, scoping out the main entrance and checking the other two from time to time. By CJ's count, there were two men left now, Kowalski and one other. He couldn't say for sure that the second man of the tunnel team, the guy on the ladder, hadn't been Kowalski, but it was a safe bet. Kowalski was most unlikely to have volunteered his own services to sniff CJ out of the tunnel. Besides, he was a trained sniper, a standout even amongst the accomplished shooters in the Ranger Regiment. He'd be out there somewhere, squinting through the eyepiece of a telescopic sight with the last member of his troop watching his back and scanning the adits with field glasses. Their most likely location was somewhere amongst those concrete blocks. Kowalski might have traded elevation for the security of concrete, but CJ was doubtful. The bare hills offered little in the way of cover.

CJ stood back from the entrance of the adit, still in the safety of the tunnel, and scoped out the area just outside it. There was a flat crawl space, then a mound of boulders that obscured his view of the clearing but also offered protection from snipers below. He crawled out on his belly as far as the boulders. The spotter would be scanning all three mine entrances plus any others they'd found. CJ had just seconds to stick his head above the boulders, figure out where they were and duck back down again before his head was blown off.

"He's down there somewhere, boy." The voice was accompanied by the sound of a gun cocking. "But I'm up here. So toss it."

CJ skidded his pistol off to one side.

There was the thump of feet landing behind him.

"Hands on the back of your head. Face in the dirt."

"I got him." He paused, waiting for instructions back through his headset.

CJ was cursing his mistake. Sure. With two men left, the sniper team was the best play. But he hadn't factored their radio link into the equation. Kowalski was the lone sniper. He'd gotten that right. But he'd deployed his last man as a remote spotter and offensive scout, and the guy had earned his keep by scaling the bluff in double time and hiding in bushes directly above the upper adit. That gave him control of that entrance and a direct line of sight down the slope and across the clearing to the adit on the north slope. With Kowalski's sights on the main adit, they had all three entrances to the mine locked down tight. The man turned his attention back to the tunnel, never taking his eyes off CJ for more than a split second, waving his M16 and flashlight into its darkness.

"No sign of them," he said. Then, "Got it."

He kicked CJ in the ribs.

"On your feet, asshole." He stepped back. Out of reach but close enough to guarantee the shot. "If it was my call, I'd blow your brains out. But Kowalski wants to flush those bitches out. So we're going to burn you alive unless they oblige." CJ got to his feet. "Keep your hands on the back of your head." It was his first good look at the guy. Ex-military. But not so obviously. He had a ponytail trailing out the back of a baseball cap and tattoos on his neck. "Now turn around and head on down."

CJ was stepping out from behind the protection of the boulders when a shot rang out and he threw himself to the ground. That was when it hit him. Not the bullet. But the sound. Not the crackling thwack of Kowalski's sniper rifle, but a dull thud. Then another. He rolled over. And that was when it finally came. The sniper shot. All sharp edges. Three sounds rolled into one. The explosion driving the bullet out of the barrel at supersonic speed, the zap as it cut through the air, and the sloosh of flesh as it blasted through Enya's chest. She jerked back and hit the rock wall, her .38 skidding at the feet of ponytail, who was lying in a dead heap next to CJ. He scrambled across and scooped her up, laying her in the half-light inside the tunnel entrance. The bullet had ripped through her chest, tearing a hole in her back. It had missed her heart, but that was incidental. If she'd been shot in the driveway of a hospital, she might have had a chance. But here she had minutes.

"I can't feel anything," she said.

"That's good." He smiled, hugging her close enough to smother his tears in her hair. He couldn't let her see them. Not tears. She couldn't take that with her. Not sadness. The last glow of life that burned itself into her retinas had to be a smile. However much it hurt him.

"I'm afraid," she said, her face whitening, edged with blue.

"Don't be." He stroked her hair. "Your brother will

forgive you."

Her eyes opened wide. "You know," she said.

He nodded. He'd always known. He didn't doubt that Declan had grown a conscience when he'd witnessed atrocities and realized that he'd been conned. But her brother was way too smart to think he could leak something that big and stay alive. But his idealistic sister? That geeky girl who escaped in Hollywood romcoms and dreamed of killing monsters in galaxies far, far away. That sentimental twin who saw her brother getting sucked deeper into Tratfors mire. She'd do it. On an impulse. CJ had never believed her payback story. All those years waiting for him to emerge from a coma—that had never made sense. Revenge didn't last that long. It outgrew itself. But guilt? That lasted forever.

"He wanted to stop, but he couldn't. I wanted to help him. I was careful, but…"

There was blood trickling from her mouth. CJ kissed her, wiping it up with his lips.

She'd made a mistake. Just like she had today. A mistake born of her nature. Everything they'd suffered. Alex. Declan. And his own years of pain. It all came down to Enya, and she'd carried the weight of it ever since. She was so goddamn smart. But for one split second, her heart had swamped her head. And it was over.

"Declan forgives you," CJ said. "And so does Alex."

"And you…" She mouthed the words, her eyes finding tears at last.

He kissed her forehead. "I always did."

She went to speak, her voice barely a whisper. He ducked his head, his ear at her mouth to catch the words she whispered, and then she was gone. He held her tight against him, burying his head in her neck, his smile abandoned, his tears flowing. When he looked up, Leila was standing there, looking down at them pistol at hand, her face ashen.

"Shit," she said, looking at Enya and back at CJ. "Are you okay?"

"We're going to need a fire," he said. "There are some flammables back there in those old cans. Kerosene, chemicals."

"What for?"

"It's almost sunset. Kowalski will have military-grade night vision or thermal imaging. Maybe both. After dark we'll be like targets on a rifle range. Thermal is heat-based. Right now these rocks have been baking in the sun all day, so there's not much contrast. But when they cool, you'll get thermal crossover. It'll mess up the image. He'll know all this stuff. So as the light fades, he'll switch to night vision first and then go thermal after dark. But there's a window when none of them is optimal. And we're going to mess them up even more."

"So you want me to get stuff that burns?"

"Can you?" He looked back at Enya. "I need a minute."

She nodded and taking the flashlight, she disappeared down the tunnel.

CJ crawled outside and fetched his pistol and ponytail's M16. Back in the tunnel, he crouched next to Enya and swept his hand through her hair and down onto her neck, where his fingers found her gold locket.

TWENTY-FIVE

The scene was black-and-white, stillness and bare rocks, otherwordly, like a lunar movie set waiting for a man in a spacesuit to hop into frame. But there was no hopping spaceman. Just something glowing white and trailing black smoke as it was tossed over the boulders up by the mine entrance where they were holed up. Kowalski looked up over his rifle's night vision scope. It was not yet dark, but light was fading. He watched the something tumble down onto the rocky slope below the adit. A jacket or some old sack they'd found in the tunnel. They must have found some oil, too, because it was burning. Not brightly. Smoldering, more like. And billowing clouds of black smoke. He went back to the scope. The smoke was getting dispersed by the breeze, but not enough of it to make a difference. In fact, the breeze was making it worse. Building a wall of particles to diffuse what little contrast there was and graying everything out. He took a thermal imaging monocular out of the bag at his elbow and tried his luck. No better. Rocks and boulders and sheets of gravel. All heated up to different temperatures and now cooling at different rates, with a white-hot glowing ember trailing filaments of wriggling heat in and around them all.

Great.

He set the monocular aside and went back to the scope on his Remington bolt-action rifle. It was mounted in a makeshift shelter built around the concrete blocks using bits of corrugated metal and broken timbers, so it looked like part of the collapsed structure.

It was a clusterfuck.

Seven men dead. Or else they were lying somewhere wishing they were dead. He'd had to call it in on the satellite phone. Short and sweet. *Help.* That was the gist of it. An immeasurable blot on his copybook. Tratfors had simple rules. Create a solution and execute it. Use whatever resources you need. Break any laws. Do anything you want. Except fail. That was the only codicil. The failure clause. Fail and you've swapped one problem for two. Fail and you become the problem. And one that someone else will be assigned to solve. They were masters of the cover-up, able to call in markers signed by powerful corporate clients and compromised intelligence and law enforcement officers. Trails of dead bodies had to be avoided wherever possible although they were manageable at a push. Failure was not.

Kowalski was thinking about that call.

It was a mistake.

At first light, there'd be a chopper hovering overhead with a fully equipped SWAT team. And there was every chance that the first bullet fired would be at him. The best case would be a happy outcome before dawn. Brink and Rose both dead. Killing them was the only task at hand. Thanks to Preston's wily gambit in Vegas, they had a complete picture. The bug planted in Leila Rose's bag wasn't just a transponder. It was a mic, and it had survived long enough to do its job. The cloud server, the hard drive, the encrypted key. They had the whole picture. They didn't catch the password. But they didn't need it. They already knew what was in that vault. They just had to find out who else knew and kill them.

Brink, O'Brien, Rose.

One down. Now all he had to do was kill Brink and Rose and this clusterfuck and all the botched operations that led up to it would all be forgotten. The situation was recoverable. They were pinned down. They had an M16 now. But so did he. And he also had the Remington, and at this range—less than five hundred yards—when the smoke cleared and the heat dissipated enough to use the thermal imaging scope, he could chop them down with laser-like precision.

He went back to the scope and cleared his head.

Patience.

A few minutes later, he got what he was waiting for. Brink.

The movement was clear even through swishing smoke. His head flashed between two boulders, and a burst of gunfire kicked up the dirt all around Kowalski's concrete hidey-hole. He returned the fire, a single shot pinging off a boulder way too late. So they'd spotted him. Not that it would help them any. It would take extremely good fortune to sneak a round through his improvised fortress. But they'd be emboldened by their new weapon, so they were sure to try again. And so they did. That head again. A sliver between the rocks and a short burst of fire. But this time Kowalski was ready and on target. A direct hit. A splash. Brink got kicked backwards, and Kowalski could see the black stain of his blood on the rocks behind him even through the gray smoke. That wasn't there before. He could see his M16 too, slithering aside on top of the boulders as Brink fell backwards. Kowalski was watching the M16 when it mysteriously disappeared as if of its own volition by sliding off the rocks.

Leila Rose.

She must have sneaked a hand up and grabbed it.

A security blanket. That was all it was. Now that Brink was dead, she was finished. She'd make a deal for sure. Things were looking up. The job was not yet wrapped up, but with Brink dead, the rest was easy. And killing him felt wonderful. It made Kowalski realize that there was so much more to this than simple accounting. He'd always hated the bastard. He was British. That didn't help. And something else. Something that had been there even before he'd humiliated him at the country club and escaped from West Coast Drum, leaving enough dead bodies to kick off aftershocks that were still rumbling through Kowalski's life. Something that went back to Iraq. Him and Solo. Jarhead buddies. A Cockney dick and a California prick. The comedy duo on everyone's best buddy list.

"Who's there?"

He lurched around and went for his pistol, but he pulled his hand up short. The voice was close, but not that close. It was coming from his headset lying on the ground nearby. Leila Rose must have found the headset on that ponytailed dickhead Morse. Great. Now they could cut a deal. A short-term deal.

"Hey, Leila. Long way from the news desk, eh?"

"I've got want you want. The hard drive and the key."

"So bring them on down."

"Sure. I'll do that right away. Why don't you step out into the open, so I know where to find you? And if you could pull your pants down and stick that sniper rifle up your ass that would be a big help too."

Kowalski chuckled.

"So we got a Mexican standoff. What next? Let me help you with that. First light, they'll be a chopper here with guys who don't do much talking. At least you've got a chance with me." He waited, but there was no response. "Leila?"

She made him wait, then said, "Brink and O'Brien are dead. I just want to get out of this."

"Either you trust me, or I trust you. If I get the hard drive and the key, it's mission over for me."

"You're such an asshole. You think I'm stupid."

"We don't have to make this personal. How about you hide the stuff somewhere up there, then come down? You've got the M16. I'll slide on out of this hole and we can meet up in the middle of the clearing here. Brink left the keys of your Range Rover in the ignition. If you tell me where you hid the stuff, I can take the keys up there with me. And if I find it, I'll toss them down to you."

"I don't know." She was wavering. She wanted off that mountain. She wanted out of all this.

"Or you can wait for the SWAT team."

"I'll get back to you."

He didn't push it. Let her stew. Think about that chopper. The morning chorus. Gunfire and grenades. She'd think herself into the wrong decision sooner or later. That was the problem with most people. Weak. If they wanted something enough, they rationalized it every which way until it added up to the answer they needed.

A few minutes later, she was back on the comms.

"I hid it," she said. "And no way you'll ever find it without me. But I'm not going to tell you where it is. Not until you're up here."

He thought about that. Maybe he could afford to take some risk. What were the chances that a well-known TV network correspondent would gun him down? If he showed some trust, she'd do the same. All he needed was a clean shot.

"I want to see Brink. Pull him out in the open. I want to make sure he's dead."

"You think I'm stupid," she said again. "So you can shoot me."

"Then I won't get the hard drive."

"Maybe you don't want it. Maybe I was wrong about that."

"So let's wait on the chopper."

Another round of silence. Then he saw movement through the smoke. The light was fading fast now. The rocks would be cooling. The thermal imaging would work, but it wouldn't show the visual detail he needed to ID the body. Brink and Morse were about the same size, so their dead—but still warm—bodies would show the same on thermal. He had to stick with the night scope. If he got lucky, Leila Rose would hoist Brink up above the rocks like a scarecrow and hold him there long enough for Kowalski to ID him and get a kill shot on her.

Perfect.

But none of that happened.

Instead a body slid over the boulder. She had to be pushing it with a stick, keeping herself out of sight behind the rock. It certainly looked like him—Brink minus the top of his head.

How's that for brain surgery, dickhead?

Kowalski enjoyed the moment as the body slopped over the boulders and fell onto the slope. It rolled slowly at first, then picked up momentum and tumbled down the mountain, catching the smoky fire and poking it back to life. Some oily scraps of cloth stuck to the body and trailed tinselly sparks and embers until the body crashed into the rocks above the main adit and disappeared from his view.

That was it. That was what he'd asked for.

But it didn't feel right.

"Show me Morse," he said. "Out in the open."

"Screw you," she said. But a few minutes later, another body appeared. She wasn't dragging it out in the open but shunting it over the boulder like the first one. Smart. That way he couldn't get the shot in. But his eyes went back to the scope anyway. The fire was almost burned out, but there was still smoke trailing back and forth in front of her. She was heaving the body, shoving it off the edge of the boulders, one hand on his ponytail the other on his belt. Kowalski almost had her when her head and shoulders appeared above the body as she struggled to wrestle it over the edge. But then it was gone. He couldn't take the risk. If he missed, their deal making days were over. She'd bury herself in the mine and he'd have to wait until the chopper turned up at dawn. So long as she was talking, there was a chance of settling it all before then. He watched the body tumble down the slope through the night scope, its face and belly blacked out with blood, until it crashed into the ridge of boulders above the bluff with the other body.

"Okay," he said. "Let's do a deal." He waited, but there was no response. "Leila, are we going to do this or not?"

The answer came minutes later. Her voice somber, resigned.

"I'm stupid. You're going to kill me anyway."

"Last chance, Leila. I want that drive. More than I want you dead."

"But I've seen what you've done. I've seen what's in those files. And now this. How can you let me live?"

"Expediency. I've got to get the drive. Don't flatter yourself. You're not so important."

But Leila wasn't buying, and the line went dead.

CJ had long since run out of letters in his planning acronym. But beyond PACE, he could always add TC for TOTALLY CRAZY. He opened his eyes. Passing out was not part of the plan, but that was why it was called crazy. It was pretty much bound to go wrong.

So how long had he been out?

Minutes? Hours? It had been perfect up to then. Leila Rose had delivered an Academy Award performance, teasing Kowalski until he popped the question.

It had to come from him.

Habeas corpus.

Let me see the bodies.

It was not the most obvious scenario. But switching clothes and watches was never going to be enough. So CJ had scalped the dead man. Then Leila had blown the top off his head with her 9mm, blotching the rocks behind CJ with the dead man's blood while CJ was blasting rounds at Kowalski and supposedly getting shot. He'd attached thin strips of cloth to Ponytail's scalp before tying it on his own head. With that much hair flopping around and the black smoke from the stinkpot fire muddling the picture, he was gambling that Kowalski could never make out the difference. It was bold and brazen, and way out there even by Crazy James standards. And the critical point was that the ask had to come from Kowalski. It had to be his idea. All that had played out perfectly. The risk of Kowalski shooting the dead bodies on their way down was real enough, but slight. He wanted that deal with Leila, and she was barely playing along. He couldn't risk firing a shot her way—at least, not unless he was sure of killing her. Besides, even if either of those bodies was still alive, then the bouncing down the mountain would surely have finished them off. And that was where the calculation had gone awry. With his pain tolerance set to default numb, CJ figured that rolling down a mountain was a big improvement on the alternatives. *Stay loose and relaxed*, he told himself. *Stunt men do this stuff all the time*. He'd lose some skin. That was a given. Pick up some bruises. Maybe even a fracture. A small one. Temporary stuff. But somewhere down that bumpy slope, he'd cracked his head on a rock. And even with the added safety helmet of a borrowed scalp, it had knocked him out.

He moved tentatively—nothing big broken—and oriented himself. He was tucked behind the ridge of boulders at the bottom of the slope directly over the main adit. That part had worked. He was invisible to Kowalski in his sniper nest and Kowalski was stuck there. Leila had an M16, a rifle that could shoot eight-inch groups or better at that distance in the hands of a trained Marine. That wasn't Leila, but Kowalski was highly unlikely to put her to the test.

The dead man was lying next to CJ. He grabbed his arm and swapped watches. The dead man had his pistol too. It was stuck down his pants. CJ tucked his hand under his belt and pulled it out. He felt woozy, not in pain, but concussed. He stared at the pistol, struggling to keep it in focus. He couldn't risk peeking over the rocks, so he had to hope that Leila had kept the faith and was looking for his movement to trigger the next phase. He was still dizzy, but his head was as good as it was going to get. So he unhooked the scalp from under his chin, tossed it aside and crawled along the ridge to an arroyo, a dry watercourse cut in the rocks. It was a few feet deep, a crawlspace to conceal his approach. And that was vital. It was dark now. Kowalski would be cruising up and down the slope with his thermal imaging scope. Most of the time, he'd be focused on the boulders in front of the upper adit, waiting for Leila to sneak out in the dark. But now and again, he'd go back down the slope to the main entrance below, then scoot over to the adit in the northern slope, figuring that she might cut back into the mine and try her luck at another exit. With all that wandering, he might catch CJ's approach. Not in the arroyo, but at the bottom where it flattened out into a wash plain of gravel. That was a twenty-to-thirty-yard shooting gallery. An easy shot for Kowalski. But CJ was counting on being lucky. And counting on Leila Rose.

Kowalski had all but given up when Leila's voice rattled the comms into life.

"You win, Kowalski. I'm coming down. But before

I do, I want to tell you something. Or even better, I'll show it to you."

Kowalski roamed the rocks with his scope, looking for the white blob of her head.

Show him what?

He was expecting her to hold something up.

The hard drive? A white flag?

Then he saw her. A splash of heat at the end of the rocks. Barely that. No head. Just hands. Sticking her gun out over the rocks and shooting blind like a raghead insurgent. Three bursts. Short on the first and wide on the second. But the third was spot-on. Kowalski ducked below the concrete block as bullets shredded wood and pocked holes in the metal of his makeshift hide.

"Did you get the message?" she said. "The message is—I know how to shoot."

Kowalski pulled his face out of the dirt and curled in closer to his concrete block, his finger sliding back into the trigger guard.

Another bullet.

Thwack.

Kowalski screamed, hitting the trigger of the Remington by reflex, blasting its lethal round somewhere north of the Pole Star. He dropped the rifle and rolled over grabbing his knee. And there he was— back from the dead yet again—CJ Brink staring down at him.

Kowalski dived under his jacket, going for his pistol, and CJ put a second shot in his shoulder. Then he shot him twice more. Once in each elbow. Kowalski howled, writhing like a snake stuck with a pitchfork. CJ searched him, tossing aside his pistol and a Bowie knife. Leila was hurrying down the slope and kicking up a few stones on the way. She was carrying Enya's satchel and the M16. CJ waved to her to come on over. But she went to the Rover instead, and after scraping open the damaged door, she got in behind the wheel. CJ looked back at Kowalski. He really didn't want an audience for what he was about to do. But it looked like he was going to have one. Leila started the Range Rover and drove over, and CJ left Kowalski in his bunker and went to meet her. The Tratfors vehicles were still there where he'd ambushed them at the entrance of the clearing, the SUV studded with bullet holes and leaking gas in a steady drip. Undriveable. And the truck had fared no better. It had gotten the worst of the grenade blast and had one wheel buckled and a tire in shreds. CJ stood between the vehicles at the trailhead, waiting for Leila, who switched on the headlights as she approached, her face disappearing in a wall of glare. She was gunning the engine. He waved his hand to slow her down and was dumbfounded when she sped up. He went to shout. To stop her. But it was too late. He dived to the side, his feet close enough to feel the draft of tires churning gravel and spitting stones as she tore past. He scrambled to his feet. But she was gone. He looked down the trail, more numb than betrayed.

Leila?

His mind reeled in speculation, but the smell of gas brought him back. The drip from the Tratfors SUV had become a rivulet streaming at his feet. He thought back to the ambush. He hadn't shot up that tank. His shots were targeted. It was Leila's distraction fire. She had to keep Kowalski pinned down while he was sneaking out of the arroyo and coming up behind him.

But her shots had strayed wide and hit that tank. It might have been inadvertent. But after sending him sprawling in the dirt, it looked more like part of a plan to make a clean getaway.

But why? Panic? Some hidden agenda?

He went back to Kowalski.

"Shit," Kowalski said, looking up at him with rheumy, bloodshot eyes. "You're one dumb lucky bastard, Brink. I thought you'd gone with her." He started to laugh, his round belly pumping breathless snickers between sniffles of pain.

CJ whirled back towards the trail.

C is for contingency.

Tratfors had the same playbook.

So what if Brink or one of the women got to their vehicle and tried to escape?

They had it covered.

The explosion cracked open the night with a lick of flame and a thunderous roar, its echo punctuated by the crashing and tinkling of metal and glass. So that was Leila. Now the hard drive was gone. And so was the person who could take that data and do the most damage with it. Questions were stacking up in CJ's head, and all of them started with the word why. But now wasn't the time for answers, so he let them all roll on by. She'd made the choice. There was just one regret. He hadn't seen it coming. Kowalski was right. He might have been in that Range Rover. He might have been up there with Leila and those other bits and pieces tumbling out of the sky. He turned back to Kowalski, and the Tratfors man read his fate on CJ's face.

No more snickers.

CJ picked up Kowalski's Bowie blade and crouched

over him, his whisper-soft voice as sharp-edged as the blade in his hand.

"I held Alex's head by the hair like this." He grabbed a handful of Kowalski's hair and jerked his head back, exposing his throat. "I ran with it through the streets of Baghdad. And when they found me, I was holding it against my chest." He edged closer. "The reason I spent years in hell and Alex and Declan were murdered is because Enya O'Brien was a good person. She had a conscience. But she was also a bit of a fumbler."

Kowalski's face lit up. "We thought it was him. We didn't know the dumb asshole was sharing ops with his sister. I was told to get rid of him. But not you guys. Not you and Alex. That's why I worked it out like I did. The militia rounds you up. Nobody gets hurt. They separate you guys and we rescue you. O'Brien gets worked on till we know who he shared the data with. Then he gets killed accidentally. The leak gets plugged and everyone's a hero."

"I get it. And if I was a generous man, I'd blame Enya and let you go. If she hadn't blown the whistle, Declan and Alex would still be alive. And I'd be normal. More or less. But I'm not a generous man. I'm a steel-souled bastard. Or so I've been told. And I'm thoughtful too. And so are those guys in the militia. They'd never agree to a bullshit plan like that. Staging a bungled rescue mission where only one captive gets killed. It's too complicated. They like simple. Beat the crap out of O'Brien till he talks, then stage a bungled rescue mission where they kill all the hostages. That'd work. You guys roll up and fire a couple of shots. They shoot us all and bugger off down a tunnel. Simple."

"No, no…"

CJ shut him up, cracking him on the forehead with the butt of the knife. "Enya is innocent because she had nothing but good in her heart. You're guilty because you had nothing but evil in yours. That country club. What's the membership? Two hundred thousand, three hundred?"

"What?"

"I was in a hospice. Guys with no legs. No arms. One guy had no balls. I watched him one night in the cafeteria. Sitting with his wife, holding hands across the table. So they get that. And you get the country club." Kowalski was shaking, his eyes swiveling around looking for rescuers that were never going to show. CJ jerked his head back to arch up his throat towards the blade. "I'm holding you to account for the death of Alex Solo. For Enya. For all of them. I'm going to saw your head off with your own blade. I'm going to carry it up there onto that road and stick it on a post where you can watch the passing traffic."

Kowalski screamed as CJ dropped the knife to his throat and cut.

But he stopped.

A voice.

Alex?

No. A memory. A feeling. A splinter of steel jammed in a synapse.

He bit the knife deeper into Kowalski's throat. But something was wrong. He rocked on his heels. Dizzy. Confused. Kowalski's face was rippling like it was underwater. CJ steadied himself. Fighting it. Blood was spilling from Kowalski's throat, but all his main cables were still intact.

Just cut him.

He was pushing himself to do it.

But no. That voice. It was stopping him. That wasn't a splinter of steel. CJ jerked himself up on his feet and tossed the knife aside, staring down at Kowalski.

"Alex had the best of this country beating inside him," he said. "He loved it. He loved his family, his buddies. He was a hero and he died like one." CJ stopped, choking up, his eyes lifting up to the sky. "But you're just a dog." He pulled the pistol from his belt and shot Kowalski through the head in a single motion.

He stood awhile after that, not so much thinking as collecting, all the bits of himself strewn around the mine and the trails he'd traveled since arriving in America. There was only one thing left to do. Something that stuck in his head as he ranged over the day's events. Enya. He couldn't leave her like that. Not in a tunnel with rats. He climbed the slope to the upper adit and carried her down. Her locket was gone. No surprise. He'd left it there as a test for Leila. Now it was a mushed nugget scattered with her remains, a little gold returned to hills that had yielded so much of it. He dragged the driver from the Tratfors SUV and tossed his body aside, putting Enya's body in his place. He jammed dry timbers underneath it to catch the dripping gas, then searched the pockets of the dead men and found a smoker. He used his lighter to fire the dribbling gas before stepping clear and watching it flame, floodlighting the arena and dancing shadows on the slopes all around it. And as its light faded, so did the stars, bleached out of the sky by the hint of the new day. The dawn was sure to bring a Tratfors cleanup crew. There'd be a chopper zooming in over the ridge within the hour. CJ considered the arsenal littering the site. He had the pistol tucked in his belt and an extra magazine, not that a 9mm would help much in that situation. But the Remington was another proposition. He slung it over his shoulder and headed back down the trail.

Leila Rose had made it halfway back to the road. The Rover's twisted frame and chassis was tossed up on the slope, its aluminum engine dumped in the dirt, pieces of bodywork scattered on the hills. There was no sign of Leila, and no sign of the laptop or the hard drive. He walked up the hill to the north, sat down and surveyed the blast scene below. He looked back over the interlocking spurs of the trail to the arena where Enya's pyre was still glowing in the half-light of dawn.

She'd never trusted Leila. She'd seen the upside in having her on the team, but there was always something holding her back. He'd dismissed it as rivalry, two strong women thrown together in a crisis both reaching for the controls. But something at the end had made him wonder. He pulled the memory card from his pocket. He'd popped it out of the locket when Leila had gone looking for kindling for their smoke bomb. He held it up to his face, staring at it like it was a photograph, something worth looking at, not just black plastic. This was the future, the new weapon for the postnuclear world. Truth and lies coded in zeros and ones. He put it back in his pocket and stood up, and he was heading back down the trail when he heard that voice again.

"Alex?"

He whipped around, eyes scouring the spurs back towards the mine, but there was nobody there. No Alex. Just a sense of him lingering. His warrior's heart. He turned and strode off, then stopped.

For sure he'd heard that voice.

And not just with his ears. Every cell in his body was tingling with it, the hairs on his neck standing to attention like proud Marines. He looked back at the clearing. The wind was kicking up, squeezing more life out of Enya's pyre, its flames lighting anew, its heat swirling curlicues of dust and smoke skyward. He watched them as they traced patterns in the light of the fire. Then something big caught. Flammable. Not an explosion but getting there. The air cracked with it, and flame reached up into the last of the darkness and the first of the light. And there was Alex. Not Alex the victim, his severed head sedately carried at his chest. This was Alex whole, Alex as CJ remembered him when they'd first met. He was in combat gear. Desert camouflage. Locked and loaded. And as the dust and smoke swirled, Alex grew larger than life, towering over the flames at his feet, his spectral flesh coming alive and glowing with a strength that stretched beyond this world.

"Hey, buddy…"

He was towering above the clearing. Fearsome. Invincible. He pointed down at CJ, arm and finger like a gun, voice booming.

"I've still got your back."

ACKNOWLEDGMENTS

The Saint of Baghdad is the story of three men who come back from the dead metaphorically. In the narrative, CJ emerges from a coma and Alex's spirit echoes from the grave, while in the real world, their creator wakes up after an authorial hibernation so long it must surely have been seen as a death. This publishing renaissance is long overdue, and it would never have happened without helping hands. I want to thank beta-readers Marcus and Shalini, editor Eliza Dee and cover designer Fiona Jayde.

Fiction writing is a creative art. The deliverable, after all, is a book. But just as an actor must create a performance, an author must perform daily or his creation will never exist. For many, that's the rub—those endless shows performed at a keyboard in front of a silent audience. I could never have written this without the drive and passion of my wife, Elizabeth, whose confidence in me never falters. So for that, and so much more, I thank her most of all.

9 781916 009523